OLD MAN SAVARIN STORIES

Literature of Canada

Poetry and Prose in Reprint

Douglas Lochhead, General Editor

Old Man Savarin Stories

Tales of Canada and Canadians

Edward William Thomson

Introduction by Linda Sheshko

UNIVERSITY OF TORONTO PRESS

© University of Toronto Press 1974
Toronto and Buffalo
Printed in Canada
Reprinted in 2018
ISBN (casebound) 0-8020-2077-1
ISBN 978-0-8020-6207-9 (paper)
LC 73-91557

Literature of Canada 10
The illustration used on the jacket is by Charles W. Jefferys and is taken
from the edition of *Old Man Savarin Stories* used in this reprint.
(Toronto: Gundy 1917).

This book has been published with the assistance of a grant from the
Ontario Arts Council.

Preface

Yes, there is a Canadian literature. It does exist. Part of the evidence to support these statements is presented in the form of reprints of the poetry and prose of the authors included in this series. Much of this literature has been long out of print. If the country's culture and traditions are to be sampled and measured, both in terms of past and present-day conditions, then the major works of both our well-known and our lesser-known writers should be available for all to buy and read. The Literature of Canada series aims to meet this need. It shares with its companion series, The Social History of Canada, the purpose of making the documents of the country's heritage accessible to an increasingly large national and international public, a public which is anxious to acquaint itself with Canadian literature — the writing itself — and also to become intimate with the times in which it grew.

DL

Edward William Thomson, 1849-1924

Linda Sheshko

Introduction

What do Edward William Thomson, Norman Duncan, Charles G.D. Roberts, Theodore Roberts, Sara Jeannette Duncan, Gilbert Parker, Arthur Stringer, and Frederick Niven have in common? All were prolific Canadian writers who contributed to a wave of new fiction between 1888 and 1914, and all took part in an exodus of Canadian writers to the great centres of writing and publishing, Boston, New York, and London.[1] The causes for this migration have been set forth by Gordon Roper in the *Literary History of Canada*, and need not concern us here. We may well be curious, however, as to why a man like Thomson, who was so concerned with Canadian life, both as writer and as political commentator, chose to spend a decade of his life in Boston. His personality and circumstances at the time may help to illuminate this decision.

The son of William Thomson and Margaret Hamilton Foley was born on the family farm in York Township on 12 February 1849. 'Aikenshaw,' the 200-acre Thomson homestead, cultivated until the 1870s by the labour of escaped slaves, was later absorbed into the city of Toronto, but Thomson's United Empire Loyalist roots ran deep in Ontario soil. His grandfather, Colonel Edward Thomson, served at Detroit and Queenston Heights during the War of 1812, and later distinguished himself in the legislature of Upper Canada, defeating William Lyon Mackenzie in an 1836 election in York. During the period of political and social agitation which preceded Confederation in Canada and during the American Civil War, Thomson was educated mainly at Brantford and Trinity College School, then at Weston, Ontario.

At the age of fourteen, while visiting an uncle in Philadelphia, young Thomson met the man who became his lifelong hero: 'One day as he stood in front of a pastry store munching a cheese cake, a tall man placed his hand on the boy's shoulder and asked: "Good, sonny?" The man was Abraham Lincoln, then bowed by war's burdens.'[2] This chance encounter seems to explain why Thomson, at fifteen, ran away to serve with the 3rd and 5th Pennsylvania Cavalry during the Virginia Campaigns of 1864-5, until his parents obtained his discharge on the grounds that he was a British subject and under age. Upon his return, 'Willie' enlisted with the Queen's Own Rifles, and took part in the skirmish at Ridgeway during the Fenian Raid of June 1866.

After his discharge from the Queen's Own Rifles in September 1867, the young man settled down to study civil engineering for five years. His studies were interrupted in the autumn of 1869 by a memorable trip to Fort Garry (Winnipeg) with Joseph Howe, the newly appointed Secretary of State for the provinces. From 1872 to 1878, Thomson worked as a land surveyor, mainly in lumbering and railway building. In 1873, while employed as a civil engineer on the construction of the Carillon Canal, around the rapids of the Ottawa River, he met and married Adelaide St-Denis, daughter of Alexandre St-Denis, of Pointe Fortune, Quebec. Thomson's letters reveal little of his wife, but Henry Morgan speaks of her in *The Canadian Men and Women of the Time* as 'a lady of high intellectual attainments, who has herself won no inconsiderable reputation as a writer.'[3]

The marriage was a romantic one — in fact, or so says local tradition, an elopement, the wealthy Pointe Fortune merchant who owned the brick house and high garden playing the part of irate parent. Perhaps Mr St-Denis thought his future son-in-law too adventurous in spirit ... or perhaps the trouble was that the suitor looked forward to the precarious profession of literature. At all events the young couple took matters into their own hands. In later years the Thomsons spent many of their summers in the Pointe Fortune house...[4]

In December 1878 Thomson became an editorial writer for the Toronto *Globe* under the editorship of George Brown. His entry into political journalism was probably facilitated by his family's political connections: 'one of his relatives ... had been in the fifties a sort of runner-up to George Brown as leader of the Liberals.' The next twelve years were spent with the *Globe*, apart from a two-year interval as a land surveyor, during the Winnipeg real estate 'boom.' The boom's collapse left him, in his own words, 'with the street between two corner lots,'[5] and he returned to journalism, first as the *Globe's* Montreal correspondent, then as its chief editorial writer. J.W. Dafoe, later to become the editor of the *Manitoba Free Press* (subsequently renamed the *Winnipeg Free Press*) and an influential figure in western Canada, met Thomson in Montreal and later remembered him as 'a brown-bearded, stalwart, active young man of thirty-five, intensely interested in life, literature, politics and human beings.'[6] It was also during his time in Montreal that 'Petherick's Peril' won him a $500 prize in a competition for the best adventure story, sponsored by the *Youth's Companion* of Boston.

As a commentator on the Canadian political scene Thomson transcended narrow party loyalties. Bred a Tory in his father's family tradition, he broke away after the 'Pacific Scandal' and followed Alexander Mackenzie. In 1891 he resigned from the

Globe because he detected a threat of 'annexation' in the Liberal policy of 'unrestricted reciprocity' with the United States, the key issue of the 1891 election, and conducted a free-lance campaign against reciprocity in the columns of sympathetic newspapers. In 1911, however, Thomson strongly supported the Taft-Fielding reciprocity compact. Laurier and reciprocity were defeated in the 1911 election, after a campaign in which the opponents of reciprocity shrewdly capitalized on Canadians' fear of being swallowed up by a hungry American republic. Such anxiety had been voiced in a *Globe* editorial of 1 June 1871: 'we are divided only by an imaginary boundary ... from a people ... [who] have before now proved themselves aggressive – a people who believe in "manifest destiny," "universal sovereignty," and other ideas not very reassuring to their neighbours.'[7]

After the election, Thomson was open to the offer of a position as revising editor and short story writer for the *Youth's Companion*, where he remained from 1891 to 1901. In November 1892, a letter to Ethelwyn Wetherald, the Canadian poet, contrasted Boston with the Toronto he had left:

> No, I have no wish to see a stone of Toronto again. You know I always detested the narrow, bigoted, canting spirit of that active Belfast, where I had the misfortune to belong to a political crew whose personnel I always detested. It was the misfortune of my life to like the Tories individually and their general way of thinking, while believing their politics to be in the main idiotic and ill calculated. And being a Globe man cut me off from nearly all the people in the world for whom I cared a cuss.

Here, Glory to God, I never meet a Methodist except in wolf's clothing, when he's just as agreeable as a pagan. Boston, so far as I know it by keeping company, is pagan to the heart's core — and vastly stronger in all good qualities, kindness, generosity, tolerance, geniality than any place debauched by 'the prevalent superstitions.'

Boston men, as I know them, are pretty accurately sketched as 'men who were born in the Congregational Church, have pews in the Unitarian Church, and go to the woods on Sunday.' The city is bookish and critical in art, music and literature, without being productive of much of anything valuable ... The Companion's owner is a most pious Baptist, but as genial and good as if he were not a Christian at all.[8]

Thomson had been brought up a Scottish Methodist, and as a friend later recalled, 'he used to say that although he had long been an agnostic, he never could quite rid himself of the Methodist creed that "the mortal sins were drinking and wenching and the venial sins lying and cheating." '[9]

Although Thomson enjoyed Boston, at certain times he felt a twinge of the *canadien errant*, as he revealed in a letter to Archibald Lampman, on 24 May 1892: 'Because this is the Queen's birthday, the sun rose gloriously this morning and has shone pretty steadily all the forenoon ... Yet the people here are not celebrating to any great extent — rebels! What a sense of exile in seeing no *Union Jacks* nor hearing any fire crackers or anvils to-day! I feel the strangeness of this land today more than ever before ... This day has been a day of banging and tooting and hooraying and picknicking with us *Canucks* ever since the beginning of things.'[10]

It appears that by the time he returned to Canada in 1901, Boston had lost its charm for him: 'Goodness! what a delightful place is Montreal compared with Boston. Of all the disgusting places and people, the worst is the place of literary coteries, and gabble-gabble about books and art and music by people who really don't know literature, etc., nearly as well as do the better educated inhabitants of country villages...'[11]

Thomson's ten years with the *Youth's Companion* were devoted to the relatively trifling task of revising manuscripts to meet the journal's standards of wholesomeness and vigorous action. The humorous story 'Miss Minnely's Management' treats his occupation satirically: 'George Renwick substituted "limb" for "leg," "intoxicated" for "drunk," and "undergarment" for "shirt," in "The Converted Ringmaster," a short-story of commerce, which he was revising for "The Family Blessing." ' Thomson's letters rarely mention his work, except when enticing Lampman to try Boston and the *Companion*, as a lesser evil than 'the infernal hole Ottawa' and the civil service.

Thomson and Lampman had been friends since the publication of *Among the Millet* (1888), when Thomson wrote an editorial in the *Globe* urging the government to recognize and foster Canadian genius by promoting men like Lampman to higher positions in the civil service. They corresponded regularly from 1891 until the year before Lampman's death in 1899, at the age of thirty-seven. Thomson thus became a corresponding member of what Claude Bissell has called 'the family compact of intellectuals and literary men that ... grew up in Central Canada during the later part of the Nineteenth Century.'[12] Though Thomson's letters to Lampman and to Ethelwyn Wetherald are reticent on the subject of his work, they reveal much of his personality, literary tastes, and the quality of his friendship.

Thomson's comments on contemporary writing are fresh, shrewd, and utterly unpretentious. A widely-read man, his taste in fiction inclined toward the realistic treatment of common life, and he tried to apply something of the vision of Howells, James, and Zola to the Canadian scene. In poetry, he expressed particular admiration for Walt Whitman and Matthew Arnold: 'I think I should have killed myself many years ago but for his poems' (letter to Wetherald, 11 Mar. 1889 – Bourinot). He regarded Lampman as a poet of genius, and continually sustained him with canny professional advice, discriminating praise, and honest, yet gentle, criticism, for which the poet had great respect. Duncan Campbell Scott, their mutual friend, said of Thomson in his introduction to the 1925 edition of Lampman's *Lyrics of Earth*: 'He was a prince of friends whose helpfulness was inexhaustible and whose courage often understayed Lampman's ship when it was in stress of weather ... The contact with a mind like Mr Thomson's was specially valuable to him. He found there something that his own mind lacked – a robust quality, knowledge and experience of life, and he found there sympathy that was broadly based on actualities, as sensitive as a woman's, as charitable and as tender. I am certain that Lampman made full use of this friendship and that it was of peculiar influence and comforting effect.'[13]

Fifteen years after Lampman's death, Thomson was still striving to enhance his friend's reputation. He reported for the *Boston Evening Transcript* of 14 March 1914 the gathering in Ottawa of 'a company of Intellectuals' in Lampman's honour, during which 'a Canadian fellow of the Royal Society of Literature of the

United Kingdom' — quite likely Thomson himself, who had been elected FRSL in 1909 — 'contended that Lampman must be regarded as a poet of the greater English Literature.'[14]

In his letters to Ethelwyn Wetherald, which also contain solid professional advice and encouragement, Thomson seems less absorbed in the task of keeping high the spirits of his correspondent, and hence freer to express his own moods and philosophy. He emerges as a man who has achieved strength through arduous struggle with himself and the human condition:

> But I won't go into the slough any deeper. Only this, there is steady satisfaction in facing the fact of our helplessness, our nothingness, our being in the hand of the Master of the Show...
> Don't imagine that this way of thinking prevents my being a 'kicker.' Nay, verily. But it does help one to make light of the whips and scorns of time, etc.; it helps one to rise (occasionally) superior to pique, to resentment, to petty memories of having been attacked. Well, I began life with a devil of a temper, a great capacity for hating and taking revenge, a considerable power of wounding (though I say it myself) — and I hate nobody, I often take thought in time and refrain from striking back ... I'm not as bad as I used to be, and whatever improvement there is in Yours Affectionately is due to having acquired a habit of looking at the Cosmos as an illusion and myself and other appearances as 'bubbles.' [18 Apr. 1889 — UNB]

Thomson's personal advice, like his poetic criticism, is calculated not to hurt — it has the ring of painful experience: 'The thing is to be yourself, true to your perceptions, your vision. But scorn blinds the soul. My God, how long I was in learning this – and learned it too late. Nothing is truly seen except as from the inside, i.e., with sympathy' (10 Dec. 1909 – UNB). Miss Wetherald, eight years Thomson's junior, once spoke with casual contempt of her rural neighbours; his response revealed a deep respect and affection for ordinary people, which are reflected both in his stories and in his simple, 'homely' manner of speaking: 'Because you have books and have a fine taste in literature, you scorn your neighbours and call them "moujiks!" Many a year I fooled away in this sort of scorn. It is, in fact, the merest conceit ... I've heard better talk, and better literary talk, outside of literary circles than in them ... and you would find this truth out for yourself if you had a year in Boston, or any other place where the *poseurs* of literature do their act ... I'm so deaf I learn little now by talk and am perforce much a reader, but Lord, I could never be bothered reading a book, if I could live with and hear my fellow men and women' (13 Aug. 1896 – Bourinot).

The correspondence continues after Thomson's return to Canada in 1901, and affords valuable glimpses of his life during a score of busy, influential years. From Montreal he wrote:

> I have returned to political journalism after ten years of disgust with Y.C. publishers and an overdose of literararism as she is exhibited in Boston. I am working for the *Montreal Star* and probably shall soon have my say in its columns which I am trying to make independent of party, and essentially in favour of Canadian independence under the Crown. I like this work, coming to it fresh and full of ideas that have been growing in me during the eleven years of exile. Still I mean to write some fiction – if I had a year's money ahead I would

> certainly tackle my long projected novel — [15 Oct.
> 1902 — Bourinot]

The expatriate's return was preceded by that of his only son, Bernard St-Denis Thomson, a Harvard graduate in Law. In March 1895, Thomson had written to Lampman: 'Bernie insists that he will go back to Canada when he takes his degree, next June.' Bernard married an Ottawa girl, Ethel Wright, and later served for many years on the editorial staff of the *New York Times*. Their son, Edward Wright Thomson, lived in Boston.[15]

Later in 1902, Thomson moved to Ottawa as Canadian correspondent for the *Boston Evening Transcript*. While contributing to the *Transcript* many illuminating articles on Canada's internal and external affairs, Thomson renewed his friendships with a number of distinguished Canadian statesmen. Laurier was an old friend, and Thomson's respect for him was founded on a most realistic perception of his methods: 'He is an iron man, most resolute, quite unbendible or -able in having his way, and as smooth as the smoothest lady's — we'll say skin. He yields on unessentials with perfect grace and good-will, stands fire like a mud fort, and bears no animosity unless you really thwart him. Then he does not hate you, but he will carefully remember, and not hurt you one little bit, unless it be to his political advantage. He bamboozles me most sweetly, often. I know when he does it, and he knows I know. Still, I am bamboozled, which is the main thing' (letter to Wetherald, 24 Feb. 1911 — UNB). In the same letter, Thomson remarks of Henri Bourassa, the French-Canadian nationalist leader: 'He is a good fellow abominably wronged by party liars. Still, he is no angel ... He means to be the straightest of politicians, but it is not possible to be absolutely straight in politics, save in intention. ... Politics is the most complicated of human games, and that is why it is so interesting.'

In addition to his political influence, this was also the period of Thomson's greatest recognition in literature. After the well-received appearance in 1895 of *Old Man Savarin and Other Stories*, he published 'This of Aucassin and Nicolette,' a verse translation, and three books for boys: *Smoky Days* and *Walter Gibbs, the Young Boss* in 1896, and *Between Earth and Sky and Other Strange Stories of Deliverance* in 1897. A decade passed before the appearance of the poem *Peter Ottawa* (1908) and *The Many Mansioned House and Other Poems* (1909), which was published in England and the United States with the title *When Lincoln Died and Other Poems*. Thomson's volume of poetry led to his election to the Royal Society of Literature in 1909, and to the Royal Society of Canada in 1910. One of his poems, 'Aspiration,' was selected for the *Oxford Book of Victorian Verse* by Sir Arthur Quiller-Couch – to whom Thomson dedicated *Old Man Savarin Stories: Tales of Canada and Canadians* (1917).

In spite of these honours, however, failing health and distress concerning the war diluted Thomson's enjoyment of later life. In 1911 he wrote to Miss Wetherald: 'Every month I become surer that everybody should be asphyxiated at about 60 years, for what sense to go on getting duller and duller?'[16] Mrs Thomson died in 1921, and in 1923, after being injured in an automobile accident in Saskatchewan, Thomson retired from journalism and returned to Boston, where he spent his last months in the home of his grandson. He died on 5 March 1924.

One difficulty in assessing the literary and journalistic reputation of a man of Thomson's versatility is the profusion of categories applied to him by different biographers. For instance, Lorne Pierce's literary history classifies him as 'poet and humorist,' and the *Globe's* obituary notice (7 Mar. 1924) hailed him as a 'Noted Canadian Political Writer and Poet,' while the *Dictionary of American Biography* considered him an 'editor, author, poet,'[17] and Henry Morgan, a 'poet; story writer; journalist' — perhaps reversing the real order of his interests.

As the *Transcript's* Canadian correspondent, Thomson achieved considerable stature: 'He wrote with editorial license, illuminating his columns by his long observations in history and statecraft. His letters were widely quoted in Canada, and his standing among public men was high and enviable.'[18] The writer's political attitudes, contrary to the usual order of things, became steadily more radical with the years. Ardent, uncompromising, and mildly rebellious, he took controversial stands on the radical issues of the day, such as free trade and Canadian nationalism, without party bias: 'The fairness of Mr Thomson's discussion of public questions is attested by the fact that two writings, as many will remember, were constantly quoted or reprinted by the newspaper organs of each of the opposing political parties.'[19] Sir Wilfred Laurier must have had high regard for his friend's objectivity and knowledge of constitutional matters, for after the Boer War, 'when during the discussions about a constitution for the Union of South Africa, Botha asked Laurier to recommend somebody who could give him an impartial appraisement of the workings of Canada's Federal Constitution, he recommended Thomson, who did a good job and got a handsome fee for his work.'[20]

Thomson's work in these years seems to have effected a successful blend of journalism and literature: the *Transcript's* notice of his death speaks of his letters as 'revealing in their epigrammatic style and independent flavor the best examples in journalistic literature of the highest type.' In *English-Canadian Literature* (1913; reprinted in the Literature of Canada series 1973), T.G. Marquis records: 'He is widely known as a sound writer on political questions and also as a writer of excellent verse. He is seen at his best in his stories...'[21] J.W. Dafoe, writing shortly after Thomson's death, mourns the loss to Canadian literature of the novels, essays, and reminiscences he *might* have written, had not old age and the lack of financial resources prevented. 'The explanation of this tragic — the word is not too strong — failure fully to express himself is: Journalism, that fleeting imitation of literature which gives its devotees successes of the minute at the cost of foregoing more enduring satisfactions.' The 'long projected novel' of which he wrote to Miss Wetherald was not the only long-planned task left unfulfilled. Another was

the writing, in the form of recollections and comments, of what would have been a political history of his own times. One can recall his comment on Sir John Willison's book of that character, not in the least in disparagement, that he could beat Sir John by 20 years of time, covering not only the early years of the Dominion but a period before Confederation — for Thomson, as has been said, was brought up in a political environment and knew many of the Upper Canadian figures of that time. He wanted two or three years of leisure to write this book; and friends of his conspired with the powers that be to get him a position in the civil service where his duties would be nominal, thus giving him his chance. But the sturdy spirit of the veteran rejected the offer of a sinecure. He would not consider it. Thus the book never got itself written.

What was thereby lost is suggested by an article which he wrote for the *Transcript* in February, 1919, following the death of Sir Wilfrid Laurier. In this he drew upon his recollections and quoting also from private memoranda compiled years before prepared what has been justly described as an 'historic document of great importance.' This was made up largely of a remarkable talk between Laurier and Thomson in 1903 about the duties of political leaders, the relations between Canada and the Empire, the future of Canada.[22]

Turning to Thomson's reputation for what he *did* write, we are told that: 'He was long acknowledged and aclaimed as undisputably the leading Canadian short story writer.'[23] The *Literary History of Canada* identifies him as 'one of the most skilful storytellers of the Canadian writers of his day...' In his review of *Old Man Savarin* for Goldwin Smith's *The Week* (9 Aug. 1895), Archibald Lampman praises the freshness and simplicity of Thomson's style: 'Mr Thomson is not one of those writers who depend for the success of their pieces upon a studied deftness in the use of language or the piling up of artificial phraseology. His mode of expressing himself is very simple — often extraordinarily simple, but it is the kindly offspring of genuine conception, and direct spontaneous feeling, and sometimes in his easy way he will give forth a stroke of imagery containing a world of meaning in a single phrase, often something particularly apt to the Canadian ear...' Desmond Pacey, though critical of Thomson's flawed craftsmanship, notes that 'his work stands out from that of his

Canadian contemporaries in the late nineteenth century by virtue of the realistic observation which it incorporates.'[24] Thomson thus emerges as a transitional figure between the nineteenth-century historical romances, and the realistic trends of the twentieth century, while keeping alive the humorous strain in Canadian fiction between its initiation by Haliburton and its revival by Leacock.

The entry on Thomson in Morgan's *Canadian Men and Women of the Time* (1898) reports that: 'He has been called the best literary critic Canada has ever possessed.' This statement derives from a letter to Morgan from Thomas Stinson Jarvis, a Canadian lawyer and novelist.[25] Jarvis's reasons for thinking so highly of Thomson's critical powers may relate, at least in part, to a long and commendatory letter concerning Jarvis's novel *Geoffrey Hampstead*, written by Thomson for the *Globe* of 23 September 1890, perhaps as part of his policy of encouraging younger writers. Here, as in his tribute to Lampman twenty-five years later, Thomson insists that rigorous standards of international taste must be applied to Canadian literature, arguing that an indulgent attitude to all things Canadian disparages the best of our writers.

Old Man Savarin Stories: Tales of Canada and Canadians (1917) resembles *Old Man Savarin and Other Stories* (1895) in that it reprints twelve of the fourteen stories in the earlier volume, with the addition of a nostalgic poem, 'The Canadian Abroad,' and five tales: 'Dour Davie's Drive,' 'Petherick's Peril,' 'The Swartz Diamond,' 'Boss of the World,' and 'Miss Minnely's Management.'

xxi

The change in title points to Thomson's increasing awareness of his role as interpreter of Canadians and Americans to each other. As he explained in *Canadian Sentiment for Canada, The Republic, and Great Britain* (1905), Thomson considered himself from youth a citizen of both countries: 'The Canadian has sometimes been called "a man without a country" and sometimes the man with more country than he can manage. It would be more correct to define him as the man of three countries, his motherland, his brotherland, and his own land, but always the man of Canada first.'[26] The need for such 'interpretation' was the greater during this period of Canadian fear and distrust of American institutions.

A further clue to the intent of Thomson's stories is supplied by a half-title in the 1895 collection, 'Off-Hand Stories,' which reflects both their casual style and the sense they convey of being *told*, rather than *written*. Thomson employs the device of an old narrator telling his tale to a young listener in 'The Privilege of the Limits,' 'Old Man Savarin,' 'Great Godfrey's Lament,' 'Petherick's Peril,' and 'The Swartz Diamond,' while first person narrators appear in 'The Waterloo Veteran,' 'The Ride by Night,' 'A Turkey Apiece,' and 'Boss of the World.' Only eight of the seventeen stories employ omniscient narration.

The sense of immediacy thus established is complemented by the stories' emphasis on vigorous action, and their retrospective focus. Like the poems of his contemporary, W.H. Drummond, Thomson's tales convey an impression of the author as a vital man of action, deeply familiar with the land and the work he depicts. With the same affectionate familiarity, the Canadian stories interpret and preserve the speech and character of certain local 'types' encountered in the author's earlier life: the Glengarry Scot, the lumberman, river-driver, and *habitant* of the

Ottawa Valley. M.O. Hammond has pointed out Thomson's preference for characters of strong individuality, humour, honesty, and above all, obstinacy: 'Thomson possessed it in large measure himself, and apparently admired it in others.'[27] Stubbornness certainly proves to be a dominant force in 'Privilege of the Limits,' 'John Bedell,' 'Old Man Savarin,' 'McGrath's Bad Night,' and 'Dour Davie's Drive.' Though many of Thomson's characters are comically portrayed, in his use of dialect, as in Drummond's, the intent is not to burlesque, but to record. Both writers helped to meet the contemporary demand for local colour stories and sketches of French-Canadian life, which rivalled the historical romance in popularity.[28]

Thomson's tales are also linked with the tradition of the *raconteur* by their predominantly reminiscent focus. With the exception of his commentary on contemporary governments in 'Boss of the World,' the stories dwell on past experiences, while Thomson's journalism, letters, and poems relate to his later observation of public affairs. In selecting historical areas, moreover, Thomson leans toward the crises of war — the aftermath of the American Revolutionary War, the Civil War, the Boer War, — rather than the events of peace: a choice dictated in part by his own experience, and by the young audience for which many of the tales were written.

The opening story, 'Privilege of the Limits,' deals with the collision between a traditional and a modern system of justice. The unwritten law of the Glengarry Scottish community is founded upon the 'Hielan' word of honor.' Dougal Stewart forfeits the settlement's sympathy by taking his complaint to the courts, for his neighbours make a sharp distinction between 'law play' and 'justice.' There is pride, obstinacy, and some sharp dealing between Stewart and McTavish, but the community is so wholly in sympathy with the latter that when he escapes without violating the letter of the law, it rallies to prevent the constables from recapturing him. The second court hearing puts the law in a different light: justice is joined with humour, as the judge calls McTavish 'a Hielan' gentleman with a very nice sense of honor.' Ultimately, it is through a legal technicality that he is freed, gleeful at having cost Stewart more in keep than in debt.

'The Waterloo Veteran,' set in a small UEL settlement beside Lake Erie, traces Canadian involvement in the wars of the Empire, from the declaration of war in the Crimea to the Sepoy Mutiny. The fierce pride of the old soldier, John Locke, so dignifies his trade of fishmonger that he marches at the head of the victory parade, 'rejoicing at the fresh glory of the race and the union of English-speaking men unconsciously celebrated and symbolized by the little rustic parade.' The nature and importance of UEL sentiment is elucidated in 'John Bedell, UE Loyalist,' which also demonstrates that Canadians 'inherited, not the benefits, but the bitterness of the Revolution.'[29] The Niagara River, which exerts such fascination on the passionate Bedell, is almost a character in the story: the stage upon which 'true love' wins out, it also leads Bedell to the revelation which precedes his death: 'now that the deed to be done was as clear before him as the face of the Almighty God. In accepting it the darker passions that had swayed his stormy life fell suddenly away from their hold on his soul ... how poor seemed hate! how mean and poor seemed all but Love and Loyalty!' Both stories put forward the ideals of military heroism, self-sacrifice, and devotion to 'England, Queen, and Duty.'

In 'Old Man Savarin,' as in Drummond's 'Da Stove-Pipe Hole,' a crotchety old man is bested by being placed in an awkward physical predicament, from which only his young adversary can release him. Once again, the law is presented as a tool for the rich and cunning, which overthrows tradition and established right; but, as in 'Privilege of the Limits,' the combination of poetic justice and a sense of humour triumphs. The story presents French Canadians as a rather sensible group, for as Mme Paradis explains, '*Canadien* hain't nev' fool 'nuff for fight, M'sieu, only if dey is got drunk' – and hence the epic battle without a blow. Here and in other stories, Thomson's sympathetic treatment of French-Canadian characters demonstrates his remoteness from certain attitudes of the *Globe*, which, under George Brown, frequently became an organ of anti-French-Canadian sentiment.

'Great Godfrey's Lament' is a strange story of mixed race, recounted by the last of the McNeils. The ruined stone house, built seemingly for giants by the patriarch Hector McNeil, recalls the tumbledown mansion which inspired F.P. Grove's *Fruits of the Earth*. Angus manifests a curious reverence for Godfrey, the only white son of seven, and a contempt for his Indian heritage: 'The rest of us were all just Indians – ay, Indians, Aleck McTavish. Brown we were, and the desire of us was all for the woods and the river. Godfrey had white sense like my father, and often we saw the same look in his eyes. My God, but we feared our father!' The brothers finally attempt to share their dual heritage, but as the empty house testifies, the family's real heritage is death.

In 'McGrath's Bad Night,' the father of a family so large the children are numbered rather than named brings his children to the verge of starvation through his stubborn violation of 'the immutable law of supply and demand.' John Pontiac, the polar opposite to 'Old Man Savarin,' generously relieves the family's desperate situation with food and a new job – 'a story which in an American or English magazine, or one of ours now would seem completely and viciously sentimental, and which was simply a true vision of pioneer virtue and that neighbourliness necessary in a new country.'[30]

'Shining Cross of Rigaud' is another tale of poverty, this time in a French-Canadian setting, but without the optimism of the previous story. Mini, the saintly child of a huge family, tries with pathetic futility to save his tiny sister from the neglect of his cruel mother. Through Angélique's death, she is released from suffering, and Mini experiences a vision of 'mysterious happiness,' from which he awakens to familiar squalour. This painful awakening is repeated when the child climbs Rigaud Mountain in quest of 'the vision and the radiant space about the shining cross.' The dreadful disillusionment of the real cross contrasts both with Mini's vision of it and with the pastoral scene and the pious people it overlooks. For Mini, as for Daniel in Gabrielle Roy's *The Tin Flute*, death is the only escape from his situation.

'Dour Davie's Drive' returns to the Glengarry setting, and demonstrates once again the cohesiveness of the Scottish settlement, as it responds to Pinnager's 'make or break' situation. Through Davie, the story emphasizes physical courage and endurance, combined with obstinacy, in contrast to the cowardice of Narcisse Larocque, a French Canadian contemptuously dismissed as a non-'white.' (This represents Thomson's closest approach to the kind of French-Canadian portrayal which one finds, for example, in Ralph Connor's *The Man from Glengarry*.)

'Petherick's Peril' employs the narrative device of an old man storyteller talking to a callow young man, whom he accosts with Ancient Mariner-like urgency. Petherick's tale skilfully provokes a concrete realization of the physical sensations of terror and relief, while pointing to the sustaining effect of faith in Providence. Frazer's reaction to the story is to internalize Petherick's experience so thoroughly that he has nightmares about it. Through the old man's words, he has been forced to confront his own mortality.

'Little Baptiste' deals with a poor French-Canadian family's attitudes to Providence, while waiting for the father to return with his winter's wages. Their credit cut off by the English storekeeper, 'the vampire of the little hamlet,' mild conflict arises between the generations: the grandmother's total faith in Providence contradicts the anxiety of Baptiste and his mother, as the old lady insists: 'The young people think too much, for sure. Trust in the good God, I say.' While Baptiste, like Huckleberry Finn, relies on the river for fish and salvage to keep the family going, he is troubled by inner conflict. Externally, his saintliness intimidates his mother; internally, 'Often the simplicity and sentimentality of his mother and grandmother gave him strange pangs at heart; they seemed to be the children, while he felt very old.' The windfall of lumber salvage which brings them cash confirms the grandmother's wisdom, and restores Little Baptiste's shaken faith in Providence.

'Red-Headed Windego' draws a comic opposition between the common sense, 'scientific' attitude of the young English-Canadian surveyor and the superstitious gullibility of his French-Canadian team. Blazing a line through uncharted lumber country, the group encounters the trail of a 'Windego,' derived from Algonquin words meaning 'evil spirit' or 'cannibal': 'The concept denoted by *Weetigo* and *Wendigo* varies from a personified Evil Spirit to a supernatural creature of which there are many, all having fearful characteristics including an insatiable appetite for human beings.'[31] In spite of their terror, Tom's bold pursuit of the 'monster' shames his men into following: 'Though the sun was sinking in clear blue, the aspect of the wilderness, gray and white and severe, touched the impressionable men with deeper melancholy. They felt lonely, masterless, mean.' Needless to say, the 'scientific explanation' triumphs over the terrors of the wilderness.

The three Civil War stories which follow leave little doubt about Thomson's sympathy for the North — an attitude which, contemporary scholarship tells us, was far from universal in Canada:

> As has often been remarked, Canadians were deeply divided in their attitudes toward the contestants in the Civil War, and careful study of this division of opinion has disclosed little pattern to it. There was nothing so simple as a liberal identification with the North, or a conservative sympathy for the South. Instead, both liberals and conservatives were at odds within themselves in a most bewildering and complex way. Moreover, opinion shifted quite radically at different stages of the war. ... It is much more accurate to speak of 'anti-Southern' or 'anti-Northern' feelings. What gave Canadian opinion this peculiar twist was, in part at least, the underlying lack of sympathy for American institutions, South or North, that was by this time firmly established as part of the Canadian political culture.[32]

In 'The Ride by Night,' an unidentified narrator recounts the words of Adam Baines, who was, like Thomson, 'one of the fifty-three thousand Canadians who served Abraham Lincoln's cause in the Civil War. Indeed, he was in the army less than a year.' The meaning of the heroic ride in which the boy took part in March 1865 remains obscure to him: 'To this day I do not know where we went, nor precisely what for. Soldiers are seldom informed of the meaning of their movements.' That rumours of Lee's surrender are flying as Baines recovers in hospital, however, hints at the possibly decisive role of his message.

By contrast, 'Drafted' views the mud and blood of battle through the homesick eyes of a young volunteer who, like the men of St-Henri in *The Tin Flute*, has enlisted in order to relieve his family's poverty. Through Harry, the oppressive noise, rain, and mud of cavalry life are concretely rendered: 'He was sustained by no mature sense that this too would pass; it was with a certain bodily despair that he felt chafed and compressed by his rough garments, and pitied himself.' Harry's persistent vision of both sides as 'American' and yearning for peace is expressed in the tragedy of his lost brother Jack: 'Both sides — I was on both sides all the time. I loved them all, North and South, all — but the Union most. O God, it was so hard!'

'A Turkey Apiece,' the rather touching tale of a company's selfless satisfaction in allowing a dying boy to maintain his dream, also takes place in the rain and mud near Fort Hell, Virginia. That the narrator is reminded of his youthful experience by a headline in the files of New York newspapers for 1864 suggests a possible origin for the story.

The narrator of 'The Swartz Diamond,' like the surveyor in 'Red-Headed Windego,' is the sole English Canadian in a French-Canadian company engaged on the side of Empire in the Boer War. The company is commanded by Lieutenant Deschamps, who is 'a gentleman. Because I was of another race he always treated me with more than the consideration due to a good non-com. Or possibly it was because he knew I had been advocate in Montreal before joining the mounted Canadian contingent.' Sergeant McTavish's sense of separateness is underlined during the old

Boer's description of the Kaffirs' attack: ' "But no hunger could have driven them against a Boer laager. They mistook the wagons for the wagons of Englishmen." The French Canadians smiled unoffended, but my jaws snapped.'

The company of Canadians is struck by the resemblance between the South African veldt and the landscape of home — 'late June's high moon seemed pouring down a Canadian wintriness' — but their encounter with Swartz teaches them that the signs (vultures) and skills (burning dry dung) of the land must be learned.

Arthur Lower speaks of 'the intoxication of loyalty to Great Britain with which English Canada responded to the Boer War.'[33] That Thomson's response was less — or more — than intoxicated is suggested by his portrayal of the Boers' superior knowledge of their land, and their superior sagacity, as Swartz distracts his captors' attention with the fascinating 'tale within the tale,' which presents his cousin Vassell in a sharply satiric light, while his men surround them: 'And again we, whose senses were trained but to the narrow spaces between Canadian woodlands, heard nothing but a sudden louder tumult of gathered horses, the hoofs of the vedettes, and the tinkle of the spruit.'

'Boss of the World,' in its humorous treatment of the dilemma confronting the inventor of the Ultimate Weapon, appears to reflect a slightly ambivalent attitude to science on Thomson's part. The narrator is accosted on a Boston streetcorner in May 1915 by a fellow-Canadian: 'About one-tenth of the people of Boston are British Canadians, mostly from the Maritime Provinces, an acquisitive prudent folk who see naught to be gained by correcting casual acquaintances who mistake them for down-east Yankees.' Adam Bemis confides in his fellow-expatriate the comic agony of decision he is suffering — which provides Thomson the occasion for many sly digs at contemporary governments. Bemis has reservations about both England and Ireland, for what would prevent them from using the Odistor against each other? Though his first impulse was to entrust his weapon to Washington, on condition that it 'leave Canada alone,' he is reluctant to do so 'while the pro-German microbe is active' there. Bemis would prefer to sell his invention to Canada, if Laurier were still in power: 'But he's got no government, now. Ontario folks beat him last election, for being too reasonable' — presumably a reference to the election of 1911. Entangled by the obstacles to achieving 'a World Power animated by liberalism and dominated by conscience,' Adam can only resign himself to the contemplation of his unrealized potential 'Bossdom.'

In 'Miss Minnely's Management' it seems clear that some resemblance is intended between George Renwick, the cynical revising editor of *The Family Blessing*, and Edward W. Thomson of the *Youth's Companion*. In an obvious parallel to Thomson's resignation from the *Globe*, Renwick 'threw up his political editorship of "The Daily Reflex" in disgust at its General Manager's sudden reversal of policy.' Feeling himself reduced to a 'life of intellectual shame' amid the oppressive wholesomeness and 'cordiality' of the *Blessing*, George sardonically applies his touchstones of taste: 'Will it please Mothers?' 'Lady schoolteachers?' 'Ministers of the Gospel?'

The title's ironic meaning is manifested when George is disillusioned of his disillusionment. Renwick's cynicism is shaken by his first encounter with Miss Minnely: 'he had thought of its famous Editress and Sole Proprietress as one "working a graft" on the Plain People by consummate sense of the commercial value of

cordial cant. Now he had to conceive of her as perfectly ingenuous.' Even after Renwick's 'conversion,' however, he harbours
lingering doubts: 'Might it not be they had managed him with an
irony as profound as the ingenuousness they had appeared to
evince?'

There is a subtle ambiguity of tone in 'Miss Minnely's Management,' for while Miss Minnely herself is portrayed with shades of
irony, yet neither is Thomson's attitude to Renwick wholly
approving: reference is made to the young man's 'too sophisticated heart,' and Thomson would hardly have approved such contempt for 'gobemouches.' In fact, we may discern a greater com-
plexity of tone in common among the last three stories of the
collection — all of which date from after Thomson's return to
Canada in 1901.

'The short story has shared in the disadvantage of other types of
literature and of culture as a whole in Canada,' Raymond Knister
observes in the preface to his 1928 anthology. 'It emerged, as the
short story in the United States did, in a spirited emulation at
best, or a shallow imitativeness at worst, of foreign models. This
was natural in the case, unless we had managed without a literature for a few hundred years until we evolved a national consciousness of our own.' To this we may add the words of one who
knew our author in his Ottawa days: 'Most of Thomson's pre-
decessors were provincial in outlook, or still strongly influenced
by the European life they had left behind. He was a man of the
New World...'[34] — and he set the imprint of his mind, restless and
temperamental, warm and unconventional, upon the development
of the short story in Canada.

NOTES

1 Gordon Roper, 'New Forces: New Fiction, 1880-1920,' *Literary History of Canada: Canadian Literature in English*, gen. ed. Carl F. Klinck (Toronto 1965) 262, 268
2 M.O. Hammond, 'Edward William Thomson,' *Queen's Quarterly* XXXVIII (Jan. 1931) 126
3 H.J. Morgan, ed., *The Canadian Men and Women of the Time* rev. ed. (Toronto 1912) 1099
4 J.G. Wales, 'An Experience Rich in Color and Character of Carillon — Pointe Fortune Neighbourhood,' *Lachute Watchman* (24 Jan. 1957). Quoted in A.S. Bourinot, ed., *Letters of Edward William Thomson to Archibald Lampman* (Ottawa 1957) 29
5 Hammond, 127
6 J.W. Dafoe, 'E.W. Thomson: Canadian Journalist and Poet,' *Manitoba Free Press* (7 Apr. 1924) 7, col. 1
7 Quoted in R.C. Brown, 'Canadian Opinion After Confederation, 1867-1914,' *Canada Views the United States*, ed. S.F. Wise and R.C. Brown (Toronto 1972) 109
8 Copy of letter in the Archives, University Library, University of New Brunswick
9 A.S. Bourinot, ed., *Edward William Thomson (1849-1924): A Bibliography with Notes and some Letters* (Ottawa 1955) 2
10 A.S. Bourinot, ed., *The Letters of Edward William Thomson to Archibald Lampman (1891-1897)* (Ottawa 1957) 7. For a vivid account of Victoria Day celebrations in a small Ontario town of this time, see the opening chapters of Sara Jeannette Duncan's *The Imperialist* (1904)
11 Hammond, 128
12 Bourinot, *Letters* 30
13 Bourinot, *Bibliography* 3
14 Bourinot, *Letters* 43
15 Ibid., 19-20
16 Bourinot, *Bibliography* 23
17 Dumas Malone, ed., *Dictionary of American Biography* XVIII (New York 1936) 483

18 Hammond, 124
19 W.E. MacLellan, 'E.W. Thomson,' *Dalhousie Review* II, 3 (Oct. 1922) 374
20 J.A. Stevenson, quoted in Bourinot, *Bibliography* 2-3
21 T.G. Marquis, *English-Canadian Literature* (Toronto 1913) 562. Reprinted in the Literature of Canada series 1973
22 Dafoe, 'E.W. Thomson: Canadian Journalist and Poet,' 7, col. 1-3
23 MacLellan, 374
24 Desmond Pacey, ed., *A Book of Canadian Stories* (Toronto 1947) xxi
25 10 Mar. 1895. Items 4420-3, National Archives of Canada, papers of Henry J. Morgan
26 Bourinot, *Bibliography* 17
27 Hammond, 132
28 Gordon Roper et al., 'The Kinds of Fiction, 1880-1920,' *Literary History of Canada* (Toronto 1965) 288
29 A.R.M. Lower, *Canadians in the Making: A Social History of Canada* (Toronto 1958) 135
30 Raymond Knister, ed., *Canadian Short Stories* (Toronto 1928) xix
31 W.S. Avis, ed., 'Weetigo,' *A Dictionary of Canadianisms on Historical Principles* (Toronto 1967) 841
32 S.F. Wise, 'The Annexation Movement and its Effect on Canadian Opinion, 1837-1867,' *Canada Views the United States* 82-3
33 Lower, 348
34 Hammond, 123

Select Bibliography

WORKS

Old Man Savarin and Other Stories Toronto: Briggs 1895, 289p

Smoky Days New York: Crowell 1896, 108p

Walter Gibbs, the Young Boss and other Stories Toronto: Briggs 1896, 361p

Between Earth and Sky and Other Strange Stories of Deliverance Toronto: Briggs 1897, 297p

Old Man Savarin Stories: Tales of Canada and Canadians Toronto: Gundy 1917, 344p

This of Aucassin and Nicolette (verse translation) Boston: Copeland 1896, 78p

Peter Ottawa Toronto: [n.p.] 1905, 16p

The Many Mansioned House and Other Poems Toronto: Briggs, 1909, 151p

When Lincoln Died and Other Poems Boston: Houghton 1909, 146p

Canadian Sentiment for Canada, The Republic, and Great Britain (address to Intercolonial Club, Boston) Boston: E. Dunn 1905, 31p

'Sane Imperialism' (editorial), *Montreal Daily Star* (14 Oct. 1924), 10

CRITICISM

Bourinot, Arthur Stanley, ed. *Edward William Thomson (1849-1924): A Bibliography with Notes and Some Letters* Ottawa: Bourinot 1955, 28p

Bourinot, Arthur Stanley, ed. *The Letters of Edward William Thomson to Archibald Lampman (1891-1897), with Notes, a Bibliography, and Other Material on Thomson and Lampman* Ottawa: Bourinot 1957, 49p

Dafoe, John W. 'E.W. Thomson: Canadian Journlist and Poet,' *Manitoba Free Press* (7 Apr. 1924), 7. Mainly reprinted in Bourinot, *Letters* 1-2, 26-8

Hammond, M.O. 'Edward William Thomson,' *Queen's Quarterly* XXXVIII (Jan. 1931) 123-39

Klinck, Carl F., gen. ed. *Literary History of Canada: Canadian Literature in English.* Toronto: University of Toronto Press 1965

MacLellan, W.E. 'E.W. Thomson,' *Dalhousie Review* II, 3 (Oct. 1922) 334, 374-5

Pacey, Desmond *Creative Writing in Canada* Toronto: Ryerson 1952

Old Man Savarin Stories

Tales of Canada and Canadians

Edward William Thomson

To

Sir A.T. Quiller-Couch

who
'gave me the good word'
in season

'I've a friend over the sea'

CONTENTS

THE CANADIAN ABROAD

When the croon of a rapid is heard on the
      breeze,
  With the scent of a pine-forest gloom,
Or the edge of the sky is of steeple-top trees,
  Set in hazes of blueberry bloom,
Or a song-sparrow sudden from quietness trills
  His delicate anthem to me,
Then my heart hurries home to the Ottawa
      hills,
  Wherever I happen to be.

When the veils of a shining lake vista unfold,
  Or the mist towers dim from a fall,
Or a woodland is blazing in crimson and gold,
  Or a snow-shroud is covering all,
Or there's honking of geese in the darkening
      sky,
  When the spring sets hepatica free,
Then my heart's winging north as they never
      can fly,
  Wherever I happen to be.

When the swallows slant curves of bewildering
      joy
  As the cool of the twilight descends,
And rosy-cheek maiden and hazel-hue boy
  Listen grave while the Angelus ends
In a tremulous flow from the bell of a shrine,
  Then a faraway mountain I see,
And my soul is in Canada's evening shine,
  Wherever my body may be.

PRIVILEGE OF THE LIMITS

"Yes, indeed, my grandfather wass once in jail," said old Mrs. McTavish, of the county of Glengarry, in Ontario, Canada; "but that wass for debt, and he wass a ferry honest man whateffer, and he would not broke his promise —no, not for all the money in Canada. If you will listen to me, I will tell chust exactly the true story about that debt, to show you what an honest man my grandfather wass.

"One time Tougal Stewart, him that wass the poy's grandfather that keeps the same store in Cornwall to this day, sold a plough to my grandfather, and my grandfather said he would pay half the plough in October, and the other half whateffer time he felt able to pay the money. Yes, indeed, that was the very promise my grandfather gave.

"So he was at Tougal Stewart's store on the first of October early in the morning pefore the shutters wass taken off, and he paid half chust exactly to keep his word. Then the crop wass

15

ferry pad next year, and the year after that
one of his horses wass killed py lightning, and
the next year his brother, that wass not rich
and had a big family, died, and do you think
wass my grandfather to let the family be disgraced without a good funeral?   No, indeed.
So my grandfather paid for the funeral, and
there was at it plenty of meat and drink for
eferypody, as wass the right Hielan' custom
those days; and after the funeral my grandfather did not feel chust exactly able to pay
the other half for the plough that year either.

"So, then, Tougal Stewart met my grandfather in Cornwall next day after the funeral,
and asked him if he had some money to spare.

" 'Wass you in need of help, Mr. Stewart?'
says my grandfather, kindly.   'For if it's in
any want you are, Tougal,' says my grandfather, 'I will sell the coat off my back, if there
is no other way to lend you a loan'; for that
wass always the way of my grandfather with
all his friends, and a bigger-hearted man there
never wass in all Glengarry, or in Stormont,
or in Dundas, moreofer.

" 'In want!' says Tougal—'in want, Mr.
McTavish!' says he, very high.   'Would you
wish to insult a gentleman, and him of the

name of Stewart, that's the name of princes
of the world?' he said, so he did.

"Seeing Tougal had his temper up, my
grandfather spoke softly, being a quiet, peace-
able man, and in wonder what he had said to
offend Tougal.

" 'Mr. Stewart,' says my grandfather, 'it
wass not in my mind to anger you whatefer.
Only I thought, from your asking me if I
had some money, that you might be looking
for a wee bit of a loan, as many a gentleman
has to do at times, and no shame to him at
all,' said my grandfather.

" 'A loan?' says Tougal, sneering. 'A loan,
is it? Where's your memory, Mr. McTavish?
Are you not owing me half the price of the
plough you've had these three years?'

" 'And wass you asking me for money for
the other half of the plough?' says my grandfather, very astonished.

" 'Just that,' says Tougal.

" 'Have you no shame or honor in you?'
says my grandfather, firing up. 'How could I
feel able to pay that now, and me chust yesterday been giving my poor brother a funeral fit
for the McTavishes' own grand-nephew, that
wass as good chentleman's plood as any

Stewart in Glengarry. You saw the expense
I wass at, for there you wass, and I thank you
for the politeness of coming, Mr. Stewart,'
says my grandfather, ending mild, for the
anger would never stay in him more than a
minute, so kind was the nature he had.

" 'If you can spend money on a funeral like
that, you can pay me for my plough,' says
Stewart; for with buying and selling he wass
become a poor creature, and the heart of a
Hielan'man wass half gone out of him, for all
he wass so proud of his name of monarchs and
kings.

"My grandfather had a mind to strike him
down on the spot, so he often said; but he
thought of the time when he hit Hamish
Cochrane in anger, and he minded the pen-
ances the priest put on him for breaking the
silly man's jaw with that blow, so he smothered
the heat that wass in him, and turned away
in scorn. With that Tougal Stewart went to
court, and sued my grandfather, puir mean
creature.

"You might think that Judge Jones—him
that wass judge in Cornwall before Judge
Jarvis that's dead—would do justice. But no,
he made it the law that my grandfather must

pay at once, though Tougal Stewart could not
deny what the bargain wass.

" 'Your Honor,' says my grandfather, 'I
said I'd pay when I felt able. And do I feel
able now? No, I do not,' says he. It's a dis-
grace to Tougal Stewart to ask me, and himself telling you what the bargain wass,' said
my grandfather. But Judge Jones said that
he must pay, for all that he did not feel able.

" 'I will nefer pay one copper till I feel
able,' says my grandfather; 'but I'll keep my
Hielan' promise to my dying day, as I always
done,' says he.

"And with that the old judge laughed, and
said he would have to give judgment. And so
he did; and after that Tougal Stewart got out
an execution. But not the worth of a handful
of oatmeal could the bailiff lay hands on, because my grandfather had chust exactly taken
the precaution to give a bill of sale on his gear
to his neighbor, Alexander Frazer, that could
be trusted to do what was right after the law
play was over.

"The whole settlement had great contempt
for Tougal Stewart's conduct; but he wass a
headstrong body, and once he begun to do
wrong against my grandfather, he held on, for

all that his trade fell away; and finally he had my grandfather arrested for debt, though you'll understand, sir, that he was owing Stewart nothing that he ought to pay when he didn't feel able.

"In those times prisoners for debt wass taken to jail in Cornwall, and if they had friends to give bail that they would not go beyond the posts that wass around the sixteen acres nearest the jail walls, the prisoners could go where they liked on that ground. This was called 'the privilege of the limits.' The limits, you'll understand, wass marked by cedar posts painted white about the size of hitching-posts.

"The whole settlement wass ready to go bail for my grandfather if he wanted it, and for the health of him he needed to be in the open air, and so he gave Tuncan Macdonnell of the Greenfields, and Æneas Macdonald of the Sandfields, for his bail, and he promised, on his Hielan' word of honor, not to go beyond the posts. With that he went where he pleased, only taking care that he never put even the toe of his foot beyond a post, for all that some prisoners of the limits would chump ofer them and back again, or maybe swing round them, holding by their hands.

"Efery day the neighbors would go into Cornwall to give my grandfather the good word, and they would offer to pay Tougal Stewart for the other half of the plough, only that vexed my grandfather, for he wass too proud to borrow, and, of course, every day he felt less and less able to pay on account of him having to hire a man to be doing the spring plóughing and seeding and making the kale-yard.

"All this time, you'll mind, Tougal Stewart had to pay five shillings a week fòr my grandfather's keep, the law being so that if the debtor swore he had not five pounds' worth of property to his name, then the creditor had to pay the five shillings, and, of course, my grandfather had nothing to his name after he gave the bill of sale to Alexander Frazer. A great diversion it was to my grandfather to be reckoning up that if he lived as long as his father, that was hale and strong at ninety-six, Tougal would need to pay five or six hundred pounds for him, and there was only two pound five shillings to be paid on the plough.

"So it was like that all summer, my grandfather keeping heartsome, with the neighbors coming in so steady to bring him the news of

the settlement. There he would sit, just inside
one of the posts, for to pass his jokes, and tell
what he wished the family to be doing next.
This way it might have kept going on for
forty years, only it came about that my grandfather's youngest child—him that was my
father—fell sick, and seemed like to die.

"Well, when my grandfather heard that bad
news, he wass in a terrible way, to be sure, for
he would be longing to hold the child in his
arms, so that his heart was sore and like to
break. Eat he could not, sleep he could not:
all night he would be groaning, and all day he
would be walking around by the posts, wishing
that he had not passed his Hielan' word of
honor not to go beyond a post; for he thought
how he could have broken out like a chentleman, and gone to see his sick child, if he had
stayed inside the jail wall. So it went on three
days and three nights pefore the wise thought
came into my grandfather's head to show him
how he need not go beyond the posts to see his
little sick poy. With that he went straight to
one of the white cedar posts, and pulled it up
out of the hole, and started for home, taking
great care to carry it in his hands pefore him,
so he would not be beyond it one bit.

"My grandfather wass not half a mile out of Cornwall, which was only a little place in those days, when two of the turnkeys came after him.

" 'Stop, Mr. McTavish,' says the turnkeys.

" 'What for would I stop?' says my grandfather.

" 'You have broke your bail,' says they.

" 'It's a lie for you,' says my grandfather, for his temper flared up for anybody to say he would broke his bail. 'Am I beyond the post?' says my grandfather.

"With that they run in on him, only that he knocked the two of them over with the post, and went on rejoicing, like an honest man should, at keeping his word and overcoming them that would slander his good name. The only thing pesides thoughts of the child that troubled him was questioning whether he had been strictly right in turning round for to use the post to defend himself in such a way that it was nearer the jail than what he wass. But when he remembered how the jailer never complained of prisoners of the limits chumping ofer the posts, if so they chumped back again in a moment, the trouble went out of his mind.

"Pretty soon after that he met Tuncan

Macdonnell of Greenfields, coming into Cornwall with the wagon.

" 'And how is this, Glengatchie?' says Tuncan. 'For you were never the man to broke
your bail.'

"Glengatchie, you'll understand, sir, is the
name of my grandfather's farm.

" 'Never fear, Greenfields,' says my grandfather, 'for I'm not beyond the post.'

"So Greenfields looked at the post, and he
looked at my grandfather, and he scratched his
head a wee, and he seen it was so; and then
he fell into a great admiration entirely.

" 'Get in with me, Glengatchie—it's proud
I'll be to carry you home'; and he turned his
team around. My grandfather did so, taking
great care to keep the post in front of him all
the time; and that way he reached home. Out
comes my grandmother running to embrace
him; but she had to throw her arms around
the post and my grandfather's neck at the same
time, he was that strict to be within his promise.
Pefore going ben the house, he went to the
back end of the kale-yard which was farthest
from the jail, and there he stuck the post; and
then he went back to see his sick child, while
all the neighbors that came round was glad to

see what a wise thought the saints had put into
his mind to save his bail and his promise.

"So there he stayed a week till my father got
well. Of course the constables came after my
grandfather, but the settlement would not let
the creatures come within a mile of Glengatchie. You might think, sir, that my grandfather would have stayed with his wife and
weans, seeing the post was all the time in the
kale-yard, and him careful not to go beyond
it; but he was putting the settlement to a great
deal of trouble day and night to keep the constables off, and he was fearful that they might
take the post away, if ever they got to Glengatchie, and give him the name of false, that
no McTavish ever had. So Tuncan Greenfields and Æneas Sandfield drove my grandfather back to the jail, him with the post behind
him in the wagon, so as he would be between
it and the jail. Of course Tougal Stewart
tried his best to have the bail declared for-
feited; but old Judge Jones only laughed, and
said my grandfather was a Hielan' gentleman,
with a very nice sense of honor, and that was
chust exactly the truth.

"How did my grandfather get free in the
end? Oh, then, that was because of Tougal

Stewart being careless—him that thought he
knew so much of the law. The law was, you
will mind, that Tougal had to pay five shillings
a week for keeping my grandfather in the
limits. The money wass to be paid efery
Monday, and it wass to be paid in lawful
money of Canada, too. Well, would you belief
that Tougal paid in four shillings in silver one
Monday, and one shilling in coppers, for he
took up the collection in church the day pefore,
and it wass not till Tougal had gone away that
the jailer saw that one of the coppers was a
Brock copper,—a medal, you will understand,
made at General Brock's death, and not lawful
money of Canada at all. With that the jailer
came out to my grandfather.

" 'Mr. McTavish,' says he, taking off his hat,
'you are a free man, and I'm glad of it.' Then
he told him what Tougal had done.

" 'I hope you will not have any hard feelings
toward me, Mr. McTavish,' said the jailer;
and a decent man he wass, for all that there
wass not a drop of Hielan' blood in him. 'I
hope you will not think hard of me for not
being hospitable to you, sir,' says he; 'but it's
against the rules and regulations for the jailer
to be offering the best he can command to the

prisoners. Now that you are free, Mr. Mc-Tavish,' says the jailer, 'I would be a proud man if Mr. McTavish of Glengatchie would do me the honor of taking supper with me this night. I will be asking your leave to invite some of the gentlemen of the place, if you will say the word, Mr. McTavish,' says he.

"Well, my grandfather could never bear malice, the kind man he was, and he seen how bad the jailer felt, so he consented, and a great company came in, to be sure, to celebrate the occasion.

"Did my grandfather pay the balance on the plough? What for should you suspicion, sir, that my grandfather would refuse his honest debt? Of course he paid for the plough, for the crop was good that fall.

" 'I would be paying you the other half of the plough now, Mr. Stewart,' says my grandfather, coming in when the store was full.

" 'Hoich, but you are the honest McTavish!' says Tougal, sneering.

"But my grandfather made no answer to the creature, for he thought it would be unkind to mention how Tougal had paid out six pounds four shillings and eleven pence to keep him in on account of a debt of two pound five that never was due till it was paid."

THE WATERLOO VETERAN

Is Waterloo a dead word to you? the name
of a plain of battle, no more? Or do you
see, on a space of rising ground, the little long-
coated man with marble features, and un-
quenchable eyes that pierce through rolling
smoke to where the relics of the old Guard
of France stagger and rally and reach fiercely
again up the hill of St. Jean toward the
squares, set, torn, red, re-formed, stubborn,
mangled, victorious beneath the unflinching
will of him behind there,—the Iron Duke of
England?

Or is your interest in the fight literary? and
do you see in a pause of the conflict Major
O'Dowd sitting on the carcass of Pyramus
refreshing himself from that case-bottle of
sound brandy? George Osborne lying yonder,
all his fopperies ended, with a bullet through
his heart? Rawdon Crawley riding stolidly
behind General Tufto along the front of the
shattered regiment where Captain Dobbin
stands heartsick for poor Emily?

Or maybe the struggle arranges itself in

your vision around one figure not named in
history or fiction,—that of your grandfather,
or his father, or some old dead soldier of the
great wars whose blood you exult to inherit,
or some grim veteran whom you saw tottering
to the rollcall beyond when Queen Victoria was
young and you were a little boy.

For me the shadows of the battle are so
grouped round old John Locke that the his-
torians, story-tellers, and painters may never
quite persuade me that he was not the centre
and real hero of the action.   The French
cuirassiers in my thought-pictures charge again
and again vainly against old John; he it is
who breaks the New Guard; upon the ground
that he defends the Emperor's eyes are fixed
all day long.   It is John who occasionally
glances at the sky with wonder if Blucher has
failed them.   Upon Shaw the Lifeguardsman,
and John, the Duke plainly most relies, and
the words that Wellington actually speaks
when the time comes for advance are, "Up,
John, and at them!"

How fate drifted the old veteran of Waterloo into our little Canadian Lake Erie village
I never knew.   Drifted him?   No; he ever
marched as if under the orders of his com-

mander. Tall, thin, white-haired, close-shaven,
and always in knee-breeches and long stock-
ings, his was an antique and martial figure.
"Fresh white-fish" was his cry, which he delivered as if calling all the village to fall in
for drill.

So impressive was his demeanor that he dig-
nified his occupation. For years after he disappeared, the peddling of white-fish by horse
and cart was regarded in that district as pecu-
liarly respectable. It was a glorious trade
when old John Locke held the steelyards and
served out the glittering fish with an air of
distributing ammunition for a long day's
combat.

I believe I noticed, on the first day I saw
him, how he tapped his left breast with a proud
gesture when he had done with a lot of cus-
tomers and was about to march again at the
head of his horse. That restored him from
trade to his soldiership—he had saluted his
Waterloo medal! There beneath his thread-
bare old blue coat it lay, always felt by the
heart of the hero.

"Why doesn't he wear it outside?" I once
asked.

"He used to," said my father; "till Hiram

Beaman, the druggist, asked him what he'd 'take for the bit of pewter.' "

"What did old John say, sir?"

" 'Take for the bit of pewter!' said he, looking hard at Beaman with scorn. 'I've took better men's lives nor ever yours was for to get it, and I'd sell my own for it as quick as ever I offered it before.'

" 'More fool you,' said Beaman.

" 'You're nowt,' said old John, very calm and cold, 'you're nowt but walking dirt.' From that day forth he would never sell Beaman a fish; he wouldn't touch his money."

It must have been late in 1854 or early in 1855 that I first saw the famous medal. Going home from school on a bright winter afternoon, I met old John walking very erect, without his usual fish-supply. A dull round white spot was clasped on the left breast of his coat.

"Mr. Locke," said the small boy, staring with admiration, "is that your glorious Waterloo medal?"

"You're a good little lad!" He stooped to let me see the noble pewter. "War's declared against Rooshia, and now it's right to show it. The old regiment's sailed, and my only son is with the colors."

Then he took me by the hand and led me into the village store, where the lawyer read aloud the news from the paper that the veteran gave him. In those days there was no railway within fifty miles of us. It had chanced that some fisherman brought old John a later paper than any previously received in the village.

"Ay, but the Duke is gone," said he, shaking his white head, "and it's curious to be fighting on the same side with another Boney."

All that winter and the next, all the long summer between, old John displayed his medal. When the report of Alma came, his remarks on the French failure to get into the fight were severe. "What was they *ever,* at best, without Boney?" he would inquire. But a letter from his son after Inkermann changed all that.

"Half of us was killed, and the rest of us clean tired with fighting," wrote Corporal Locke. "What with a bullet through the flesh of my right leg, and the fatigue of using the bayonet so long, I was like to drop. The Russians was coming on again as if there was no end to them, when strange drums came sounding in the mist behind us. With that we closed up and faced half-round, thinking they had outflanked us and the day was gone, so there was nothing more to do but make out to die hard, like the sons of Waterloo men. You would have been pleased to see the looks of what was left of the old regiment, father. Then all of a sudden a French column came up the rise out of the mist, screaming, *'Vive l'Empereur!'* their drums beating the charge. We gave them room, for we were too dead tired to go first. On they went like mad at the Russians, so that was the end of a hard morning's work. I was down,—fainted with loss of blood,—but I will soon be fit for duty again. When I came to myself there was a Frenchman pouring brandy down my throat, and talking in his gibberish as kind as any Christian. Never a word will I say agin them red-legged French again."

"Show me the man that would!" growled old John. "It was never in them French to act cowardly. Didn't they beat all the world, and even stand up many's the day agen ourselves and the Duke? They didn't beat,—it wouldn't be in reason,—but they tried brave enough, and what more'd you ask of mortal men?"

With the ending of the Crimean War our

village was illuminated. Rows of tallow
candles in every window, fireworks in a vacant
field, and a torchlight procession! Old John
marched at its head in full regimentals,
straight as a ramrod, the hero of the night.
His son had been promoted for bravery on the
field. After John came a dozen gray militia-
men of Queenston Heights, Lundy's Lane,
and Chippewa; next some forty volunteers of
'37. And we boys of the U. E. Loyalist settlement cheered and cheered, thrilled with an intense vague knowledge that the old army of
Wellington kept ghostly step with John, while
aerial trumpets and drums pealed and beat
with rejoicing at the fresh glory of the race
and the union of English-speaking men unconsciously celebrated and symbolized by the
little rustic parade.

After that the old man again wore his medal
concealed. The Chinese War of 1857 was
too contemptible to celebrate by displaying his
badge of Waterloo.

Then came the dreadful tale of the Sepoy
mutiny—Meerut, Delhi, Cawnpore! After the
tale of Nana Sahib's massacre of women and
children was read to old John he never smiled,
I think. Week after week, month after month,

as hideous tidings poured steadily in, his face became more haggard, gray, and dreadful. The feeling that he was too old for use seemed to shame him. He no longer carried his head high, as of yore. That his son was not marching behind Havelock with the avenging army seemed to cut our veteran sorely. Sergeant Locke had sailed with the old regiment to join Outram in Persia before the Sepoys broke loose. It was at this time that old John was first heard to say, "I'm 'feared something's gone wrong with my heart."

Months went by before we learned that the troops for Persia had been stopped on their way and thrown into India against the mutineers. At that news old John marched into the village with a prouder air than he had worn for many a day. His medal was again on his breast.

It was but the next month, I think, that the village lawyer stood reading aloud the account of the capture of a great Sepoy fort. The veteran entered the post-office, and all made way for him. The reading went on:—

"The blowing open of the Northern Gate was the grandest personal exploit of the attack. It was performed by native sappers, covered by the fire of two regiments, and headed by Lieutenants Holder and Dacre, Sergeants Green, Carmody, Macpherson, and Locke."

The lawyer paused. Every eye turned to the face of the old Waterloo soldier. He straightened up to keener attention, threw out his chest, and tapped the glorious medal in salute of the names of the brave.

"God be praised, my son was there!" he said. "Read on."

"Sergeant Carmody, while laying the powder, was killed, and the native havildar wounded. The powder having been laid, the advance party slipped down into the ditch to allow the firing party, under Lieutenant Dacre, to do its duty. While trying to fire the charge he was shot through one arm and leg. He sank, but handed the match to Sergeant Macpherson, who was at once shot dead. Sergeant Locke, already wounded severely in the shoulder, then seized the match, and succeeded in firing the train. He fell at that moment, literally riddled with bullets."

"Read on," said old John, in a deeper voice. All forbore to look twice upon his face.

"Others of the party were falling, when the mighty gate was blown to fragments, and the waiting regiments of infantry, under Colonel Campbell, rushed into the breach."

There was a long silence in the post-office, till old John spoke once more.

"The Lord God be thanked for all his dealings with us! My son, Sergeant Locke, died well for England, Queen, and Duty."

Nervously fingering the treasure on his breast, the old soldier wheeled about, and marched proudly straight down the middle of the village street to his lonely cabin.

The villagers never saw him in life again. Next day he did not appear. All refrained from intruding on his mourning. But in the evening, when the Anglican minister heard of his parishioner's loss, he walked to old John's home.

There, stretched upon his straw bed, he lay in his antique regimentals, stiffer than At Attention, all his medals fastened below that of Waterloo above his quiet heart. His right hand lay on an open Bible, and his face wore an expression as of looking for ever and ever upon Sergeant Locke and the Great Commander who takes back unto Him the heroes He fashions to sweeten the world.

JOHN BEDELL, U. E. LOYALIST[1]

"A RENEGADE! A rebel against his king! A black-hearted traitor! You dare to tell me that you love George Winthrop! Son of canting, lying Ezra Winthrop! By the Eternal, I'll shoot him on sight if he comes this side!"

While old John Bedell was speaking, he tore and flung away a letter, reached for his long rifle on its pins above the chimney-place, dashed its butt angrily to the floor, and poured powder into his palm.

"For Heaven's sake, father! You would not! You could not! The war is over. It would be murder!" cried Ruth Bedell, sobbing.

"Wouldn't I?" He poured the powder in. "Yes, by gracious, quicker'n I'd kill a rattlesnake!" He placed the round bullet on the

[1] The United Empire Loyalists were American Tories who forsook their homes and property after the Revolution in order to live in Canada under the British Flag. It is impossible to understand Canadian feeling for the Crown at the present day without understanding the U. E. Loyalist spirit, which, though Canadians are not now unfriendly to the United States, is still the most important political force in the Dominion, and holds it firmly in allegiance to the Crown.

little square of greased rag at the muzzle of his
rifle. "A rank traitor—bone and blood of
those who drove out loyal men!"—he crowded
the tight lead home, dashed the ramrod into
place, looked to the flint. "Rest there,—wake
up for George Winthrop!" and the fierce old
man replaced rifle and powder-horn on their
pegs.

Bedell's hatred for the foes who had beaten
down King George's cause, and imposed the
alternative of confiscation or the oath of allegiance on the vanquished, was considered intense, even by his brother Loyalists of the
Niagara frontier.

"The Squire kind o' sees his boys' blood
when the sky's red," said they in explanation.
But Bedell was so much an enthusiast that he
could almost rejoice because his three stark
sons had gained the prize of death in battle.
He was too brave to hate the fighting-men he
had so often confronted; but he abhorred the
politicians, especially the intimate civic enemies
on whom he had poured scorn before the armed
struggle began. More than any he hated Ezra
Winthrop, the lawyer, arch-revolutionist of
their native town, who had never used a
weapon but his tongue. And now his Ruth,

the beloved and only child left to his exiled age, had confessed her love for Ezra Winthrop's son! They had been boy and girl, pretty maiden and bright stripling together, without the Squire suspecting—he could not, even now, conceive clearly so wild a thing as their affection! The confession burned in his heart like veritable fire,—a raging anguish of mingled loathing and love. He stood now gazing at Ruth dumbly, his hands clenched, head sometimes mechanically quivering, anger, hate, love, grief, tumultuous in his soul.

Ruth glanced up—her father seemed about to speak—she bowed again, shuddering as though the coming words might kill. Still there was silence,—a long silence. Bedell stood motionless, poised, breathing hard—the silence oppressed the girl—each moment her terror increased—expectant attention became suffering that demanded his voice—and still was silence—save for the dull roar of Niagara that more and more pervaded the air. The torture of waiting for the words—a curse against her, she feared—overwore Ruth's endurance. She looked up suddenly, and John Bedell saw in hers the beloved eyes of his dead wife, shrinking with intolerable fear. He groaned heavily, flung up his hands despairingly, and strode out toward the river.

How crafty smooth the green Niagara sweeps toward the plunge beneath that perpetual white cloud above the Falls! From Bedell's clearing below Navy Island, two miles above the Falls, he could see the swaying and rolling of the mist, ever rushing up to expand and overhang. The terrible stream had a profound fascination for him, with its racing eddies eating at the shore; its long weeds, visible through the clear water, trailing close down to the bottom; its inexorable, eternal, onward pouring. Because it was so mighty and so threatening, he rejoiced grimly in the awful river. To float, watching cracks and ledges of its flat bottom-rock drift quickly upward; to bend to his oars only when white crests of the rapids yelled for his life; to win escape by sheer strength from points so low down that he sometimes doubted but the greedy forces had been tempted too long; to stake his life, watching tree-tops for a sign that he could yet save it, was the dreadful pastime by which Bedell often quelled passionate promptings to revenge his exile. "The Falls is bound to get the Squire, some day," said the banished set-

tlers. But the Squire's skiff was clean built
as a pickerel, and his old arms iron-strong.
Now when he had gone forth from the beloved
child, who seemed to him so traitorous to his
love and all loyalty, he went instinctively to
spend his rage upon the river.

Ruth Bedell, gazing at the loaded rifle, shuddered, not with dread only, but a sense of having been treacherous to her father. She had
not told him all the truth. George Winthrop
himself, having made his way secretly through
the forest from Lake Ontario, had given her
his own letter asking leave from the Squire to
visit his newly made cabin. From the moment
of arrival her lover had implored her to fly
with him. But filial love was strong in Ruth
to give hope that her father would yield to the
yet stronger affection freshened in her heart.
Believing their union might be permitted, she
had pledged herself to escape with her lover if
it were forbidden. Now he waited by the hickory wood for a signal to conceal himself or
come forward.

When Ruth saw her father far down the
river, she stepped to the flagstaff he had raised
before building the cabin—his first duty being
to hoist the Union Jack! It was the largest

flag he could procure; he could see it flying
defiantly all day long; at night he could hear
its glorious folds whipping in the wind; the hot
old Loyalist loved to fancy his foeman cursing
at it from the other side, nearly three miles
away. Ruth hauled the flag down a little, then
ran it up to the mast-head again.

At that, a tall young fellow came springing
into the clearing, jumping exultantly over
brush-heaps and tree-trunks, his queue wag-
gling, his eyes bright, glad, under his three-cor-
nered hat. Joying that her father had yielded,
he ran forward till he saw Ruth's tears.

"What, sweetheart!—crying? It was the
signal to come on," cried he.

"Yes; to see you sooner, George. Father
is out yonder. But no, he will never, never
consent."

"Then you will come with me, love," he said,
taking her hands.

"No, no; I dare not," sobbed Ruth. "Father
would overtake us. He swears to shoot you on
sight! Go, George! Escape while you can!
Oh, if he should find you here!"

"But, darling love, we need not fear. We
can escape easily. I know the forest path.
But—" Then he thought how weak her pace.

"We might cross here before he could come up!" cried Winthrop, looking toward where the Squire's boat was now a distant blotch.

"No, no," wailed Ruth, yet yielding to his embrace. "This is the last time I shall see you forever and forever. Go, dear,—good-bye, my love, my love."

But he clasped her in his strong arms, kissing, imploring, cheering her,—and how should true love choose hopeless renunciation?

.   .   .   .

Tempting, defying, regaining his lost ground, drifting down again, trying hard to tire out and subdue his heart-pangs, Bedell dallied with death more closely than ever. He had let his skiff drift far down toward the Falls. Often he could see the wide smooth curve where the green volume first lapses vastly on a lazy slope, to shoulder up below as a huge calm billow, before pitching into the madness of waves whose confusion of tossing and tortured crests hurries to the abyss. The afternoon grew toward evening before he pulled steadily home, crawling away from the roarers against the cruel green, watching the ominous cloud with some such grim humor as if under observation by an overpowering but baffled enemy.

Approaching his landing, a shout drew Bedell's glance ashore to a group of men excitedly gesticulating. They seemed motioning him to watch the American shore. Turning, he saw a boat in midstream, where no craft then on the river, except his own skiff, could be safe, unless manned by several good men. Only two oars were flashing. Bedell could make out two figures indistinctly. It was clear they were doomed,—though still a full mile above the point whence he had come, they were much farther out than he when near the rapids. Yet one life might be saved! Instantly Bedell's bow turned outward, and cheers flung to him from ashore.

At that moment he looked to his own landing-place, and saw that his larger boat was gone. Turning again, he angrily recognized it, but kept right on—he must try to rescue even a thief. He wondered Ruth had not prevented the theft, but had no suspicion of the truth. Always he had refused to let her go out upon the river—mortally fearing it for *her*.

Thrusting his skiff mightily forward,—often it glanced, half-whirled by up-whelming and spreading spaces of water,—the old Loyalist's heart was quit of his pangs, and sore only with

certainty that he must abandon one human soul
to death. By the time that he could reach the
larger boat his would be too near the rapids for
escape with three!

When George Winthrop saw Bedell in pursuit, he bent to his ash-blades more strongly,
and Ruth, trembling to remember her father's
threats, urged her lover to speed. They feared
the pursuer only, quite unconscious that they
were in the remorseless grasp of the river.
Ruth had so often seen her father far lower
down than they had yet drifted that she did not
realize the truth, and George, a stranger in the
Niagara district, was unaware of the length of
the cataracts above the Falls. He was also
deceived by the stream's treacherous smooth-
ness, and instead of half-upward, pulled
straight across, as if certainly able to land anywhere he might touch the American shore.

Bedell looked over his shoulder often. When
he distinguished a woman, he put on more
force, but slackened soon—the pull home would
tax his endurance, he reflected. In some sort
it was a relief to know that one *was* a woman;
he had been anticipating trouble with two men
equally bent on being saved. That the man
would abandon himself bravely, the Squire

took as a matter of course. For a while he
thought of pulling with the woman to the
American shore, more easily to be gained from
the point where the rescue must occur. But
he rejected the plan, confident he could win
back, for he had sworn never to set foot on that
soil unless in war. Had it been possible to save
both, he would have been forced to disregard
that vow; but the Squire knew that it was impossible for him to reach the New York shore
with two passengers—two would overload his
boat beyond escape. Man or woman—one
must go over the Falls.

Having carefully studied landmarks for his
position, Bedell turned to look again at the
doomed boat, and a well-known ribbon caught
his attention! The old man dropped his oars,
confused with horror. "My God, my God! it's
Ruth!" he cried, and the whole truth came with
another look, for he had not forgotten George
Winthrop.

"Your father stops, Ruth. Perhaps he is in
pain," said George to the quaking girl.

She looked back. "What can it be?" she
cried, filial love returning overmasteringly.

"Perhaps he is only tired." George affected
carelessness,—his first wish was to secure his

bride,—and pulled hard away to get all advantage from Bedell's halt.

"Tired! He is in danger of the Falls, then!" screamed Ruth. "Stop! Turn! Back to him!"

Winthrop instantly prepared to obey. "Yes, darling," he said, "we must not think of ourselves. We must go back to save him!" Yet his was a sore groan at turning; what Duty ordered was so hard,—he must give up his love for the sake of his enemy.

But while Winthrop was still pulling round, the old Loyalist resumed rowing, with a more rapid stroke that soon brought him alongside.

In those moments of waiting, all Bedell's life, his personal hatreds, his loves, his sorrows, had been reviewed before his soul. He had seen again his sons, the slain in battle, in the pride of their young might; and the gentle eyes of Ruth had pleaded with him beneath his dead wife's brow. Into those beloved, unforgotten, visionary eyes he looked with an encouraging, strengthening gaze,—now that the deed to be done was as clear before him as the face of Almighty God. In accepting it the darker passions that had swayed his stormy life fell suddenly away from their hold on his soul. How trivial had been old disputes! how good at heart

old well-known civic enemies! how poor seemed
hate! how mean and poor seemed all but Love
and Loyalty!

Resolution and deep peace had come upon
the man.

The lovers wondered at his look. No wrath
was there. The old eyes were calm and cheerful, a gentle smile flickered about his lips. Only
that he was very pale, Ruth would have been
wholly glad for the happy change.

"Forgive me, father," she cried, as he laid
hand on their boat.

"I do, my child," he answered. "Come now
without an instant's delay to me."

"Oh, father, if you would let us be happy!"
cried Ruth, heart-torn by two loves.

"Dear, you shall be happy. I was wrong,
child; I did not understand how you loved him.
But come! You hesitate! Winthrop, my son,
you are in some danger. Into this boat instantly! both of you! Take the oars, George.
Kiss me, dear, my Ruth, once more. Good-
bye, my little girl. Winthrop, be good to her.
And may God bless you both forever!"

As the old Squire spoke, he stepped into the
larger boat, instantly releasing the skiff. His
imperative gentleness had secured his object

without loss of time, and the boats were apart
with Winthrop's readiness to pull.

"Now row! Row for her life to yonder
shore! Bow well up! Away, or the Falls will
have her!" shouted Bedell.

"But you!" cried Winthrop, bending for his
stroke. Yet he did not comprehend Bedell's
meaning. Till the last the old man had spoken
without strong excitement. Dread of the river
was not on George; his bliss was supreme in
his thought, and he took the Squire's order for
one of exaggerated alarm.

"Row, I say, with all your strength!" cried
Bedell, with a flash of anger that sent the
young fellow away instantly. "Row! Concern
yourself not for me. I am going home. Row!
for her life, Winthrop! God will deliver you
yet. Good-bye, children. Remember always
my blessing is freely given you."

"God bless and keep you forever, father!"
cried Ruth, from the distance, as her lover
pulled away.

They landed, conscious of having passed a
swift current, indeed, but quite unthinking of
the price paid for their safety. Looking back
on the darkling river, they saw nothing of the
old man.

"Poor father!" sighed Ruth, "how kind he was! I'm sore-hearted for thinking of him at home, so lonely."

Left alone in the clumsy boat, Bedell stretched with the long, heavy oars for his own shore, making appearance of strong exertion. But when he no longer feared that his children might turn back with sudden understanding, and vainly, to his aid, he dragged the boat slowly, watching her swift drift down—down toward the towering mist. Then as he gazed at the cloud, rising in two distinct volumes, came a thought spurring the Loyalist spirit in an instant. He was not yet out of American water! Thereafter he pulled steadily, powerfully, noting landmarks anxiously, studying currents, considering always their trend to or from his own shore. Half an hour had gone when he again dropped into slower motion. Then he could see Goat Island's upper end between him and the mist of the American Fall.

Now the old man gave himself up to intense curiosity, looking over into the water with fascinated inquiry. He had never been so far down the river. Darting beside their shadows, deep in the clear flood, were now larger fishes than he had ever taken, and all moved up as if hurrying to escape. How fast the long trailing, swaying, single weeds, and the crevices in flat rock whence they so strangely grew, went up stream and away as if drawn backward. The sameness of the bottom to that higher up interested him—where then *did* the current begin to sweep clean? He should certainly know that soon, he thought, without a touch of fear, having utterly accepted death when he determined it were base to carry his weary old life a little longer, and let Ruth's young love die. Now the Falls' heavy monotone was overborne by terrible sounds—a mingled clashing, shrieking, groaning, and rumbling, as of great bowlders churned in their beds.

Bedell was nearing the first long swoop downward at the rapids' head when those watching him from the high bank below the Chippewa River's mouth saw him put his boat stern with the current and cease rowing entirely, facing fairly the up-rushing mist to which he was being hurried. Then they observed him stooping, as if writing, for a time. Something flashed in his hands, and then he knelt with head bowed down. Kneeling, they prayed, too.

Now he was almost on the brink of the

cascades. Then he arose, and, glancing backward to his home, caught sight of his friends
on the high shore. Calmly he waved a farewell.
What then? Thrice round he flung his hat,
with a gesture they knew full well. Some had
seen that exultant waving in front of ranks of
battle. As clearly as though the roar of waters
had not drowned his ringing voice, they knew
that old John Bedell, at the poise of death,
cheered thrice, "Hurrah! Hurrah! Hurrah
for the King!"

They found his body a week afterward, floating with the heaving water in the gorge below
the Falls. Though beaten almost out of recognition, portions of clothing still adhered to it,
and in a waistcoat pocket they found the old
Loyalist's metal snuff-box, with this inscrip-
tion scratched by knife-point on the cover:
"God be praised, I die in British waters!
JOHN BEDELL."

OLD MAN SAVARIN

OLD Ma'ame Paradis had caught seventeen small doré, four suckers, and eleven channel-catfish before she used up all the worms in her tomato-can. Therefore she was in a cheerful and loquacious humor when I came along and offered her some of my bait.

"Merci; non, M'sieu. Dat's 'nuff fishin' for me. I got too old now for fish too much. You like me make you present of six or seven doré? Yes? All right. Then you make me present of one quarter dollar."

When this transaction was completed, the old lady got out her short black clay pipe, and filled it with *tabac blanc*.

"Ver' good smell for scare mosquitoes," said she. "Sit down, M'sieu. For sure I like to be here, me, for see the river when she's like this."

Indeed the scene was more than picturesque. Her fishing-platform extended twenty feet from the rocky shore of the great Rataplan Rapid of the Ottawa, which, beginning to tumble a mile to the westward, poured a roar-

ing torrent half a mile wide into the broader,
calm brown reach below. Noble elms towered
on the shores. Between their trunks we could
see many whitewashed cabins, whose doors of
blue or green or red scarcely disclosed their
colors in that light.

The sinking sun, which already touched the
river, seemed somehow the source of the vast
stream that flowed radiantly from its blaze.
Through the glamour of the evening mist and
the maze of June flies we could see a dozen
men scooping for fish from platforms like that
of Ma'ame Paradis.

Each scooper lifted a great hoop-net set on
a handle some fifteen feet long, threw it easily
up stream, and swept it on edge with the current to the full length of his reach. Then it
was drawn out and at once thrown upward
again, if no capture had been made. In case
he had taken fish, he came to the inshore edge
of his platform, and upset the net's contents
into a pool separated from the main rapid by
an improvised wall of stones.

"I'm too old for scoop some now," said
Ma'ame Paradis, with a sigh.

"You were never strong enough to scoop,
surely," said I.

"No, eh? All right, M'sieu. Then you hain't nev' hear 'bout the time Old Man Savarin was catched up with. No, eh? Well, I'll tol' you 'bout that." And this was her story as she told it to me.

.   .   .   .

"Der was fun dose time. Nobody ain't nev' catch up with dat old rascal ony other time since I'll know him first. Me, I'll be only fifteen den. Dat's long time 'go, eh? Well, for sure, I ain't so old like what I'll look. But Old Man Savarin was old already. He's old, old, old, when he's only thirty; an' *mean— baptême!* If de old Nick ain' got de hottest place for dat old stingy—yes, for sure!

"You'll see up dere where Frawce Seguin is scoop? Dat's the Laroque platform by right. Me, I was a Laroque. My fader was use for scoop dere, an' my gran'fader—the Laroques scoop dere all de time since ever dere was some Rapid Rataplan. Den Old Man Savarin he's buyed the land up dere from Felix Ladoucier, an' he's told my fader, 'You can't scoop no more wisout you pay me rent.'

" 'Rent!' my fader say. *'Saprie!* Dat's my fader's platform for scoop fish! You ask anybody.'

" 'Oh, I'll know all 'bout dat,' Old Man Savarin is say. 'Ladoucier let you scoop front of his land, for Ladoucier one big fool. De lan's mine now, an' de fishin' right is mine. You can't scoop dere wisout you pay me rent.'

" '*Baptême!* I'll show you 'bout dat,' my fader say.

"Next mawny he is go for scoop same like always. Den Old Man Savarin is fetch my fader up before de magistrate. De magistrate make my fader pay nine shillin'!

" 'Mebbe dat's learn you one lesson,' Old Man Savarin is say.

"My fader swear pretty good, but my moder say: 'Well, Narcisse, dere hain' no use for take it out in *malediction.* De nine shillin' is paid. You scoop more fish—dat's the way.'

"So my fader he is go out early, early nex' mawny. He's scoop, he's scoop. He's catch plenty fish before Old Man Savarin come.

" 'You ain't got 'nuff yet for fishin' on my land, eh? Come out of dat,' Old Man Savarin is say.

" '*Saprie!* Ain't I pay nine shillin' for fish here?' my fader say.

" '*Oui*—you pay nine shillin' for fish here *wisout* my leave. But you ain't pay nothin' for fish here *wis* my leave.   You is goin' up before de magistrate some more.'

"So he is fetch my fader up anoder time. An' de magistrate make my fader pay twelve shillin' more!

" 'Well, I s'pose I can go fish on my fader's platform now,' my fader is say.

"Old Man Savarin was laugh. 'Your honor, dis man tink he don't have for pay me no rent, because you'll make him pay two fines for trespass on my land.'

"So de magistrate told my fader he hain't got no more right for go on his own platform than he was at the start.   My fader is ver' angry.   He's cry, he's tear his shirt; but Old Man Savarin only say, 'I guess I learn you one good lesson, Narcisse.'

"De whole village ain't told de old rascal how much dey was angry 'bout dat, for Old Man Savarin is got dem all in debt at his big store. He is grin, grin, and told everybody how he learn my fader two good lesson. An' he is told my fader: 'You see what I'll be goin' for do wis you if ever you go on my land again wisout you pay me rent.'

" 'How much you want?' my fader say.

" 'Half de fish you catch.'

" '*Monjee!* Never!'

" 'Five dollar a year, den.'

" '*Saprie,* no. Dat's too much.'

" 'All right. Keep off my lan,' if you hain't want anoder lesson.'

" 'You's a tief,' my fader say.

" 'Hermidas, make up Narcisse Laroque bill,' de old rascal say to his clerk. 'If he hain't pay dat bill to-morrow, I sue him.'

"So my fader is scare mos' to death. Only my moder she's say, '*I'll* pay dat bill, me.'

"So she's take the money she's saved up long time for make my weddin' when it come. An' she's paid de bill. So den my fader hain't scare no more, an' he is shake his fist good under Old Man Savarin's ugly nose. But dat old rascal only laugh an' say, 'Narcisse, you like to be fined some more, eh?'

" '*Tort Dieu.* You rob me of my place for fish, but I'll take my platform anyhow,' my fader is say.

" 'Yes, eh? All right—if you can get him wisout go on my land. But you go on my land, and see if I don't learn you anoder. lesson,' Old Savarin is say.

"So my fader is rob of his platform, too. Nex' ting we hear, Frawce Seguin has rent dat platform for five dollars a year.

"Den de big fun begin. My fader an Frawce is cousin. All de time before den dey was good friend. But my fader he is go to Frawce Seguin's place an' he is told him, 'Frawce, I'll goin' lick you so hard you can't nev' scoop on my platform.'

"Frawce only laugh. Den Old Man Savarin come up de hill.

" 'Fetch him up to de magistrate an' learn him anoder lesson,' he is say to Frawce.

" 'What for?' Frawce say.

" 'For try to scare you.'

" 'He hain't hurt me none.'

" 'But he's say he will lick you.'

" 'Dat's only because he's vex,' Frawce say.

" '*Baptême! Non!*' my fader say. 'I'll be goin' for lick you good, Frawce.'

" 'For sure?' Frawce say.

" '*Saprie!* Yes; for sure.'

" 'Well, dat's all right den, Narcisse. When you goin' for lick me?'

" 'First time I'll get drunk. I'll be goin' for get drunk dis same day.'

" 'All right, Narcisse. If you goin' get drunk for lick me, I'll be goin' get drunk for lick you'—*Canadien* hain't nev' fool 'nuff for fight, M'sieu, only if dey is got drunk.

"Well, my fader he's go on old Marceau's hotel, an' he's drink all day. Frawce Seguin he's go cross de road on Joe Maufraud's hotel, an' *he's* drink all day. When de night come, dey's bose stand out in front of de two hotel for fight.

"Dey's bose yell an' yell for make de oder feller scare bad before dey begin. Hermidas Laronde an' Jawnny Leroi dey's hold my fader for fear he's go 'cross de road for keel Frawce Seguin dead. Pierre Seguin an' Magloire Sauve is hold Frawce for fear he's come 'cross de road for keel my fader dead. And dose men fight dat way 'cross de road, till dey hain't hardly able for stand up no more.

"My fader he's tear his shirt and he's yell, 'Let me at him!' Frawce he's tear his shirt and he's yell, 'Let me at him!' But de men hain't goin' for let dem loose, for fear one is strike de oder ver' hard. De whole village is shiver 'bout dat offle fight—yes, seh, shiver bad!

"Well, dey's fight like dat for more as four hours, till dey hain't able for yell no more, an' dey hain't got no money left for buy wheeskey for de crowd. Den Marceau and Joe Maufraud tol' dem bose it was a shame for two cousins to fight so bad. An' my fader he's say he's ver' sorry dat he lick Frawce so hard, and dey's bose sorry. So dey's kiss one anoder good—only all their close is tore to pieces.

"An' what you tink 'bout Old Man Savarin? Old Man Savarin is just stand in front of his store all de time, an' he's say: 'I'll tink I'll fetch 'him *bose* hup to de magistrate, an' I'll learn him *bose* a lesson.'

"Me, I'll be only fifteen, but I hain't scare 'bout dat fight same like my moder is scare. No more is Alphonsine Seguin scare. She's seventeen, an' she wait for de fight to be all over. Den she take her fader home, same like I'll take my fader home for bed. Dat's after twelve o'clock of night.

"Nex' mawny early my fader he's groaned and he's groaned: 'Ah—ugh—I'm sick, sick, me. I'll be goin' for die dis time, for sure.'

" 'You get up an' scoop some fish,' my moder she's say, angry. 'Den you hain't be sick no more.'

" 'Ach—ugh—I'll hain't be able. Oh, I'll be so sick. An' I hain' got no place for scoop fish now no more. Frawce Seguin has rob my platform.'

" 'Take de nex' one lower down,' my moder she's say.

" 'Dat's Jawnny Leroi's.'

" 'All right for dat. Jawnny he's hire for run timber to-day.'

" 'Ugh—I'll not be able for get up. Send for M'sieu le Curè—I'll be goin' for die for sure.'

" '*Misère,* but dat's no *man!* Dat's a drunk pig,' my moder she's say, angry. 'Sick, eh? Lazy, lazy—dat's so. An' dere hain't no fish for de little chilluns, an' it's Friday mawny.' So my moder she's begin for cry.

"Well, M'sieu, I'll make de rest short; for de sun is all gone now. What you tink I do dat mawny? I take de big scoop-net an' I'll come up here for see if I'll be able for scoop some fish on Jawnny Leroi's platform. Only dere hain't nev' much fish dere.

"Pretty quick I'll look up and I'll see Alphonsine Seguin scoop, scoop on my fader's old platform. Alphonsine's fader is sick, sick, same like my fader, an' all de Seguin boys is too little for scoop, same like my brudders is too little. So dere Alphonsine she's scoop, scoop for breakfas'.

"What you tink I'll see some more? I'll

see Old Man Savarin. He's watchin' from de corner of de cedar bush, an I'll know ver' good what he's watch for. He's watch for catch my fader go on his own platform. He's want for learn my fader anoder lesson. *Saprie!* dat's make me ver' angry, M'sieu!

"Alphonsine she's scoop, scoop plenty fish. I'll not be scoop none. Dat's make me more angry. I'll look up where Alphonsine is, an' I'll talk to myself:—

" 'Dat's my fader's platform,' I'll be say. 'Dat's my fader's fish what you catch, Alphonsine. You hain't nev' be my cousin no more. It is mean, mean for Frawce Seguin to rent my fader's platform for please dat old rascal Savarin.' Mebby I'll not be so angry at Alphonsine, M'sieu, if I was able for catch some fish; but I hain't able—I don't catch none.

"Well, M'sieu, dat's de way for long time— half-hour mebby. Den I'll hear Alphonsine yell good. I'll look up de river some more. She's try for lift her net. She's try hard, hard, but she hain't able. De net is down in de rapid, an' she's only able for hang on to de hannle. Den I'll know she's got one big sturgeon, an' he's so big she can't pull him up.

"*Monjee!* what I care 'bout dat! I'll laugh me. Den I'll laugh good some more, for I'll want Alphonsine for see how I'll laugh big. And I'll talk to myself:—

" 'Dat's good for dose Seguins,' I'll say. 'De big sturgeon will pull away de net. Den Alphonsine she will lose her fader's scoop wis de sturgeon. Dat's good 'nuff for dose Seguins! Take my fader platform, eh?'

"For sure, I'll want for go an' help Alphonsine all de same—she's my cousin, an' I'll want for see de sturgeon, me. But I'll only just laugh, laugh. *Non, M'sieu;* dere was not one man out on any of de oder platform dat mawny for to help Alphonsine. Dey was all sleep ver' late, for dey was all out ver' late for see de offle fight I told you 'bout.

"Well, pretty quick, what you tink? I'll see Old Man Savarin goin' to my fader's platform. He's take hold for help Alphonsine, an' dey's bose pull, and pretty quick de big sturgeon is up on de platform. I'll be more angry as before.

"Oh, *tort Dieu!* What you tink come den? Why, dat Old Man Savarin is want for take de sturgeon!

"First dey hain't speak so I can hear, for

de Rapid is too loud.   But pretty quick dey's
bose angry, and I hear dem talk.

"'Dat's my fish,' Old Man Savarin is say.
'Didn't I save him?   Wasn't you goin' for lose
him, for sure?'

"Me—I'll laugh good.   Dass *such* an old
rascal.

"'You get off dis platform, quick!' Alphonsine she's say.

"'Give me my sturgeon,' he's say.

"'Dat's a lie—it hain't your sturgeon.   It's
my sturgeon,' she's yell.

"'I'll learn you one lesson 'bout dat,' he's
say.

"Well, M'sieu, Alphonsine she's pull back
de fish just when Old Man Savarin is make one
grab.   An' when she's pull back, she's step to
one side, an' de old rascal he is grab at de fish,
an' de heft of de sturgeon is make him fall on
his face, so he's tumble in de Rapid when
Alphonsine let go de sturgeon.   So der's Old
Man Savarin floating in de river—and *me!*
I'll don' care eef he's drown one bit!

"One time he is on his back, one time he is
on his face, one time he is all under de water.
For sure he's goin' for be draw into de *culbute*
an' get drown' dead, if I'll not be able for

scoop him when he's go by my platform. I'll want for laugh, but I'll be too much scare.

"Well, M'sieu, I'll pick up my fader's scoop and I'll stand out on de edge of de platform. De water is run so fast, I'm mos' 'fraid de old man is boun' for pull me in when I'll scoop him. But I'll not mind for dat, I'll throw de scoop an' catch him; an' for sure, he's hold on good.

"So dere's de old rascal in de scoop, but when I'll get him safe, I hain't able for pull him in one bit. I'll only be able for hold on an' laugh, laugh—he's look *ver'* queer! All I can do is to hold him dere so he can't go down de *culbute*. I'll can't pull him up if I'll want to.

"De old man is scare ver' bad. But pretty quick he's got hold of de cross-bar of de hoop, an' he's got his ugly old head up good.

" 'Pull me in,' he say, ver' angry.

" 'I'll hain't be able,' I'll say.

"Jus' den Alphonsine she's come 'long, an' she's laugh so she can't hardly hold on wis me to de hannle. I was laugh good some more. When de old villain see us have fun, he's yell: 'I'll learn you bose one lesson for this. Pull me ashore!'

" 'Oh! you's learn us bose one lesson, M'sieu Savarin, eh?' Alphonsine she's say. 'Well, den, us bose will learn M'sieu Savarin one lesson first. Pull him up a little,' she's say to me.

"So we pull him up, an' den Alphonsine she's say to me: 'Let out de hannle, quick'— and he's under de water some more. When we stop de net, he's got hees head up pretty quick.

" '*Monjee!* Ill be drown' if you don't pull me out,' he's mos' *cry*.

" 'Ver' well—if you's drown, your family be ver' glad,' Alphonsine she's say. 'Den they's got all your money for spend quick, quick.'

"M'sieu, dat scare him offle. He's begin for cry like one baby.

" 'Save me out,' he's say. 'I'll give you any-thing I've got.'

" 'How much?' Alphonsine she's say.

"He's tink, and he's say, 'Quarter dollar.'

"Alphonsine an' me is laugh, laugh.

" 'Save me,' he's cry some more. 'I hain't fit for die dis mawny.'

" 'You hain't fit for live no mawny,' Alphon-sine she's say. 'One quarter dollar, eh? Where's my sturgeon?'

" 'He's got away when I fall in,' he's say.

" 'How much you goin' give me for lose my big sturgeon?' she's ask.

" 'How much you'll want, Alphonsine?'

" 'Two dollare.'

" 'Dat's too much for one sturgeon,' he's say. For all he was not feel fit for die, he was more 'fraid for pay out his money.

" 'Let him down some more,' Alphonsine she's say.

" 'Oh, *misère, misère!* I'll pay de two dollare,' he's say when his head come up some more.

" 'Ver' well, den,' Alphonsine she's say; 'I'll be willin' for save you, *me*. But you hain't scooped by *me*. You's in Marie's net. I'll only come for help Marie. You's her sturgeon'; an' Alphonsine she's laugh an' laugh.

" 'I didn't lost no sturgeon for Marie,' he's say.

" 'No, eh?' I'll say mysef. 'But you's steal my fader's platform. You's take his fishin' place. You's got him fined two times. You's make my moder pay his bill wis *my* weddin' money. What you goin' pay for all dat? You tink I'll be goin' for mos' kill mysef pullin' you out for noting? When you ever do someting for anybody for noting, eh, M'sieu Savarin?'

" 'How much you want?' he's say.

" 'Ten dollare for de platform, dat's all.'

" 'Never—dat's robbery,' he's say, an' he's begin to cry like *ver'* li'll baby.

" 'Pull him hup, Marie, an' give him some more,' Alphonsine she's say.

"But de old rascal is so scare 'bout dat, dat he's say he's pay right off. So we's pull him up near to de platform, only we hain't big 'nuff fool for let him out of de net till he's take out his purse an' pay de twelve dollare.

"*Monjee,* M'sieu! If ever you see one angry old rascal! He not even stop for say: 'T'ank you for save me from be drown' dead in the *culbute!'* He's run for his house an' he's put on dry clo'es, and' he's go up to de magistrate first ting for learn me an' Alphonsine one big lesson.

"But de magistrate hain' ver' bad magistrate. He's only laugh an' he's say:—

" 'M'sieu Savarin, de whole river will be laugh at you for let two young girl take eet out of smart man like you like dat. Hain't you tink your life worth twelve dollare? Didn't dey save you from de *culbute? Monjee!* I'll

tink de whole river not laugh so ver' bad if you
pay dose young girl one hunder dollare for
save you so kind.'

" 'One hunder dollare!' he's mos' cry.
'Hain't you goin' to learn dose girl one lesson
for take advantage of me dat way?'

" 'Didn't you pay dose girl yoursef? Didn't
you took out your purse yoursef? Yes, eh?
Well, den, I'll goin' for learn you one lesson
yourself, M'sieu Savarin,' de magistrate is say.
'Dose two young girl is ver' wicked, eh? Yes,
dat's so. But for why? Hain't dey just do to
you what you been doin' ever since you was in
beesness? Don' I know? You hain' never yet
got advantage of nobody wisout you rob him
all you can, an' dose wicked young girl only
act just like you give dem a lesson all your
life.'

"An' de best fun was de whole river *did*
laugh at M'sieu Savarin. An' my fader and
Frawce Seguin is laugh most of all, till he's
catch hup wis bose of dem anoder time. You
come for see me some more, an' I'll tol' you
'bout dat."

GREAT GODFREY'S LAMENT

"Hark to Angus! Man, his heart will be sore the night! In five years I have not heard him playing 'Great Godfrey's Lament,'" said old Alexander McTavish, as with him I was sitting of a June evening, at sundown, under a wide apple-tree of his orchard-lawn.

When the sweet song-sparrows of the Ottawa valley had ceased their plaintive strains, Angus McNeil began on his violin. This night, instead of "Tullochgorum" or "Roy's Wife" or "The March of the McNeils," or any merry strathspey, he crept into an unusual movement, and from a distance came the notes of an exceeding strange strain blent with the meditative murmur of the Rataplan Rapids.

I am not well enough acquainted with musical terms to tell the method of that composition in which the wail of a Highland coronach seemed mingled with such mournful crooning as I had heard often from Indian voyageurs north of Lake Superior. Perhaps that fancy sprang from my knowledge that Angus McNeil's father had been a younger son of the chief of the McNeil clan, and his mother a daughter of the greatest man of the Cree nation.

"Ay, but Angus is wae," sighed old Mc-Tavish. "What will he be seeing the now? It was the night before his wife died that he played yon last. Come, we will go up the road. He does be liking to see the people gather to listen."

We walked, maybe three hundred yards, and stood leaning against the ruined picket-fence that surrounds the great stone house built by Hector McNeil, the father of Angus, when he retired from his position as one of the "Big Bourgeois" of the famous Northwest Fur Trading Company.

The huge square structure of four stories and a basement is divided, above the ground floor, into eight suites, some of four, and some of five rooms. In these suites the fur-trader, whose ideas were all patriarchal, had designed that he and his Indian wife, with his seven sons and their future families, should live to the end of his days and theirs. That was a dream at the time when his boys were all under nine years old, and Godfrey little more than a baby in arms.

The ground-floor is divided by a hall twenty-

five feet wide into two long chambers, one intended to serve as a dining-hall for the multitude of descendants that Hector expected to
see round his old age, the other as a withdraw-
ing-room for himself and his wife, or for festive
occasions. In this mansion Angus McNeil
now dwelt alone.

He sat out that evening on a balcony at the
rear of the hall, whence he could overlook the
McTavish place and the hamlet that extends a
quarter of a mile further down the Ottawa's
north shore. His right side was toward the
large group of French-Canadian people who
had gathered to hear him play. Though he
was sitting, I could make out that his was a
gigantic figure.

"Ay—it will be just exactly 'Great Godfrey's Lament,'" McTavish whispered. "Weel
do I mind him playing yon many's the night
after Godfrey was laid in the mools. Then he
played it no more till before his ain wife died.
What is he seeing now? Man, it's weel kenned
he has the second sight at times. Maybe he
sees the pit digging for himself. He's the last
of them."

"Who was Great Godfrey?" I asked, rather
loudly.

Angus McNeil instantly cut short the "La-ment," rose from his chair, and faced us.

"Aleck McTavish, who have you with you?" he called imperiously.

"My young cousin from the city, Mr. Mc-Neil," said McTavish, with deference.

"Bring him in. I wish to spoke with you, Aleck McTavish. The young man that is not acquaint with the name of Great Godfrey Mc-Neil can come with you. I will be at the great door."

"It's strange-like," said McTavish, as we went to the upper gate. "He has not asked me inside for near five years. I'm feared his wits is disordered, by his way of speaking. Mind what you say. Great Godfrey was most like a god to Angus."

When Angus McNeil met us at the front door I saw he was verily a giant. Indeed, he was a wee bit more than six and a half feet tall when he stood up straight. Now he was stooped a little, not with age, but with con-sumption,—the disease most fatal to men of mixed white and Indian blood. His face was dark brown, his features of the Indian cast, but his black hair had not the Indian lankness. It curled tightly round his grand head.

Without a word he beckoned us on into the vast withdrawing room. Without a word he seated himself beside a large oaken centre-table, and motioned us to sit opposite.

Before he broke silence, I saw that the windows of that great chamber were hung with faded red damask; that the heads of many a bull moose, buck, bear, and wolf grinned among guns and swords and claymores from its walls; that charred logs, fully fifteen feet long, remained in the fireplace from the last winter's burning; that there were three dim portraits in oil over the mantel; that the room contained much frayed furniture, once sumptuous of red velvet; and that many skins of wild beasts lay strewn over a hard-wood floor whose edges still retained their polish and faintly gleamed in rays from the red west.

That light was enough to show that two of the oil paintings must be those of Hector Mc-Neil and his Indian wife. Between these hung one of a singularly handsome youth with yellow hair.

"Here my father lay dead," cried Angus McNeil, suddenly striking the table. He stared at us silently for many seconds, then again struck the table with the side of his

clenched fist. "He lay here dead on this table
—yes! It was Godfrey that straked him out
all alone on this table. You mind Great Godfrey, Aleck McTavish."

"Well I do, Mr. McNeil; and your mother
yonder,—a grand lady she was." McTavish
spoke with curious humility, seeming wishful,
I thought, to comfort McNeil's sorrow by exciting his pride.

"Ay—they'll tell hereafter that she was just
exactly a squaw," cried the big man, angrily.
"But grand she was, and a great lady, and a
proud. Oh, man, man! but they were proud,
my father and my Indian mother. And Godfrey was the pride of the hearts of them both.
No wonder; but it was sore on the rest of us
after they took him apart from our ways."

Aleck McTavish spoke not a word, and big
Angus, after a long pause, went on as if almost
unconscious of our presence:—

"White was Godfrey, and rosy of the cheek
like my father; and the blue eyes of him would
match the sky when you'll be seeing it up
through a blazing maple on a clear day of
October. Tall, and straight, and grand was
Godfrey, my brother. What was the thing
Godfrey could not do? The songs of him

hushed the singing-birds on the tree, and the fiddle he would play to take the soul out of your body. There was not white one among us till he was born.

"The rest of us all were just Indians—ay, Indians, Aleck McTavish. Brown we were, and the desire of us was all for the woods and the river. Godfrey had white sense like my father, and often we saw the same look in his eyes. My God, but we feared our father!"

Angus paused to cough. After the fit he sat silent for some minutes. The voice of the great rapid seemed to fill the room. When he spoke again, he stared past our seat with fixed, dilated eyes, as if tranced by a vision.

"Godfrey, Godfrey—you hear! Godfrey, the six of us would go over the falls and not think twice of it, if it would please you, when you were little. Oich, the joy we had in the white skin of you, and the fine ways, till my father and mother saw we were just making an Indian of you, like ourselves! So they took you away; ay, and many's the day the six of us went to the woods and the river, missing you sore. It's then you began to look on us with that look that we could not see was different from the look we feared in the blue eyes of our

father. Oh, but we feared him, Godfrey! And
the time went by, and we feared and we hated
you that seemed lifted up above your Indian
brothers!"

"Oich, the masters they got to teach him!"
said Angus, addressing himself again to my
cousin. "In the Latin and the Greek they
trained him. History books he read, and stories in song. Ay, and the manners of Godfrey!
Well might the whole pride of my father and
mother be on their one white son. A grand
young gentleman was Godfrey,—Great Godfrey we called him, when he was eighteen.

"The fine, rich people that would come up
in bateaux from Montreal to visit my father
had the smile and the kind word for Godfrey;
but they looked upon us with the eyes of the
white man for the Indian. And that look we
were more and more sure was growing harder
in Godfrey's eyes. So we looked back at him
with the eyes of the wolf that stares at the bull
moose, and is fierce to pull him down, but dares
not try, for the moose is too great and lordly.

"Mind you, Aleck McTavish, for all we
hated Godfrey when we thought he would be
looking at us like strange Indians—for all that,
yet we were proud of him that he was our own

brother.   Well, we minded how he was all like
one with us when he was little; and in the calm
looks of him, and the white skin, and the yellow
hair, and the grandeur of him, we had pride,
do you understand?   Ay, and in the strength
of him we were glad.   Would we not sit still
and pleased when it was the talk how he could
run quicker than the best, and jump higher
than his head—ay, would we!   Man, there was
none could compare in strength with Great
Godfrey, the youngest of us all!

"He and my father and mother more and
more lived by themselves in this room.   Yonder
room across the hall was left to us six Indians.
No manners, no learning had we; we were no
fit company for Godfrey.   My mother was like
she was wilder with love of Godfrey the more
he grew and the grander, and never a word for
days and weeks together did she give to us.   It
was Godfrey this, and Godfrey that, and all
her thought was Godfrey!

"Most of all we hated him when she was
lying dead here on this table.   We six in the
other room could hear Godfrey and my father
groan and sigh.   We would step softly to the
door and listen to them kissing her that was
dead,—them white, and she Indian like our-

selves,—and us not daring to go in for the fear
of the eyes of our father. So the soreness was
in our hearts so cruel hard that we would not
go in till the last, for all their asking. My God,
my God, Aleck McTavish, if you saw her!
she seemed smiling like at Godfrey, and she
looked like him then, for all she was brown
as November oak-leaves, and he white that day
as the froth on the rapid.

"That put us farther from Godfrey than
before. And farther yet we were from him
after, when he and my father would be walking
up and down, up and down, arm in arm, up
and down the lawn in the evenings. They
would be talking about books, and the great
McNeils in Scotland. The six of us knew we
were McNeils, for all we were Indians, and we
would listen to the talk of the great pride and
the great deeds of the McNeils that was our
own kin. We would be drinking the whiskey
if we had it, and saying: 'Godfrey to be the
only McNeil! Godfrey to take all the pride of
the name of us!' Oh, man, man! but we hated
Godfrey sore."

Big Angus paused long, and I seemed to see
clearly the two fair-haired, tall men walking
arm in arm on the lawn in the twilight, as if

unconscious or careless of being watched and overheard by six sore-hearted kinsmen.

"You'll mind when my father was thrown from his horse and carried into this room, Aleck McTavish? Ay, well you do. But you nor no other living man but me knows what came about the night that he died.

"Godfrey was alone with him. The six of us were in yon room. Drink we had, but cautious we were with it, for there was a deed to be done that would need all our senses. We sat in a row on the floor—we were Indians— it was our wigwam—we sat on the floor to be against the ways of them two. Godfrey was in here across the hall from us; alone he was with our white father. He would be chief over us by the will, no doubt,—and if Godfrey lived through that night it would be strange.

"We were cautious with the whiskey, I told you before. Not a sound could we hear of Godfrey or of my father. Only the rapid, calling and calling,—I mind it well that night. Ay, and well I mind the striking of the great clock,—tick, tick, tick, tick, tick,—I listened and I dreamed on it till I doubted but it was the beating of my father's heart.

"Ten o'clock was gone by, and eleven was

near. How many of us sat sleeping I know
not; but I woke up with a start, and there was
Great Godfrey, with a candle in his hand, looking down strange at us, and us looking up
strange at him.

" 'He is dead,' Godfrey said.

"We said nothing.

" 'Father died two hours ago,' Godfrey said.

"We said nothing.

" 'Our father is white,—he is very white,'
Godfrey said, and he trembled. 'Our mother
was brown when she was dead.'

"Godfrey's voice was wild.

" 'Come, brothers, and see how white is our
father,' Godfrey said.

"No one of us moved.

" 'Won't you come? In God's name, come,'
said Godfrey. 'Oich—but it is very strange!
I have looked in his face so long that now I do
not know him for my father. He is like no
kin to me, lying there. I am alone, alone.'

"Godfrey wailed in a manner. It made me
ashamed to hear his voice like that—him that
looked like my father that was always silent as
a sword—him that was the true McNeil.

" 'You look at me, and your eyes are the
eyes of my mother,' says Godfrey, staring

wilder. 'What are you doing here, all so still? Drinking the whiskey? I am the same as you. I am your brother. I will sit with you, and if you drink the whiskey, I will drink the whiskey, too.'

"Aleck McTavish! with that he sat down on the floor in the dirt and litter beside Donald, that was oldest of us all.

" 'Give me the bottle,' he said. 'I am as much Indian as you, brothers. What you do I will do, as I did when I was little, long ago.'

"To see him sit down in his best,—all his learning and his grand manners as if forgotten, —man, it was like as if our father himself was turned Indian, and was low in the dirt!

"What was in the heart of Donald I don't know, but he lifted the bottle and smashed it down on the floor.

" 'God in heaven! what's to become of the McNeils! You that was the credit of the family, Godfrey!' says Donald with a groan.

"At that Great Godfrey jumped to his feet like he was come awake.

" 'You're fitter to be the head of the McNeils than I am, Donald,' says he; and with that the tears broke out of his eyes, and he cast himself into Donald's arms. Well, with that

we all began to cry as if our hearts would break.
I threw myself down on the floor at Godfrey's
feet, and put my arms round his knees the same
as I'd lift him up when he was little. There I
cried, and we all cried around him, and after a
bit I said:—

" 'Brothers, this was what was in the mind
of Godfrey. He was all alone in yonder. We
are his brothers, and his heart warmed to us,
and he said to himself, it was better to be like
us than to be alone, and he thought if he came
and sat down and drank the whiskey with us,
he would be our brother again, and not be any
more alone.'

" 'Ay, Angus, Angus, but how did you know
that?' says Godfrey, crying; and he put his
arms round my neck, and lifted me up till we
were breast to breast. With that we all put
our arms some way round one another and
Godfrey, and there we stood sighing and swaying and sobbing a long time, and no man saying a word.

" 'Oh, man, Godfrey dear, but our father is
gone, and who can talk with you now about the
Latin, and the history books, and the great
McNeils—and our mother that's gone?' says
Donald; and the thought of it was such pity
that our hearts seemed like to break.

"But Godfrey said: 'We will talk together like brothers. If it shames you for me to be like you, then I will teach you all they taught me, and we will all be like our white father.'

"So we all agreed to have it so, if he would tell us what to do. After that we came in here with Godfrey, and we stood looking at my father's white face. Godfrey all alone had straked him out on this table, with the silver-pieces on the eyes that we had feared. But the silver we did not fear. Maybe you will not understand it, Aleck McTavish, but our father never seemed such close kin to us as when we would look at him dead, and at Godfrey, that was the picture of him, living and kind.

"After that you know what happened yourself."

"Well I do, Mr. McNeil. It was Great Godfrey that was the father to you all," said my cousin.

"Just that, Aleck McTavish. All that he had was ours to use as we would,—his land, money, horses, this room, his learning. Some of us could learn one thing and some of us could learn another, and some could learn nothing, not even how to behave. What I could learn was the playing of the fiddle. Many's the hour Godfrey would play with me while the rest were all happy around.

"In great content we lived like brothers, and proud to see Godfrey as white and fine and grand as the best gentleman that ever came up to visit him out of Montreal. Ay, in great content we lived all together till the consumption came on Donald, and he was gone. Then it came and came back, and came back again, till Hector was gone, and Ranald was gone, and in ten years' time only Godfrey and I were left. Then both of us married, as you know. But our children died as fast as they were born, almost,—for the curse seemed on us. Then his wife died, and Godfrey sighed and sighed ever after that.

"One night I was sleeping with the door of my room open, so I could hear if Godfrey needed my help. The cough was on him then. Out of a dream of him looking at my father's· white face I woke and went to his bed. He was not there at all.

"My heart went cold with fear, for I heard the rapid very clear, like the nights they all died. Then I heard the music begin down stairs, here in this chamber where they were all laid out dead,—right here on this table where I will soon lie like the rest. I leave it to you to see it done, Aleck McTavish, for you are a Highlandman by blood. It was that I wanted to say to you when I called you in. I have seen himself in my coffin three nights. Nay, say nothing; you will see.

"Hearing the music that night, down I came softly. Here sat Godfrey, and the kindest look was on his face that ever I saw. He had his fiddle in his hand, and he played about all our lives.

"He played about how we all came down from the North in the big canoe with my father and mother, when we were little children and him a baby. He played of the rapids we passed over, and of the rustling of the poplar-trees and the purr of the pines. He played till the river you hear now was in the fiddle, with the sound of our paddles, and the fish jumping for flies. He played about the long winters when we were young, so that the snow of those winters seemed falling again. The ringing of our skates on the ice I could hear in the fiddle. He played through all our lives when we were young and going in the woods yonder together —and then it was the sore lament began!

"It was like as if he played how they kept

him away from his brothers, and him at his books thinking of them in the woods, and him hearing the partridges' drumming, and the squirrels' chatter, and all the little birds singing and singing. Oich, man, but there's no words for the sadness of it!"

Old Angus ceased to speak as he took his violin from the table and struck into the middle of "Great Godfrey's Lament." As he played, his wide eyes looked past us, and the tears streamed down his brown cheeks. When the woful strain ended, he said, staring past us: "Ay, Godfrey, you were always our brother."

Then he put his face down in his big brown hands, and we left him without another word.

McGRATH'S BAD NIGHT

"COME, then, childer," said Mrs. McGrath,
and took the big iron pot off. They crowded
around her, nine of them, the eldest not more
than thirteen, the youngest just big enough to
hold out his yellow crockery bowl.

"The youngest first," remarked Mrs. Mc-
Grath, and ladled out a portion of the boiled
cornmeal to each of the deplorable boys and
girls. Before they reached the stools from
which they had sprung up, or squatted again
on the rough floor, they all burned their mouths
in tasting the mush too eagerly. Then there
they sat, blowing into their bowls, glaring into
them, lifting their loaded iron spoons occasionally to taste cautiously, till the mush had somewhat cooled.

Then, *gobble-de-gobble-de-gobble,* it was all
gone! Though they had neither sugar, nor
milk, nor butter to it, they found it a remark-
ably excellent sample of mush, and wished only
that, in quantity, it had been something more.

Peter McGrath sat close beside the cooking-
stove, holding Number Ten, a girl-baby, who

was asleep, and rocking Number Eleven, who was trying to wake up, in the low, unpainted cradle. He never took his eyes off Number Eleven; he could not bear to look around and see the nine devouring the corn-meal so hungrily. Perhaps McGrath could not, and certainly he would not,—he was so obstinate,—have told why he felt so reproached by the scene. He had felt very guilty for many weeks.

Twenty, yes, a hundred times a day he looked in a dazed way at his big hands, and they reproached him, too, that they had no work.

"Where is our smooth, broad-axe handle?" asked the fingers, "and why do not the wide chips fly?"

He was ashamed, too, every time he rose up, so tall and strong, with nothing to do, and eleven children and his wife next door to starvation; but if he had been asked to describe his feelings, he would merely have growled out angrily something against old John Pontiac.

"You'll take your sup now, Peter?" asked Mrs. McGrath, offering him the biggest of the yellow bowls. He looked up then, first at her forlorn face, then at the pot. Number Nine was diligently scraping off some streaks of mush that had run down the outside; Numbers Eight, Seven, Six, and Five were looking respectfully into the pot; Numbers Four, Three, Two, and One were watching the pot, the steaming bowl, and their father at the same time. Peter McGrath was very hungry.

"Yourself had better eat, Mary Ann," he said. "I'll be having mine after it's cooler."

Mrs. McGrath dipped more than a third of the bowlful back into the pot, and ate the rest with much satisfaction. The numerals watched her anxiously but resignedly.

"Sure it'll be cold entirely, Peter dear," she said, "and the warmth is so comforting. Give me little Norah now, the darlint! and be after eating your supper."

She had ladled out the last spoonful of mush, and the pot was being scraped inside earnestly by Nine, Eight, Seven, and Six. Peter took the bowl, and looked at his children.

The earlier numbers were observing him with peculiar sympathy, putting themselves in his place, as it were, possessing the bowl in imagination; the others now moved their spoons absent-mindedly around in the pot, brought them empty to their mouths, mechanically, now and again, sucked them more or less, and still stared steadily at their father.

His inner walls felt glued together, yet indescribably hollow; the smell of the mush went up into his nostrils, and pungently provoked his palate and throat. He was famishing.

"Troth, then, Mary Ann," he said, "there's no hunger in me to-night. Sure, I wish the childer would n't leave me the trouble of eating it. Come, then, all of ye!"

The nine came promptly to his call. There were just twenty-two large spoonfuls in the bowl; each child received two; the remaining four went to the four youngest. Then the bowl was skilfully scraped by Number Nine, after which Number Seven took it, whirled a cup of water artfully round its interior, and with this put a fine finish on his meal.

Peter McGrath then searched thoughtfully in his trousers pockets, turning their corners up, getting pinches of tobacco dust out of their remotest recesses; he put his blouse pocket through a similar process. He found no pockets in his well-patched overcoat when he took it down, but he pursued the dust into its lining, and separated it carefully from little dabs of wool. Then he put the collection into an extremely old black clay pipe, lifted a coal in with his fingers, and took his supper.

It would be absurd to assert that, on this continent, a strong man could be so poor as Peter, unless he had done something very wrong or very foolish. Peter McGrath was, in truth, out of work because he had committed an outrage on economics. He had been guilty of the enormous error of misunderstanding, and trying to set at naught in his own person, the immutable law of supply and demand.

Fancying that a first-class hewer in a timber shanty had an inalienable right to receive at least thirty dollars a month, when the demand was only strong enough to yield him twenty-two dollars a month, Peter had refused to engage at the beginning of the winter.

"Now, Mr. McGrath, you're making a mistake," said his usual employer, old John Pontiac. "I'm offering you the best wages going, mind that. There's mighty little squared timber coming out this winter."

"I'm ready and willing to work, boss, but I'm fit to arn thirty dollars, surely."

"So you are, so you are, in good times, neighbor, and I'd be glad if men's wages were forty. That could only be with trade active, and a

fine season for all of us; but I couldn't take
out a raft this winter, and pay what you ask."

"I'd work extra hard. I'm not afeard of
work."

"Not you, Peter. There never was a lazy
bone in your body. Don't I know that well?
But look, now: if I was to pay you thirty, I
should have to pay all the other hewers thirty;
and that's not all. Scorers and teamsters and
road-cutters are used to getting wages in pro-
portion to hewers. Why, it would cost me a
thousand dollars a month to give you thirty!
Go along, now, that's a good fellow, and tell
your wife that you've hired with me."

But Peter did not go back. "I'm bound to
have my rights, so I am," he said sulkily to
Mary Ann when he reached the cabin. "The
old boss is getting too hard like, and set on
money. Twenty-two dollars! No! I'll go in
to Stambrook and hire."

Mary Ann knew that she might as well try
to convince a saw-log that its proper course
was up-stream, as to protest against Peter's
obstinacy. Moreover, she did think the offered
wages very low, and had some hope he might
better himself; but when he came back from
Stambrook, she saw trouble ahead. He did

not tell her that there, where his merits were
not known, he had been offered only twenty
dollars, but she surmised his disappointment.

"You'd better be after seeing the boss again,
maybe, Peter dear," she said timidly.

"Not a step," he answered. "The boss'll be
after me in a few days, you'll see." But there
he was mistaken, for all the gangs were full.

After that Peter McGrath tramped far and
wide, to many a backwoods hamlet, looking
vainly for a job at any wages. The season was
the worst ever known on the river, and before
January the shanties were discharging men,
so threatening was the outlook for lumbermen,
and so glutted with timber the markets of the
world.

Peter's conscience accused him every hour,
but he was too stubborn to go back to John
Pontiac. Indeed, he soon got it into his stupid
head that the old boss was responsible for his
misfortunes, and he consequently came to hate
Mr. Pontiac very bitterly.

After supping on his pipeful of tobacco-
dust, Peter sat, straight-backed, leaning elbows
on knees and chin on hands, wondering what on
earth was to become of them all next day. For
a man out of work there was not a dollar of

credit at the little village store; and work! why, there was only one kind of work at which money could be earned in that district in the winter.

When his wife took Number Eleven's cradle into the other room, she heard him, through the thin partition of upright boards, pasted over with newspapers, moving round in the dim red flickering fire-light from the stove-grating.

The children were all asleep, or pretending it; Number Ten in the big straw bed, where she lay always between her parents; Number Eleven in her cradle beside; Nine crosswise at the foot; Eight, Seven, Six, Five, and Four in the other bed; One, Two, and Three curled up, without taking off their miserable garments, on the "locks" of straw beside the kitchen stove.

Mary Ann knew very well what Peter was moving round for. She heard him groan, so low that he did not know he groaned, when he lifted off the cover of the meal barrel, and could feel nothing whatever therein. She had actually beaten the meal out of the cracks to make that last pot of mush. He knew that all the fish he had salted down in the summer were gone, that the flour was all out, that the last morsel of the pig had been eaten up long ago; but he went to each of the barrels as though he could not realize that there was really nothing left. There were four of those low groans.

"O God, help him! do help him! please do!" she kept saying to herself. Somehow, all her sufferings and the children's were light to her, in comparison, as she listened to that big, taciturn man groan, and him sore with the hunger.

When at last she came out, Peter was not there. He had gone out silently, so silently that she wondered, and was scared. She opened the door very softly, and there he was, leaning on the rail fence between their little rocky plot and the great river. She closed the door softly, and sat down.

There was a wide steaming space in the river, where the current ran too swiftly for any ice to form. Peter gazed on it for a long while. The mist had a friendly look; he was soon reminded of the steam from an immense bowl of mush! It vexed him. He looked up at the moon. The moon was certainly mocking him; dashing through light clouds, then jumping into a wide, clear space, where it soon became motionless, and mocked him steadily.

He had never known old John Pontiac to jeer any one, but there was his face in that moon,—Peter made it out quite clearly. He looked up the road to where he could see, on the hill half a mile distant, the shimmer of John Pontiac's big tin-roofed house. He thought he could make out the outlines of all the buildings,—he knew them so well,—the big barn, the stable, the smoke-house, the store-house for shanty supplies.

Pork barrels, flour barrels, herring kegs, syrup kegs, sides of frozen beef, hams and flitches of bacon in the smoke-house, bags of beans, chests of tea,—he had a vision of them all! Teamsters going off to the woods daily with provisions, the supply apparently inexhaustible.

And John Pontiac had refused to pay him fair wages!

Peter in exasperation shook his big fist at the moon; it mocked him worse than ever. Then out went his gaze to the space of mist; it was still more painfully like mush steam. His pigsty was empty, except of snow; it made him think again of the empty barrels in the cabin.

The children empty too, or would be to-morrow,—as empty as he felt that minute. How dumbly the elder ones would reproach him! and what would comfort the younger ones crying with hunger?

Peter looked again up the hill, through the walls of the store-house. He was dreadfully hungry.

"John! John!" Mrs. Pontiac jogged her husband. "John, wake up! there's somebody trying to get into the smoke-house."

"Eh—ugh—ah! I'm 'sleep—ugh." He relapsed again.

"John! John! wake up! There *is* somebody!"

"What—ugh—eh—what you say?"

"There's somebody getting into the smoke-house."

"Well, there's not much there."

"There's ever so much bacon and ham. Then there's the store-house open."

"Oh, I guess there's nobody."

"But there is, I'm sure. You must get up!"

They both got up and looked out of the window. The snow-drifts, the paths through them, the storehouse, the smoke-house, and the other white-washed out-buildings could be seen as clearly as in broad day. The smoke-house door was open!

Old John Pontiac was one of the kindest souls that ever inhabited a body, but this was a little too much. Still he was sorry for the man, no matter who, in that smoke-house,—some Indian probably. He must be caught and dealt with firmly; but he did not want the man to be too much hurt.

He put on his clothes and sallied forth. He reached the smoke-house; there was no one in it; there was a gap, though, where two long flitches of bacon *had* been!

John Pontiac's wife saw him go over to the store-house, the door of which was open too. He looked in, then stopped, and started back as if in horror. Two flitches tied together with a rope were on the floor, and inside was a man filling a bag with flour from a barrel.

"Well, well! this is a terrible thing," said old John Pontiac to himself, shrinking around a corner. "Peter McGrath! Oh, my! oh, my!"

He became hot all over, as if he had done something disgraceful himself. There was nobody that he respected more than that pig-headed Peter. What to do? He must punish him of course; but how? Jail?—for him with eleven children! "Oh, my! oh, my!" Old John wished he had not been awakened to see this terrible downfall.

"It will never do to let him go off with it," he said to himself after a little reflection. "I'll put him so that he'll know better another time."

Peter McGrath, as he entered the store-house, had felt that bacon heavier than the heaviest end of the biggest stick of timber he had ever helped to cant. He felt guilty, sneaking, disgraced; he felt that the literal Devil had first tempted him near the house, then all suddenly—with his own hunger pangs and thoughts of his starving family—swept him into the smoke-house to steal. But he had consented to do it; he had said he would take flour too,—and he would, he was so obstinate! And withal, he hated old John Pontiac worse than ever; for now he accused him of being the cause of his coming to this.

Then all of a sudden he met the face of Pontiac looking in at the door.

Peter sprang back; he saw Stambrook jail —he saw his eleven children and his wife—he felt himself a detected felon, and that was worst of all.

"Well, Peter, you'd ought to have come right in," were the words that came to his ears, in John Pontiac's heartiest voice. "The missis would have been glad to see you. We did go to bed a bit early, but there wouldn't have been any harm in an old neighbor like you waking us up. Not a word of that—hold on! listen to me. It would be a pity if old friends like you and me, Peter, couldn't help one another to a trifling loan of provisions without making a fuss over it." And old John, taking up the scoop, went on filling the bag as if that were a matter of course.

Peter did not speak; he could not.

"I was going round to your place to-morrow," resumed John, cheerfully, "to see if I couldn't hire you again. There's a job of hewing for you in the Conlonge shanty,—a man gone off sick. But I can't give more'n twenty-two, or say twenty-three, seeing you're an old neighbor. What do you say?"

Peter still said nothing; he was choking.

"You had better have a bit of something more than bacon and flour, Peter," he went on, "and I'll give you a hand to carry the truck home. I guess your wife won't mind seeing me with you; then she'll know that you've taken

a job with me again, you see.   Come along and
give me a hand to hitch the mare up.   I'll drive
you down."

"Ah—ah—Boss—Boss!" spoke Peter then,
with terrible gasps between.   "Boss—O, my
God, Mr. Pontiac—I can't never look you in
the face again!"

"Peter McGrath — old neighbor,"— and
John Pontiac laid his hand on the shaking
shoulder,—"I guess I know all about it; I
guess I do.   Sometimes a man is driven he don't
know how.   Now we will say no more about it.
I'll load up, and you come right along with me.
And mind, I'll do the talking to your wife."

Mary Ann McGrath was in a terrible frame
of mind.   What had become of Peter?

She had gone out to look down the road, and
had been recalled by Number Eleven's crying.
Number Ten then chimed in; Nine, too, awoke,
and determined to resume his privileges as an
infant.   One after another they got up and
huddled around her—craving, craving,—all
but the three eldest, who had been well prac-
tised in the stoical philosophy by the gradual
decrease of their rations.   But these bounced
up suddenly at the sound of a grand jangle of
bells.

Could it be? Mr. Pontiac they had no doubt
about; but was that real bacon that he laid on
the kitchen table? Then a side of beef, a can
of tea; next a bag of flour, and again an actual
keg of sirup. Why, this was almost incredible!
And, last, he came in with an immense round
loaf of bread! The children gathered about it;
old John almost sickened with sorrow for them,
and hurrying out his jackknife, passed big
hunks around.

"Well, now, Mrs. McGrath," he said during
these operations, "I don't hardly take it kindly
of you and Peter not to have come up to an old
neighbor's house before this for a bit of a loan.
It's well I met Peter to-night. Maybe he'd
never have told me your troubles—not but
what I blame myself for not suspecting how it
was a bit sooner. I just made him take a little
loan for the present. No, no; don't be talking
like that! Charity! tut! tut! it's just an advance of wages. I've got a job for Peter; he'll
be on pay to-morrow again."

At that Mary Ann burst out crying again.
"Oh, God bless you, Mr. Pontiac! it's a kind
man you are! May the saints be about your
bed!"

With that she ran out to Peter, who still

stood by the sleigh; she put the baby in his
arms, and clinging to her husband's shoulder,
cried more and more.

And what did obstinate Peter McGrath do?
Why, he cried, too, with gasps and groans that
seemed almost to kill him.

"Go in," he said; "go in, Mary Ann—go in
—and kiss—the feet of him. Yes—and the
boards—he stands on. You don't know what
he's done—for me. It's broke I am—the bad
heart of me—broke entirely—with the goodness of him. May the heavens be his bed!"

"Now, Mrs. McGrath," cried old John,
"never you mind Peter; he's a bit light-headed
to-night. Come away in and get a bite for him.
I'd like a dish of tea myself before I go home."
Didn't that touch on her Irish hospitality bring
her in quickly!

"Mind you this, Peter," said the old man,
going out then, "don't you be troubling your
wife with any little secrets about to-night;
that's between you and me. That's all I ask
of you."

Thus it comes about that to this day, when
Peter McGrath's fifteen children have helped
him to become a very prosperous farmer, his
wife does not quite understand the depth of

worship with which he speaks of old John Pontiac.

Mrs. Pontiac never knew the story of the night.

"Never mind who it was, Jane," John said, turning out the light, on returning to bed, "except this,—it was a neighbor in sore trouble."

"Stealing—and you helped him! Well, John, such a man as you are!"

"Jane, I don't ever rightly know what kind of a man I might be, suppose hunger was cruel on me, and on you, and all of us! Let us bless God that he's saved us from the terriblest temptations, and thank him most especially when he inclines our hearts—inclines our hearts —that's all."

SHINING CROSS OF RIGAUD

I

WHEN Mini was a fortnight old his mother wrapped her head and shoulders in her ragged shawl, snatched him from the family litter of straw, and, with a volley of cautionary objurgations to his ten brothers and sisters, strode angrily forth into the raw November weather. She went down the hill to the edge of the broad, dark Ottawa, where thin slices of ice were swashing together. There sat a hopeless-looking little man at the clumsy oars of a flat-bottomed boat.

"The little one's feet are out," said the man.

"So much the better! For what was another sent us?" cried Mini's mother.

"But the little one must be baptized," said the father, with mild expostulation.

"Give him to me, then," and the man took off his own ragged coat. Beneath it he had nothing except an equally ragged guernsey, and the wind was keen. The woman surrendered the child carelessly, and drawing her shawl closer, sat frowning moodily in the stern.

Mini's father wrapped him in the wretched garment, carefully laid the infant on the pea-straw at his feet, and rowed wearily away.

They took him to the gray church on the far-ther shore, whose tall cross glittered coldly in the wintry sun. There Madame Lajeunesse, the skilful washerwoman, angry to be taken so long from her tubs, and Bonhomme Hamel, who never did anything but fish for *barbotes,* met them. These highly respectable connec-tions of Mini's mother had a disdain for her inferior social status, and easily made it under-stood that nothing but a Christian duty would have brought them out. Where else, indeed, could the friendless infant have found spon-sors? It was disgraceful, they remarked, that the custom of baptism at three days old should have been violated. While they answered for Mini's spiritual development he was quiet, neither crying nor smiling till the old priest crossed his brow. Then he smiled, and that, Bonhomme Hamel remarked, was a blessed sign.

"Now he's sure of heaven when he does die!" cried Mini's mother, getting home again, and tossed him down on the straw, for a conclusion to her sentence.

But the child lived, as if by miracle. Hunger, cold, dirt, abuse, still left him a feeble vitality. At six years old his big dark eyes wore so sad a look that mothers of merry children often stopped to sigh over him, frightening the child, for he did not understand sympathy. So unresponsive and dumb was he that they called him half-witted. Three babies younger than he had died by then, and the fourth was little Angélique. They said she would be very like Mini, and there was reason why in her wretched infancy. Mini's was the only love she ever knew. When she saw the sunny sky his weak arms carried her, and many a night he drew over her the largest part of his deplorable coverings. She, too, was strangely silent. For days long they lay together on the straw, quietly suffering what they had known from the beginning. It was something near starvation.

When Mini was eight years old his mother sent him one day to beg food from Madame Leclaire, whose servant she had been long ago.

"It's Lucile's Mini," said Madame, taking him to the door of the cosey sitting-room, where Monsieur sat at *solitaire*.

"*Mon Dieu*, did one ever see such a child!"

cried the retired notary. "For the love of
Heaven, feed him well, Marie, before you let
him go!"

But Mini could scarcely eat. He trembled
at the sight of so much food, and chose a crust
as the only thing familiar.

"Eat, my poor child. Have no fear," said
Madame.

"But Angélique," said he.

"Angélique? Is it the baby?"

"Yes, Madame, if I might have something
for her."

"Poor little loving boy," said Madame, tears
in her kind eyes. But Mini did not cry; he had
known so many things so much sadder.

When Mini reached home his mother seized
the basket. Her wretched children crowded
around. There were broken bread and meat
in plenty. "Here—here—and here!" She distributed crusts, and chose a well-fleshed bone
for her own teeth. Angélique could not walk,
and did not cry, so got nothing. Mini, however, went to her with the tin pail before his
mother noticed it.

"Bring that back!" she shouted.

"Quick, baby!" cried Mini, holding it that
Angélique might drink. But the baby was not

quick enough. Her mother seized the pail and tasted; the milk was still almost warm. "Good," said she, reaching for her shawl.

"For the love of God, mother!" cried Mini, "Madame said it was for Angélique." He knew too well what new milk would trade for. The woman laughed and flung on her shawl.

"Only a little, then; only a cupful," cried Mini, clutching her, struggling weakly to restrain her. "Only a little cupful for Angélique."

"Give her bread!" She struck him so that he reeled, and left the cabin. *Then* Mini cried, but not for the blow.

He placed a soft piece of bread and a thin shred of meat in Angélique's thin little hand, but she could not eat, she was so weak. The elder children sat quietly devouring their food, each ravenously eyeing that of the others. But there was so much that when the father came he also could eat. He, too, offered Angélique bread. Then Mini lifted his hand which held hers, and showed beneath the food she had refused.

"If she had milk!" said the boy.

"My God, if I could get some," groaned the

man, and stopped as a shuffling and tumbling was heard at the door.

"She is very drunk," said the man, without amazement. He helped her in, and, too far gone to abuse them, she soon lay heavily breathing near the child she had murdered.

Mini woke in the pale morning thinking Angélique very cold in his arms, and, behold, she was free from all the suffering forever. So he *could* not cry, though the mother wept when she awoke, and shrieked at his tearlessness as hardhearted.

Little Angélique had been rowed across the great river for the last time; night was come again, and Mini thought he *must* die; it could not be that he should be made to live without Angélique! Then a wondrous thing seemed to happen. Little Angélique had come back. He could not doubt it next morning, for, with the slowly lessening glow from the last brands of fire had not her face appeared?—then her form?—and lo! she was closely held in the arms of the mild Mother whom Mini knew from her image in the church, only she smiled more sweetly now in the hut. Little Angélique had learned to smile, too, which was most wonderful of all to Mini. In their heavenly looks was a meaning of which he felt almost aware; a mysterious happiness was coming close and closer; with the sense of ineffable touches near his brow, the boy dreamed. Nothing more did Mini know till his mother's voice woke him in the morning. He sprang up with a cry of "Angélique," and gazed round upon the familiar squalor.

II

FROM the summit of Rigaud Mountain a mighty cross flashes sunlight all over the great plain of Vaudreuil. The devout *habitant,* ascending from vale to hill-top in the county of Deux Montagnes, bends to the sign he sees across the forest leagues away. Far off on the brown Ottawa, beyond the Cascades of Carillon and the Chute à Blondeau, the keen-eyed *voyageur* catches its gleam, and, for gladness to be nearing the familiar mountain, more cheerily raises the *chanson* he loves. Near St. Placide the early ploughman—while yet mist wreathes the fields and before the native Rossignol has fairly begun his plaintive flourishes —watches the high cross of Rigaud for the first glint that shall tell him of the yet unrisen sun. The wayfarer marks his progress by the bear-

ing of that great cross, the hunter looks to it
for an unfailing landmark, the weatherwise
farmer prognosticates from its appearances.
The old watch it dwindle from sight at evening
with long thoughts of the well-beloved vanished, who sighed to its vanishing through vanished years; the dying turn to its beckoning
radiance; happy is the maiden for whose bridal
it wears brightness; blessed is the child thought
to be that holds out tiny hands for the glittering cross as for a star.   Even to the most
worldly it often seems flinging beams of heaven,
and to all who love its shining that is a dark
day when it yields no reflection of immortal
meaning.

To Mini the Cross of Rigaud had as yet been
no more than an indistinct glimmering, so far
from it did he live and so dulled was he by his
sufferings. It promised him no immortal joys,
for how was he to conceive of heaven except as
a cessation of weariness, starvation, and pain?
Not till Angélique had come in the vision did
he gain certainty that in heaven she would
smile on him always from the mild Mother's
arms. As days and weeks passed without that
dream's return, his imagination was ever the
more possessed by it. Though the boy looked

frailer than ever, people often remarked with amazement how his eyes wore some unspeakable happiness.

Now it happened that one sunny day after rain Mini became aware that his eyes were fixed on the Cross of Rigaud. He could not make out its form distinctly, but it appeared to thrill toward him. Under his intent watching the misty cross seemed gradually to become the centre of such a light as had enwrapped the figures of his dream. While he gazed, expecting his vision of the night to appear in broad day on the far summit, the light extended, changed, rose aloft, assumed clear tints, and shifted quickly to a great rainbow encircling the hill.

Mini believed it a token to him. That Angélique had been there by the cross the little dreamer doubted not, and the transfiguration to that arch of glory had some meaning that his soul yearned to apprehend. The cross drew his thoughts miraculously; for days thereafter he dwelt with its shining; more and more it was borne in on him that he could always see dimly the outline of little Angélique's face there; sometimes, staring very steadily for minutes together, he could even believe that she beckoned and smiled.

"Is Angélique really there, father?" he asked one day, looking toward the hill-top.

"Yes, there," answered his father, thinking the boy meant heaven.

"I will go to her, then," said Mini to his heart.

Birds were not stirring when Mini stepped from the dark cabin into gray dawn, with firm resolve to join Angélique on the summit. The Ottawa, with whose flow he went toward Rigaud, was solemnly shrouded in motionless mist, which began to roll slowly during the first hour of his journey. Lifting, drifting, clinging, ever thinner and more pervaded by sunlight, it was drawn away so that the unruffled flood reflected a sky all blue when he had been two hours on the road. But Mini took no note of the river's beauty. His eyes were fixed on the cloudy hilltop, beyond which the sun was climbing. As yet he could see nothing of the cross, nor of his vision; yet the world had never seemed so glad, nor his heart so light with joy. *Habitants,* in their rattling *calèches,* were amazed by the glow in the face of a boy so ragged and forlorn. Some told afterward how they had half doubted the reality of his rags;

for might not one, if very pure at heart, have
been privileged to see such garments of apparent meanness change to raiment of angelic tex-
ture? Such things had been, it was said, and
certainly the boy's face was a marvel.

His look was ever upward to where fibrous
clouds shifted slowly, or packed to level bands
of mist half concealing Rigaud Hill, as the sun
wheeled higher, till at last, in mid-sky, it flung
rays that trembled on the cross, and gradually
revealed the holy sign outlined in upright and
arms. Mini shivered with an awe of expectation; but no nimbus was disclosed which his
imagination could shape to glorious signifi-
cance. Yet he went rapturously onward, firm
in the belief that up there he must see Angélique face to face.

As he journeyed the cross gradually lessened
in height by disappearance behind the nearer
trees, till only a spot of light was left, which
suddenly was blotted out too. Mini drew a
deep breath, and became conscious of the great-
ness of the hill,—a towering mass of brown
rock, half hidden by sombre pines and the delicate greenery of birch and poplar. But soon,
because the cross *was* hidden, he could figure it
all the more gloriously, and entertain all the

more luminously the belief that there were
heavenly presences awaiting him. He pressed
on with all his speed, and began to ascend the
mountain early in the afternoon.

"Higher," said the women gathering pearly-
bloomed blueberries on the steep hillside.
"Higher," said the path, ever leading the tired
boy upward from plateau to plateau,—"higher,
to the vision and the radiant space about the
shining cross!"

Faint with hunger, worn with fatigue, in the
half-trance of physical exhaustion, Mini still
dragged himself upward through the afternoon. At last he knew he stood on the summit
level very near the cross. There the child, awed
by the imminence of what he had sought, halted
to control the rapturous, fearful trembling of
his heart. Would not the heavens surely open?
What words would Angélique first say? Then
again he went swiftly forward through the
trees to the edge of the little cleared space.
There he stood dazed.

The cross was revealed to him at a few yards'
distance. With woful disillusionment Mini
threw himself face downward on the rock, and
wept hopelessly, sorely; wept and wept, till his
sobs became fainter than the up-borne long

notes of a hermit-thrush far below on the edge
of the plain.

A tall mast, with a shorter at right angles,
both covered by tin roofing-plates, held on by
nails whence rust had run in streaks,—that was
the shining Cross of Rigaud! Fragments of
newspaper, crusts of bread, empty tin cans,
broken bottles, the relics of many picnics scat-
tered widely about the foot of the cross; rude
initial letters cut deeply into its butt where the
tin had been torn away;—these had Mini seen.

The boy ceased to move. Shadows stole
slowly lengthening over the Vaudreuil cham-
paign; the sun swooned down in a glamour of
painted clouds; dusk covered from sight the
yellows and browns and greens of the August
fields; birds stilled with the deepening night;
Rigaud Mountain loomed from the plain, a
dark long mass under a flying and waning
moon; stars came out from the deep spaces
overhead, and still Mini lay where he had wept.

DOUR DAVIE'S DRIVE

PINNAGER was on snow-shoes, making a bee-line toward his field of sawlogs dark on the ice of Wolverine River. He crossed shanty roads, trod heaps of brush, forced his way through the tops of felled pines, jumped from little crags into seven feet of snow—Pinnager's men called him "a terror on snow-shoes." They never knew the direction from which he might come —an ignorance which kept them all busy with axe, saw, cant-hook, and horses over the two square miles of forest comprising his "cut."

It was "make or break" with Pinnager. He had contracted to put on the ice all the logs he might make; for every one left in the woods he must pay stumpage and forfeit. Now his axe-men had done such wonders that Pinnager's difficulty was to get his logs hauled out.

Teams were scarce that winter. The shanty was eighty miles from any settlement; ordinary teamsters were not eager to work for a small speculative jobber, who might or might not be able to pay in the spring. But Pinnager had some extraordinary teamsters, sons of farmers who neighbored him at home, and who were sure he would pay them, though he should have to mortgage his land.

The time was late February; seven feet of snow, crusted, on the level; a thaw might turn the whole forest floor to slush; but if the weather should "hold hard" for six weeks longer, Pinnager might make and not break. Yet the chances were heavily against him.

Any jobber so situated would feel vexed on hearing that one of his best teams had suddenly been taken out of his service. Pinnager, crossing a shanty road with the stride of a moose, was hailed by Jamie Stuart with the news:

"Hey, boss, hold on! Davie McAndrews' leg's broke. His load slewed at the side hill— log catched him against a tree."

"Where is he?" shouted Pinnager furiously.

"Carried him to shanty."

"Where are his horses?"

"Stable."

"Tell Aleck Dunbar to go get them out. He must take Davie's place—confound the lad's carelessness!"

"Davie says no; won't let any other man drive his horses."

"He won't? I'll show him!" and Pinnager

made a bee-line for his shanty. He was choking with rage, all the more so because he knew
that nothing short of breaking Davie McAndrews' neck would break Davie McAndrews'
stubbornness, a reflection that cooled Pinnager
before he reached the shanty.

The cook was busy about the caboose fire,
getting supper for fifty-three devourers, when
Pinnager entered the low door, and made
straight for one of the double tier of dingy
bunks. There lay a youth of eighteen, with an
unusual pallor on his weather-beaten face, and
more than the usual sternness about his formidable jaw.

"What's all this, Davie? You sure the leg's
broke? I'd 'a thought you old enough to take
care."

"You would?" said Davie grimly. "And
yourself not old enough to have yon piece of
road mended—you that was so often told about
it!"

"When you knew it was bad, the more you
should take care."

"And that's true, Pinnager. But no use in
you and me choppin' words. I'm needing a
doctor's hands on me. Can you set a bone?"

"No, I'll not meddle with it. Maybe Jock

Scott can; but I'll send you out home. A fine loss I'll be at! Confound it—and me like to break for want of teams!"

"I've thocht o' yer case, Pinnager," said Davie, with a curious judicial air. "It's sore hard for ye; I ken that well. There's me and me feyther's horses gawn off, and you countin' on us. I feel for ye, so I do. But I'll no put you to ony loss in sendin' me out."

"Was you thinking to tough it through here, Davie? No, you'll not chance it. Anyway, the loss would be the same—more, too. Why, if I send out for the doctor, there's a team off for full five days, and the expense of the doctor! Then he mightn't come. Wow, no! it's out you must go."

"What else?" said Davie coolly. "Would I lie here till spring and my leg mendin' into the Lord kens what-like shape? Would I be lettin' ony ither drive the horses my feyther entrustit to my lone? Would I be dependin' on Mr. Pinnager for keep, and me idle? Man, I'd eat the horses' heads off that way; at home they'd be profit to my feyther. So it's me and them that starts at gray the morn's morn."

"Alone!" exclaimed Pinnager.

"Just that, man. What for no?"

"You're light-headed, Davie. A lad with his leg broke can't drive three days."

"Maybe yes and maybe no. I'm for it, onyhow."

"It may snow, it may——"

"Aye, or rain, or thaw, or hail; the Lord's no in the habit o' makin' weather suit ony but himsel'. But I'm gawn; the cost of a man wi' me would eat the wages ye're owing my feyther."

"I'll lose his team, anyhow," said Pinnager, "and me needing it bad. A driver with you could bring back the horses."

"Nay, my feyther will trust his beasts to nane but himsel' or his sons. But I'll have yer case in mind, Pinnager; it's a sore needcessity you're in. I'll ask my feyther to send back the team, and another to the tail of it; it's like that Tam and Neil will be home by now. And I'll spread word how ye're needin' teams, Pinnager; it's like your neighbors will send ye in sax or eight spans."

"Man, that's a grand notion, Davie! But you can't go alone; it's clean impossible."

"I'm gawn, Pinnager."

"You can't turn out in seven feet of snow when you meet loading. You can't water or feed your horses. There's forty miles the sec-

ond day, and never a stopping-place; your
horses can't stand it."

"I'm wae for the beasts, Pinnager; but
they'll have no force but to travel dry and hungry if that's set for them."

"You're bound to go?"

"Div you tak' me for an idjit to be talkin'
and no meanin' it? Off wi' ye, man! The leg's
no exactly a comfort when I'm talkin'.'"

"Why, Davie, it must be hurting you terrible!" Pinnager had almost forgotten the
broken leg, such was Davie's composure.

"It's no exactly a comfort, I said. Get you
gone, Pinnager; your men may be idlin'. Get
you gone, and send in Jock Scott, if he's man
enough to handle my leg. I'm wearyin' just
now for my ain company."

As Davie had made his programme, so it
stood. His will was inflexible to protests.
Next morning at dawn they set him on a hay-
bed in his low, unboxed sleigh. A bag of oats
supported his back; his unhurt leg was braced
against a piece of plank spiked down. Jock
Scott had pulled the broken bones into what
he thought their place, and tied that leg up in
splints of cedar.

The sleigh was enclosed by stakes, four on

each side, all tied together by stout rope. The
stake at Davie's right hand was shortened, that
he might hang his reins there. His water-
bucket was tied to another stake, and his bag
of provisions to a third. He was warm in a
coon-skin coat, and four pairs of blankets under
or over him.

At the last moment Pinnager protested: "I
must send a man to drive. It sha'n't cost you a
cent, Davie."

"Thank you, kindly, Pinnager," said Davie
gravely. "I'll tell that to your credit at the
settlement. But ye're needin' all your help,
and I'd take shame to worsen your chances.
My feyther's horses need no drivin' but my
word."

Indeed, they would "gee," "haw," or "whoa"
like oxen, and loved his voice. Round-bar-
relled, deep-breathed, hardy, sure-footed, active, gentle, enduring, brave, and used to the
exigencies of "bush roads," they would take
him through safely if horses' wit could.

Davie had uttered never a groan after those
involuntary ones forced from him when the
log, driving his leg against a tree, had made
him almost unconscious. But the pain-sweat
stood beaded on his face during the torture of

carrying him to the sleigh. Not a sound from
his lips, though! They could guess his sufferings from naught but his hard breathing
through the nose, that horrible sweat, and the
iron set of his jaw. After they had placed him,
the duller agony that had kept him awake all
night returned; he smiled grimly, and said,
"That's a comfort."

He had eaten and drunk heartily; he seemed
strong still; but what if his sleigh should turn
over at some sidling place of the rude, lonely,
and hilly forest road?

As Davie chirruped to his horses and was off,
the men gave him a cheer; then Pinnager and
all went away to labor fit for mighty men, and
the swinging of axes and the crashing of huge
pines and the tumbling of logs from rollways
left them fancy-free to wonder how Davie could
ever brace himself to save his broken leg at the
cahots.

The terrible *cahots*—plunges in snow-roads!
But for them Davie would have suffered little
more than in a shanty bunk. The track was
mostly two smooth ruts separated by a ridge
so high and hard that the sleigh-bottom often
slid on it. Horses less sure-footed would have
staggered much, and bitten crossly at one an-

other while trotting in those deep, narrow ruts, but Davie's horses kept their "jog" amiably, tossing their heads with glee to be traveling toward home.

The clink of trace-chains, the clack of harness, the glide of runners on the hard, dry snow, the snorting of the frosty-nosed team, the long whirring of startled grouse—Davie heard only these sounds, and heard them dreamily in the long, smooth flights between *cahots*.

Overhead the pine tops were a dark canopy with little fields of clear blue seen through the rifts of green; on the forest floor small firs bent under rounding weights of snow which often slid off as if moved by the stir of partridge wings; the fine tracery of hemlocks stood clean; and birches snuggled in snow that mingled with their curling rags. Sometimes a breeze eddied downward in the aisles, and then all the undergrowth was a silent commotion of snow, shaken and falling. Davie's eyes noted all things unconsciously; in spite of his pain he felt the enchantment of the winter woods until—another *cahot!* he called his team to walk.

Never was one *cahot* without many in succession; he gripped his stake hard at each, braced his sound leg, and held on, feeling like to die with the horrible thrust of the broken one forward and then back; yet always his will ordered his desperate senses.

Eleven o'clock! Davie drew up before the half-breed Peter Whiteduck's midwood stopping-place, and briefly explained his situation.

"Give my horses a feed," he went on. "There's oats in this bag. I'll no be moved mysel'. Maybe you'll fetch me a tin of tea; I've got my own provisions." So he ate and drank in the zero weather.

"You'll took lil' drink of whiskey," said Peter, with commiseration, as Davie was starting away.

"I don't use it."

"You'll got for need some 'fore you'll see de Widow Green place. Dass twenty-tree mile."

"I will need it, then," said Davie, and was away.

Evening had closed in when the bunch of teamsters awaiting supper at Widow Green's rude inn heard sleigh-bells, and soon a shout outside:

"Come out, some one!"

That was an insolence in the teamsters' code. Come out, indeed! The Widow Green, bust-

ling about with fried pork, felt outraged. To
be called out!—of her own house!—like a dog!
—not she!

"Come out here, somebody!" Davie shouted
again.

"G' out and break his head one of you," said
fighting Moses Frost. "To be shoutin' like a
lord!" Moses was too great a personage to go
out and wreak vengeance on an unknown.

Narcisse Larocque went—to thrash anybody
would be glory for Narcisse, and he felt sure
that Moses would not, in these circumstances,
let anybody thrash him.

"What for you shout lak' dat? Call mans
hout, hey?" said Narcisse. "I'll got good mind
for broke your head, me!"

"Hi, there, men!" Davie ignored Narcisse
as he saw figures through the open door.
"Some white man come out. My leg's broke."

Oh, then the up-jumping of big men! Moses,
striding forth, ruthlessly shoved Narcisse, who
lay and cowered with legs up as a dog trying
to placate an angry master. Then Moses carried Davie in as gently as if the young stalwart
had been a girl baby, and laid him on the
widow's one spare bed.

That night Davie slept soundly for four

hours, and woke to consciousness that his leg
was greatly swollen. He madé no moan, but
lay in the darkness listening to the heavy
breathing of the teamsters on the floor. They
could do nothing for him; why should he
awaken them? As for pitying himself, Davie
could do nothing so fruitless. He fell to plans
for getting teams in to Pinnager, for this
young Scot's practical mind was horrified at
the thought that the man should fail financially
when ten horses might give him a fine profit
for his winter's work.

Davie was away at dawn, every slight jolt
giving his swollen leg pain almost unendurable,
as if edges of living bone were griding together
and also tearing cavities in the living flesh; but
he must endure it, and well too, for the teamsters had warned him he must meet "strings of
loadin' " this day.

The rule of the long one-tracked road into
the wilderness is, of course, that empty outgo-
ing sleighs shall turn out for incoming laden
ones. Turn out into seven feet of snow! Davie
trusted that incoming teamsters would handle
his floundering horses, and he set his mind to
plan how they might save him from tumbling
about on his turned-out sleigh.

About nine o'clock, on a winding road, he called, "Whoa!" and his bays stood. A sleigh piled with baled hay confronted him thirty yards distant. Four others followed closely; the load drawn by the sixth team was hidden by the woodland curve. No teamsters were visible; they must be walking behind the procession; and Davie wasted no strength in shouting. On came the laden teams, till the steam of the leaders mingled with the clouds blown by his bays. At that halt angry teamsters, yelling, ran forward and sprang, one by one, up on their loads, the last to grasp reins being the leading driver.

"Turn out, you fool!" he shouted. Then to his comrades behind, "There's a blamed idyit don't know enough to turn out for loading!"

Davie said nothing. It was not till one angry man was at his horses' heads and two more about to tumble his sleigh aside that he spoke:

"My leg is broke."

"Gah! G'way! A man driving with his leg broke! You're lying! Come, get out and tramp down snow for your horses! It's your back ought to be broke—stoppin' loadin'!"

"My leg is broke," Davie calmly insisted.

"You mean it?"

Davie threw off his blankets.

"Begor, it is broke!" "And him drivin' himself!" "It's a terror!" "Great spunk entirely!" Then the teamsters began planning to clear the way.

That was soon settled by Davie's directions: "Tramp down the crust for my horses; onhitch them; lift my sleigh out on the crust; pass on; then set me back on the road."

Half an hour was consumed by the operation —thrice repeated before twelve o'clock. Fortunately Davie came on the last "string" of teams halted for lunch by the edge of a lake. The teamsters fed and watered his horses, gave him hot tea, and with great admiration saw him start for an afternoon drive of twenty-two miles.

"You'll not likely meet any teams," they said. "The last of the 'loading' that's like to come in soon is with ourselves."

How Davie got down the hills, up the hills, across the rivers and over the lakes of that terrible afternoon he could never rightly tell.

"I'm thinkin' I was light-heided," he said afterward. "The notion was in me somehow that the Lord was lookin' to me to save Pinnager's bits of children. I'd waken out of it at the *cahots*—there was mair than enough. On the smooth my head would be strange-like, and I mind but the hinder end of my horses till the moon was high and me stoppit by McGraw's."

During the night at McGraw's his head was cleared by some hours of sound sleep, and next morning he insisted on traveling, though snow was falling heavily.

"My feyther's place is no more than a bittock ayont twenty-eight miles," he said. "I'll make it by three of the clock, if the Lord's willin', and get the doctor's hands on me. It's my leg I'm thinkin' of savin'. And mind ye, McGraw, you've promised me to send in your team to Pinnager."

Perhaps people who have never risen out of bitter poverty will not understand Davie's keen anxiety about Pinnager and Pinnager's children; but the McAndrews and Pinnagers and all their neighbors of "the Scotch settlement" had won up by the tenacious labor and thrift of many years. Davie remembered well how, in his early boyhood, he had often craved more food and covering. Pinnager and his family should not be thrown back into the gulf of poverty if Davie McAndrews' will could save them.

This day his road lay through a country thinly settled, but he could see few cabins through the driving storm. The flagging horses trotted steadily, as if aware that the road would become worse the longer they were on it, but about ten o'clock they inclined to stop where Davie could dimly see a long house and a shed with a team and sleigh standing in it. Drunken yells told him this must be Black Donald Donaldson's notorious tavern; so he chirruped his horses onward.

Ten minutes later yells and sleigh-bells were following him at a furious pace. Davie turned head and shouted; still the drunken men shrieked and came on. He looked for a place to turn out—none! He dared not stop his horses lest the gallopers, now close behind him, should be over him and his low sleigh. Now his team broke into a run at the noises, but the fresh horses behind sped faster. The men were hidden from Davie by their crazed horses. He could not rise to appeal; he could not turn to daunt the horses with his whip; their front-hoofs, rising high, were soon within twenty feet of him. Did his horses slacken, the others would be on top of him, kicking and tumbling.

The *cahots* were numerous; his yells for a

halt became so much like screams of agony that
he took shame of them, shut his mouth firmly,
and knew not what to do. Then suddenly his
horses swerved into the cross-road to the Scotch
settlement, while the drunkards galloped away
on the main road, still lashing and yelling.
Davie does not know to this day who the men
were.

Five hours later David McAndrews, the
elder, kept at home by the snowstorm, heard
bells in his lane, and looked curiously out of the
sitting-room window.

"Losh, Janet!" he said, most deliberately.
"I wasna expeckin' Davie; here he's back wi'
the bays."

He did not hurry out to meet his fourth son,
for he is a man who hates the appearance of
haste; but his wife did, and came rushing back
through the kitchen.

"It's Davie himsel'! He's back wi' his leg
broke! He's come a' the way by his lone!"

"Hoot-toot, woman! Ye're daft!"

"I'm no daft; come and see yoursel'. Wae's
me, my Davie's like to die! Me daft, indeed!
Ye'll need to send Neil straight awa' to the
village for Doctor Aberdeen."

And so dour Davie's long drive was past.

While his brother carried him in, his will was occupied with the torture, but he had scarcely been laid on his bed when he said, very respectfully—but faintly—to his father:

"You'll be sendin' Neil oot for the doctor, sir? Aye; then I'd be thankfu' if you'd give Aleck leave to tak' the grays and warn the settlement that Pinnager's needin' teams sorely. He's like to make or break; if he gets sax or eight spans in time he's a made man."

That was enough for the men of the Scotch settlement. Pinnager got all the help he needed; and yet he is far from as rich to-day as Davie McAndrews, the great Brazeau River lumberman, who walks a little lame of his left leg.

PETHERICK'S PERIL

EACH story of the Shelton Cotton Factory is fifteen feet between floors; there are seven such over the basement, and this rises six feet above the ground. The brick walls narrow to eight inches as they ascend, and form a parapet rising above the roof. One of the time-keepers of the factory, Jack Hardy, a young man about my own age, often runs along the brick-work, the practice giving him a singular delight that has seemed to increase with his proficiency in it. Having been a clerk in the works from the beginning, I have frequently used the parapet for a footpath, and although there was a sheer fall of one hundred feet to the ground, have done it with ease and without dizziness. Occasionally Hardy and I have run races, on the opposite walls, an exercise in which he invariably beats me, because I become timid with increase of pace.

Hopelessly distanced last Wednesday, while the men were off at noon, I gave up midway, and looking down, observed the upturned face of an old man gazing at me with parted lips, wide eyes, and an expression of horror so startling that I involuntarily stepped down to the bricklayer's platform inside. I then saw that the apparently frightened spectator was Mr. Petherick, who had been for some weeks paymaster and factotum for the contractors.

"What's the matter, Petherick?" I called down. He made no answer, but walking off rapidly, disappeared round the mill. Curious about his demeanor, I descended, and after some little seeking found him smoking alone.

"You quite frightened me just now, Petherick," said I. "Did you think I was a ghost?"

"Not just that," he replied.

"Did you expect me to fall, then?"

"Not just that, either," said he. The old man was clearly disinclined to talk, and apparently much agitated. I began to joke him about his lugubrious expression, when the one o'clock bell rang, and he shuffled off hastily to another quarter.

Though I puzzled awhile over the incident, it soon passed so entirely from my mind that I was surprised when, passing Petherick in the afternoon, and intending to go aloft, he said, as I went by:

"Don't do it again, Mr. Frazer!"

"What?" I stopped.

"That!" he retorted.

"Oh! You mean running on the wall," said I.

"I mean going on it at all!" he exclaimed. His earnestness was so marked that I conceived a strong interest in its cause.

"I'll make a bargain with you, Mr. Petherick. If you tell me why you advise me, I'll give the thing up!"

"Done!" said he. "Come to my cottage this evening, and I'll tell you a strange adventure of my own, though perhaps you'll only laugh that it's the reason why it sickens me to see you fooling up there."

Petherick was ready to talk when Jack and I sat down on his doorsteps that evening, and immediately launched into the following narrative:

I was born and grew to manhood near the highest cliffs of the Polvydd coast. Millions of sea-fowls make their nests along the face of those wave-worn precipices. My companions and I used to get much excitement, and sometimes a good deal of pocket money, by taking their eggs. One of us, placing his feet in a loop at the end of a rope and taking a good grip with his hands, would be lowered by the others to the nest. When he had his basket full they'd haul him up and another would go down.

Well, one afternoon I thus went dangling off. They paid out about a hundred feet of rope before I touched the ledge and let go.

You must know that most of the cliffs along that coast overhang the water. At many points one could drop six hundred feet into the sea, and then be forty or fifty feet from the base of the rock he left. The coast is scooped under by the waves, and in some places the cliff wall is as though it had been eaten away by seas once running in on higher levels. There will be an overhanging coping, then—some hundred feet down—a ledge sticking out farther than that of the top; under that ledge all will be scooped away. In some places there are three or four such ledges, each projecting farther than those above.

These ledges used to fall away occasionally, as they do yet, I am told, for the ocean is gradually devouring that coast. Where they did not project farther than the upper coping, the egg-gatherer would swing like a pendulum on the rope, and get on the rock, if not too far in, then put a rock on the loop to hold it till his return. When a ledge did project so that one could drop straight on it, he hauled down some slack and left the rope hanging. Did the wind never blow it off? Seldom, and never out of reach.

Well, the ledge I reached was like this. It was some ten feet wide; it stuck out maybe six feet farther than the cliff top; the rock wall went up pretty near perpendicular, till near the coping at the ground; but below the ledge, the cliff's face was so scooped away that the sea, five hundred feet below, ran in under it nigh fifty feet.

As I went down, thousands of birds rose from the jagged places of the precipice, circling around me with harsh screams. Soon touching the ledge, I stepped from the loop, and drawing down a little slack, walked off briskly. For fully a quarter of a mile the ledge ran along the cliff's face almost as level and even in width as that sidewalk. I remember fancying that it sloped outward more than usual, but instantly dismissed the notion, though Gaffer Pentreath, the oldest man in that countryside, used to tell us that we should not get the use of that ledge always. It had been as steady in our time as in his grandfather's, and we only laughed at his prophecies. Yet the place of an old filled fissure was marked by a line of grass, by tufts of weeds and small bushes, stretching almost as far as the ledge itself, and within a foot or so of the cliff's face.

Eggs were not so many as usual, and I went a long piece from my rope before turning back. Then I noticed the very strange conduct of the hosts of sea-fowls below. Usually there were hundreds, but now there were millions on the wing, and instead of darting forth in playful motions, they seemed to be wildly excited, screaming shrilly, rushing out as in terror, and returning in masses as though to alight, only to wheel in dread and keep the air in vast clouds.

The weather was beautiful, the sea like glass. At no great distance were two large brigs and, nearer, a small yacht lay becalmed, heaving on the long billows. I could look down her cabin stairway almost, and it seemed scarcely more than a long leap to her deck.

Puzzled by the singular conduct of the sea-birds, I soon stopped and set my back against the cliff, to rest while watching them. The day was deadly still and very warm.

I remember taking off my cap and wiping the sweat from my face and forehead with my sleeve. While doing this, I looked down involuntarily to the fissure at my feet. Instantly my blood almost froze with horror! There was a distinct crack between the inner edge of the fissure and the hard-packed, root-threaded soil with which it was filled! Forcibly I pressed back, and in a flash looked along the ledge. The fissure was widening under my eyes, the rock before me seemed sinking outward, and with a shudder and a groan and roar, the whole long platform fell crashing to the sea below! I stood on a margin of rock scarce a foot wide, at my back a perpendicular cliff, and, five hundred feet below, the ocean, now almost hidden by the vast concourse of wheeling and affrighted birds.

Can you believe that my first sensation was one of relief? I stood safe! Even a feeling of interest held me for some moments. Almost coolly I observed a long and mighty wave roll out from beneath. It went forth with a high, curling crest—a solid wall of water! It struck the yacht stern on, plunged down on her deck, smashed through her swell of sail, and swept her out of sight forever.

Not till then did my thoughts dwell entirely on my own position; not till then did I comprehend its hopelessness! Now my eyes closed convulsively, to shut out the abyss down which my glance had fallen; shuddering, I pressed hard against the solid wall at my back; an appalling cold slowly crept through me. My reason struggled against a wild desire to leap; all the demons of despair whispered me to make an instant end. In imagination I *had* leaped! I felt the swooning helplessness of falling and the cold, upward rush of air!

Still I pressed hard back against the wall of rock, and though nearly faint from terror, never forgot for an instant the death at my feet, nor the utter danger of the slightest motion. How long this weakness lasted I know not; I only know that the unspeakable horror of that first period has come to me in waking dreams many and many a day since; that I have long nights of that deadly fear; that to think of the past is to stand again on that narrow foothold; and to look around on the earth is often to cry out with joy that it widens away from my feet.

(The old man paused long. Glancing sidewise at Jack, I saw that his face was pallid. I
myself had shuddered and grown cold, so
strongly had my imagination realized the awful experience that Petherick described. At
length he resumed his story:)

Suddenly these words flashed to my brain:
"Are not two sparrows sold for a farthing?
And one of them shall not fall on the ground
without your Father. Fear not, therefore; ye
are of more value than many sparrows." My
faculties were so strained that I seemed to hear
the words. Indeed, often yet I think that I
did truly hear a voice utter them very near me.

Instantly hope arose, consciously desperate
indeed; but I became calm, resourceful, capable, and felt unaccountably aided. Careful not
to look down, I opened my eyes and gazed far
away over the bright sea. The rippled billows
told that a light outward breeze had sprung up.
Slowly, and somewhat more distant, the two
brigs moved toward the horizon. Turning my
head, I could trace the narrow stone of my
footing to where my rope dangled, perhaps
three hundred yards distant.

It seemed to hang within easy reach of the
cliff's face, and instantly I resolved and as

instantly proceeded to work toward it. No
time remained for hesitation. Night was coming on. I reasoned that my comrades thought
me killed. They had probably gone to view
the new condition of the precipice from a lower
station, and on their return would haul up and
carry off the rope. I made a move toward it.
Try to think of that journey!

Shuffling sidewise very carefully, I had not
made five yards before I knew that I could not
continue to look out over that abyss without
glancing down, and that I could not glance
down without losing my senses. You have the
brick line to keep eyes on as you walk along
the factory wall; do you think you could move
along it erect, looking down as you would have
to? Yet it is only one hundred feet high.
Imagine five more such walls on top of that
and you trying to move sidewise—incapable
of closing your eyes, forced to look down, from
end to end, yes, three times farther! Imagine
you've got to go on or jump off! Would you
not, in an ecstasy of nervous agitation, fall to
your knees, get down face first at full length,
clutch by your hands, and with your shut eyes
feel your way? I longed to lie down and hold,
but of course that was impossible.

The fact that there was a wall at my back
made it worse! The cliff seemed to press outward against me. It did, in fact, incline very
slightly outward. It seemed to be thrusting
me off. Oh, the horror of that sensation! Your
toes on the edge of a precipice, and the impla-
cable, calm mountain apparently weighting
you slowly forward.

(Beads of sweat poured out over his white
face at the horror he had called before him.
Wiping his lips nervously with the back of his
hand, and looking askant, as at the narrow
pathway, he paused long. I saw its cruel edge
and the dark gleams of its abysmal water.)

I knew that with my back to the wall I could
never reach the rope. I could not face toward
it and step forward, so narrow was the ledge.
Motion was perhaps barely possible that way,
but the breadth of my shoulders would have
forced me to lean somewhat more outward, and
this I dared not and could not do. Also, to see
a solid surface before me became an irresistible
desire. I resolved to try to turn round before
resuming the desperate journey. To do this
I had to nerve myself for one steady look at
my footing.

In the depths below the myriad sea-fowl then

rested on the black water, which, though swelling more with the rising wind, had yet an unbroken surface at some little distance from the precipice, while farther out it had begun to jump to whitecaps, and in beneath me, where I could not see, it dashed and churned with a faint, pervading roar that I could barely distinguish. Before the descending sun a heavy bank of cloud had risen. The ocean's surface bore that appearance of intense and angry gloom that often heralds a storm, but, save the deep murmur going out from far below my perch, all to my hearing was deadly still.

Cautiously I swung my right foot before the other and carefully edged around. For an instant as my shoulder rubbed up against the rock, I felt that I must fall. I did stagger, in fact, but the next moment stood firm, face to the beetling cliff, my heels on the very edge, and the new sensation of the abyss behind me no less horrible than that from which I had with such difficulty escaped. I stood quaking. A delirious horror thrilled every nerve. The skin about my ears and neck, suddenly cold, shrank convulsively.

Wild with fear, I thrust forward my head against the rock and rested in agony. A whir

and wind of sudden wings made me conscious
of outward things again. Then a mad eagerness to climb swept away other feeling, and my
hands attempted in vain to clutch the rock.
Not daring to cast my head backward, I drew
it tortoise-like between my raised shoulders,
and chin against the precipice, gazed upward
with straining of vision from under my eye-
brows.

Far above me the dead wall stretched. Sidewise glances gave me glimpses of the projecting summit coping. There was no hope in that
direction. But the distraction of scanning the
cliff-side had given my nerves some relief; to
my memory again returned the promise of the
Almighty and the consciousness of his regard.
Once more my muscles became firm-strung.

A cautious step sidewise made me know how
much I had gained in ease and security of motion by the change of front. I made progress
that seemed almost rapid for some rods, and
even had exultation in my quick approach to
the rope. Hence came freedom to think how I
should act on reaching it, and speculation as
to how soon my comrades would haul me up.

Then the idea rushed through me that they
might even yet draw it away too soon, that

while almost in my clutch it might rise from my hands. Instantly all the terrors of my position returned with tenfold force; an outward thrust of the precipice seemed to grow distinct, my trembling hands told me that it moved bodily toward me; the descent behind me took an unspeakable remoteness, and from the utmost depth of that sheer air seemed to ascend steadily a deadly and a chilling wind. But I think I did not stop for an instant. Instead a delirium to move faster possessed me, and with quick, sidelong steps—my following foot striking hard against that before—sometimes on the point of stumbling, stretched out like the crucified, I pressed in mortal terror along.

Every possible accident and delay was presented to my excited brain. What if the ledge should narrow suddenly to nothing? Now I believed that my heels were unsupported in air, and I moved along on tip-toe. Now I was convinced that the narrow pathway sloped outward, that this slope had become so distinct, so increasingly distinct, that I might at any moment slip off into the void. But dominating every consideration of possible disaster was still that of the need for speed, and distinct amid all other terrors was that sensation of the dead wall ever silently and inexorably pressing me outward.

My mouth and throat were choked with dryness, my convulsive lips parched and arid; much I longed to press them against the cold, moist stone. But I never stopped. Faster, faster, more wildly I stepped—in a frenzy I pushed along. Then suddenly before my staring eyes was a well-remembered edge of mossy stone, and I knew that the rope should be directly behind me. Was it?

I glanced over my left shoulder. The rope was not to be seen! Wildly I looked over the other—no rope! Almighty God! and hast thou deserted me?

But what! Yes, it moves, it sways in sight! it disappears—to return again to view! There was the rope directly at my back, swinging in the now strong breeze with a motion that had carried it away from my first hurried glances. With the relief tears pressed to my eyes and, face bowed to the precipice, almost forgetful for a little time of the hungry air beneath, I offered deep thanks to my God for the deliverance that seemed so near.

(The old man's lips continued to move, but no sound came from them. We waited silent

while, with closed eyes and bent head, he remained absorbed in the recollection of that
strange minute of devoutness. It was some
moments before he spoke again:)

I stood there for what now seems a space of
hours, perhaps half a minute in reality. Then
all the chances still to be run crowded upon me.
To turn around had been an attempt almost
desperate. before, and certainly, most certainly,
the ledge was no wider where I now stood.
Was the rope within reach? I feared not.
Would it sway toward me? I could hope for
that.

But could I grasp it should I be saved?
Would it not yield to my hand, coming slowly
down as I pulled, unrolling from a coil above,
trailing over the ground at the top, running
fast as its end approached the edge, falling suddenly at last? Or was it fastened to the accustomed stake? Was any comrade near who
would summon aid at my signal? If not, and
if I grasped it, and if it held, how long should
I swing in the wind that now bore the freshness
and tremors of an imminent gale?

Again fear took hold of me, and as a desperate man I prepared to turn my face once more
to the vast expanse of water and the nothing

beyond that awful cliff. Closing my eyes, I
writhed around with I know not what motions
till again my back pressed the cliff. That was
a restful sensation. And now for the decision
of my fate! I looked at the rope. Not for a
moment could I fancy it within my reach! Its
sidewise swayings were not, as I had expected,
even slightly inward—indeed when it fell back
against the wind it swung outward as though
the air were eddying from the wall.

Now at last I gazed down steadily. Would
a leap be certain death? The water was of
immense depth below. But what chance of
striking it feet or head first? What chance
of preserving consciousness in the descent?
No, the leap would be death; that at least was
clear.

Again I turned to the rope. I was now perfectly desperate, but steady, nerved beyond
the best moments of my life, good for an effort
surpassing the human. Still the rope swayed
as before, and its motion was very regular. I
saw that I could touch it at any point of its
gyration by a strong leap.

But could I grasp it? What use if it were
not firmly secured above? But all time for hesitation had gone by. I knew too well that

strength was mine but for a moment, and that
in the next reaction of weakness I should drop
from the wall like a dead fly. Bracing myself,
I watched the rope steadily for one round, and
as it returned against the wind, jumped
straight out over the heaving Atlantic.

By God's aid I reached, touched, clutched,
held the strong line. And it held! Not absolutely. Once, twice, and again, it gave, gave,
with jerks that tried my arms. I knew these
indicated but tightening. Then it held firm
and I swung turning in the air, secure above
the waves that beat below.

To slide down and place my feet in the loop
was the instinctive work of a moment. Fortunately it was of dimensions to admit my body
barely. I slipped it over my thighs up to my
armpits just as the dreaded reaction of weakness came. Then I lost consciousness.

When I awakened my dear mother's face
was beside my pillow, and she told me that I
had been tossing for a fortnight in brain fever.
Many weeks I lay there, and when I got strong
found that I had left my nerve on that awful
cliff-side. Never since have I been able to look
from a height or see any other human being on
one without shuddering.

So now you know the story, Mr. Frazer, and have had your last walk on the factory wall.

He spoke truer than he knew. His story has given me such horrible nightmares ever since that I could no more walk on the high brickwork than along that narrow ledge of the distant Polvydd coast.

Delima made no answer. She was in doubt about the plenty which her mother-in-law spoke of. She wondered whether small André and Odillon and 'Toinette, whose heavy breathing she could hear through the thin partition, would have been sleeping so peacefully had little Baptiste not divided his share among them at supper-time, with the excuse that he did not feel very well?

Delima was young yet,—though little Baptiste was such a big boy,—and would have rested fully on the positively expressed trust of her mother-in-law, in spite of the empty flour barrel, if she had not suspected little Baptiste of sitting there hungry.

However, he was such a strange boy, she soon reflected, that perhaps going empty did not make him feel bad! Little Baptiste was so decided in his ways, made what in others would have been sacrifices so much as a matter of course, and was so much disgusted on being offered credit or sympathy in consequence, that his mother, not being able to understand him, was not a little afraid of him.

He was not very formidable in appearance, however, that clumsy boy of fourteen or so, whose big freckled, good face was now bent

over the cradle where *la petite* Seraphine lay
smiling in her sleep, with soft little fingers
clutched round his rough one.

"For sure," said Delima, observing the
baby's smile, "the good angels are very near.
I wonder what they are telling her?"

"Something about her father, of course; for
so I have always heard it is when the infants
smile in sleep," answered the old woman.

Little Baptiste rose impatiently and went
into the sleeping-room. Often the simplicity
and sentimentality of his mother and grandmother gave him strange pangs at heart; they
seemed to be the children, while he felt very
old. They were always looking for wonderful
things to happen, and expecting the saints and
le bon Dieu to help the family out of difficulties
that little Baptiste saw no way of overcoming
without the work which was then so hard to get.
His mother's remark about the angels talking
to little Seraphine pained him so much that he
would have cried had he not felt compelled to
be very much of a man during his father's absence.

If he had been asked to name the spirit hov-
ering about, he would have mentioned a very
wicked one as personified in John Conolly, the

might come home during the night or next morning, with his winter's wages.

Big Baptiste had "gone up" for Rewbell the jobber; had gone in November, to make logs in the distant Petawawa woods, and now the month was May. The "very magnificent" pig he had salted down before going away had been eaten long ago. My! what a time it seemed now to little Baptiste since that pig-killing! How good the *boudin* (the blood-puddings) had been, and the liver and tender bits, and what a joyful time they had had! The barrelful of salted pike and catfish was all gone too, —which made the fact that fish were not biting well this year very sad indeed.

Now on top of all these troubles this new danger of being turned out on the roadside! For where are they to get four dollars, or two, or one even, to stave Conolly off? Certainly his father was away too long; but surely, surely, thought the boy, he would get back in time to save his home! Then he remembered with horror, and a feeling of being disloyal to his father for remembering, that terrible day, three years before, when big Baptiste had come back from his winter's work drunk, and without a dollar, having been robbed while on a spree in Ottawa.

If that were the reason of his father's delay now, ah, then there would be no hope, unless *le bon Dieu* should indeed work a miracle for them!

While the boy thought over the situation with fear, his grandmother went to her bed, and soon afterward Delima took the little Seraphine's cradle into the sleeping-room. That left little Baptiste so lonely that he could not sit still; nor did he see any use of going to lie awake in bed by André and Odillon.

So he left the cabin softly, and reaching the river with a few steps, pushed off his flat-bottomed boat, and was carried smartly up stream by the shore eddy. It soon gave him to the current, and then he drifted idly down under the bright moon, listening to the roar of the long rapid, near the foot of which their cabin stood. Then he took to his oars, and rowed to the end of his night-line, tied to the wharf. He had an unusual fear that it might be gone, but found it all right, stretched taut; a slender rope, four hundred feet long, floated here and there far away in the darkness by flat cedar sticks,—a rope carrying short bits of line, and forty hooks, all loaded with excellent fat, wriggling worms.

That day little Baptiste had taken much trouble with his night-line; he was proud of the plentiful bait, and now, as he felt the tightened rope with his fingers, he told himself that his well-filled hooks *must* attract plenty of fish,—perhaps a sturgeon! Wouldn't that be grand? A big sturgeon of seventy-five pounds!

He pondered the Ottawa statement that "there are seven kinds of meat on the head of a sturgeon," and, enumerating the kinds, fell into a conviction that one sturgeon at least would surely come to his line. Had not three been caught in one night by Pierre Mallette, who had no sort of claim, who was too lazy to bait more than half his hooks, altogether too wicked to receive any special favors from *le bon Dieu?*

Little Baptiste rowed home, entered the cabin softly, and stripped for bed, almost happy in guessing what the big fish would probably weigh.

Putting his arms around little André, he tried to go to sleep; but the threats of Conolly came to him with new force, and he lay awake, with a heavy dread in his heart.

How long he had been lying thus he did not

know, when a heavy step came upon the plank outside the door.

"Father's home!" cried little Baptiste, springing to the floor as the door opened.

"Baptiste! my own Baptiste!" cried Delima, putting her arms around her husband as he stood over her.

"Did I not say," said the old woman, seizing her son's hand, "that the good God would send help in time?"

Little Baptiste lit the lamp. Then they saw something in the father's face that startled them all. He had not spoken, and now they perceived that he was haggard, pale, wild-eyed.

"The good God!" cried big Baptiste, and knelt by the bed, and bowed his head on his arms, and wept so loudly that little André and Odillon, wakening, joined his cry. *"Le bon Dieu* has forgotten us! For all my winter's work I have not one dollar! The concern is failed. Rewbell paid not one cent of wages, but ran away, and the timber has been seized."

Oh, the heartbreak! Oh, poor Delima! poor children! and poor little Baptiste, with the threats of Conolly rending his heart!

"I have walked all day," said the father,

"and eaten not a thing. Give me something, Delima."

"O holy angels!" cried the poor woman, breaking into a wild weeping. "O Baptiste, Baptiste, my poor man! There is nothing; not a scrap; not any flour, not meal, not grease even; not a pinch of tea!" but still she searched frantically about the rooms.

"Never mind," said big Baptiste then, holding her in his strong arms. "I am not so hungry as tired, Delima, and I can sleep."

The old woman, who had been swaying to and fro in her chair of rushes, rose now, and laid her aged hands on the broad shoulders of the man.

"My son Baptiste," she said, "you must not say that God has forgotten us, for He has not forgotten us. The hunger is hard to bear, I know,—hard, hard to bear; but great plenty will be sent in answer to our prayers. And it is hard, hard to lose thy long winter's work; but be patient, my son, and thankful, yes, thankful for all thou hast.

"Behold, Delima is well and strong. See the little Baptiste, how much a man! Yes, that is right; kiss the little André and Odillon; and see! how sweetly 'Toinette sleeps! All strong

and well, son Baptiste! Were one gone, think
what thou wouldst have lost! But instead, be
thankful, for behold, another has been given,—
the little Seraphine here, that thou hast not before seen!"

Big, rough, soft-hearted Baptiste knelt by
the cradle, and kissed the babe gently.

"It is true, *Memere*," he answered, "and I
thank *le bon Dieu* for his goodness to me."

But little Baptiste, lying wide awake for
hours afterwards, was not thankful. He could
not see that matters could be much worse. A
big hard lump was in his throat as he thought
of his father's hunger, and the home-coming
so different from what they had fondly counted
on. Great slow tears came into the boy's eyes,
and he wiped them away, ashamed even in the
dark to have been guilty of such weakness.

In the gray dawn little Baptiste suddenly
awoke, with the sensation of having slept on
his post. How heavy his heart was! Why?
He sat dazed with indefinite sorrow. Ah, now
he remembered! Conolly threatening to turn
them out! and his father back penniless! No
breakfast! Well, we must see about that.

Very quietly he rose, put on his patched
clothes, and went out. Heavy mist covered the

face of the river, and somehow the rapid seemed stilled to a deep, pervasive murmur. As he pushed his boat off, the morning fog was chillier than frost about him; but his heart got lighter as he rowed toward his night-line, and he became even eager for the pleasure of handling his fish. He made up his mind not to be much disappointed if there were no sturgeon, but could not quite believe there would be none; surely it was reasonable to expect *one,* perhaps two—why not three?—among the catfish and *doré.*

How very taut and heavy the rope felt as he raised it over his gunwales, and letting the bow swing up stream, began pulling in the line hand over hand! He had heard of cases where every hook had its fish; such a thing might happen again surely! Yard after yard of rope he passed slowly over the boat, and down into the water it sank on his track.

Now a knot on the line told him he was nearing the first hook; he watched for the quiver and struggle of the fish,—probably a big one, for there he had put a tremendous bait on and spat on it for luck, moreover. What? the short line hung down from the rope, and the baited hook rose clear of the water!

Baptiste instantly made up his mind that that hook had been placed a little too far inshore; he remembered thinking so before; the next hook was in about the right place!

Hand over hand, ah! the second hook, too! Still baited, the big worm very livid! It must be thus because that worm was pushed up the shank of the hook in such a queer way: he had been rather pleased when he gave the bait that particular twist, and now was surprised at himself; why, any one could see it was a thing to scare fish!

Hand over hand to the third,—the hook was naked of bait! Well, that was more satisfactory; it showed they had been biting, and, after all, this was just about the beginning of the right place.

Hand over hand; *now* the splashing will begin, thought little Baptiste, and out came the fourth hook with its livid worm! He held the rope in his hand without drawing it in for a few moments, but could see no reasonable objection to that last worm. His heart sank a little, but pshaw! only four hooks out of forty were up yet! wait till the eddy behind the shoal was reached, then great things would be seen. Maybe the fish had not been lying in that first bit of current.

Hand over hand again, now! yes, certainly, *there* is the right swirl! What? a *losch,* that unclean semi-lizard! The boy tore it off and flung it indignantly into the river. However, there was good luck in a *losch;* that was well known.

But the next hook, and the next, and next, and next came up baited and fishless. He pulled hand over hand quickly—not a fish! and he must have gone over half the line! Little Baptiste stopped, with his heart like lead and his arms trembling. It was terrible! Not a fish, and his father had no supper, and there was no credit at the store. Poor little Baptiste!

Again he hauled hand over hand—one hook, two, three—oh! ho! Glorious! What a delightful sheer downward the rope took! Surely the big sturgeon at last, trying to stay down on the bottom with the hook! But Baptiste would show that fish his mistake. He pulled, pulled, stood up to pull; there was a sort of shake, a sudden give of the rope, and little Baptiste tumbled over backward as he jerked his line up from under the big stone!

Then he heard the shutters clattering as Conolly's clerk took them off the store window; at half-past five to the minute that was

always done.   Soon big Baptiste would be up,
that was certain.   Again the boy began hauling
in line: baited hook! baited hook! naked hook!
baited hook!—such was still the tale.

"Surely, surely," implored little Baptiste,
silently, "I shall find some fish!"   Up! up!
only four remained!   The boy broke down.
Could it be?   Had he not somehow skipped
many hooks?   Could it be that there was to be
no breakfast for the children?   Naked hook
again!   Oh, for some fish! anything! three,
two!

"Oh, send just one for my father!—my poor,
hungry father!" cried little Baptiste, and drew
up his last hook.   It came full baited, and the
line was out of the water clear away to his outer
buoy!

He let go the rope and drifted down the
river, crying as though his heart would break.
All the good hooks useless! all the labor thrown
away! all his self-confidence come to naught!

Up rose the great sun; from around the
kneeling boy drifted the last of the morning
mists; bright beams touched his bowed head
tenderly.   He lifted his face and looked up the
rapid.   Then he jumped to his feet with sudden
wonder; a great joy lit up his countenance.

Far up the river a low, broad, white patch appeared on the sharp sky-line made by the level dark summit of the long slope of tumbling water. On this white patch stood many figures of swaying men black against the clear morning sky, and little Baptiste saw instantly that an attempt was being made to "run" a "band" of deals, or many cribs lashed together, instead of single cribs as had been done the day before.

The broad strip of white changed its form slowly, dipped over the slope, drew out like a wide ribbon, and soon showed a distinct slant across the mighty volume of the deep raft channel. When little Baptiste, acquainted as he was with every current, eddy, and shoal in the rapid, saw that slant, he knew that his first impression of what was about to happen had been correct. The pilot of the band *had* allowed it to drift too far north before reaching the rapid's head.

Now the front cribs, instead of following the curve of the channel, had taken slower water, while the rear cribs, impelled by the rush under them, swung the band slowly across the current. All along the front the standing men swayed back and forth, plying sweeps full forty feet long, attempting to swing into chan-

nel again, with their strokes dashing the dark
rollers before the band into wide splashes of
white. On the rear cribs another crew pulled
in the contrary direction; about the middle of
the band stood the pilot, urging his gangs with
gestures to greater efforts.

Suddenly he made a new motion; the gang
behind drew in their oars and ran hastily forward to double the force in front. But they
came too late! Hardly had the doubled bow
crew taken a stroke when all drew in their oars
and ran back to be out of danger. Next moment the front cribs struck the "hog's-back"
shoal.

Then the long broad band curved downward
in the centre, the rear cribs swung into the shal-
lows on the opposite side of the raft-channel,
there was a great straining and crashing, the
men in front huddled together, watching the
wreck anxiously, and the band went speedily to
pieces. Soon a fringe of single planks came
down stream, then cribs and pieces of cribs;
half the band was drifting with the currents,
and half was "hung up" on the rocks among
the breakers.

Launching the big red flat-bottomed bow
boat, twenty of the raftsmen came with wild

speed down the river, and as there had been no
rush to get aboard, little Baptiste knew that the
cribs on which the men stood were so hard
aground that no lives were in danger. It meant
much to him; it meant that he was instantly at
liberty to gather in *money!* money, in sums
that loomed to gigantic figures before his imagination.

He knew that there was an important reason
for hurrying the deals to Quebec, else the great
risk of running a band at that season would not
have been undertaken; and he knew that hard
cash would be paid down as salvage for all
planks brought ashore, and thus secured from
drifting far and wide over the lake-like expanse
below the rapid's foot. Little Baptiste plunged
his oars in and made for a clump of deals floating in the eddy near his own shore. As he
rushed along, the raftsmen's boat crossed his
bows, going to the main raft below for ropes
and material to secure the cribs coming down
intact.

"Good boy!" shouted the foreman to Baptiste. "Ten cents for every deal you fetch
ashore above the raft!"

Ten cents! he had expected but five! What
a harvest!

Striking his pike-pole into the clump of deals,—"fifty at least," said joyful Baptiste,—he soon secured them to his boat, and then pulled, pulled, pulled, till the blood rushed to his head, and his arms ached, before he landed his wealth.

"Father!" cried he, bursting breathlessly into the sleeping household. "Come quick! I can't get it up without you."

"Big sturgeon?" cried the shantyman, jumping into his trousers.

"Oh, but we shall have a good fish breakfast!" cried Delima.

"Did I not say the blessed *le bon Dieu* would send plenty fish?" observed *Memere*.

"Not a fish!" cried little Baptiste, with recovered breath. "But look! look!" and he flung open the door. The eddy was now white with planks.

"Ten cents for each!" cried the boy. "The foreman told me."

"Ten cents!" shouted his father. *"Baptême!* it's my winter's wages!"

And the old grandmother! And Delima? Why, they just put their arms round each other and cried for joy.

"And yet there's no breakfast," said Delima,

starting up. "And they will work hard, hard."

At that instant who should reach the door but Monsieur Conolly! He was a man who respected cash wherever he found it, and already the two Baptistes had a fine show ashore.

"Ma'ame Larocque," said Conolly, politely, putting in his head, "of course you know I was only joking yesterday. You can get anything you want at the store."

What a breakfast they did have, to be sure! the Baptistes eating while they worked. Back and forward they dashed till late afternoon, driving ringed spikes into the deals, running light ropes through the rings, and, when a good string had thus been made, going ashore to haul in. At that hauling Delima and *Memere,* even little André and Odillon gave a hand.

Everybody in the little hamlet made money that day, but the Larocques twice as much as any other family, because they had an eddy and a low shore. With the help of the people "the big *Bourgeois*" who owned the broken raft got it away that evening, and saved his fat contract after all.

"Did I not say so?" said *"Memere,"* at night, for the hundredth time. "Did I not say so? Yes, indeed, *le bon Dieu* watches over us all."

"Yes, indeed, grandmother," echoed little Baptiste, thinking of his failure on the nightline. "We may take as much trouble as we like, but it's no use unless *le bon Dieu* helps us. Only—I don't know what de big Bourgeois say about that—his raft was all broke up so bad."

"Ah, *oui,*" said *Memere,* looking puzzled for but a moment. "But he didn't put his trust in *le bon Dieu;* that's it, for sure. Besides, maybe *le bon Dieu* want to teach him a lesson; he'll not try for run a whole band of deals next time. You see that was a tempting of Providence; and then—the big Bourgeois is a Protestant."

RED-HEADED WINDEGO

Big Baptiste Seguin, on snow-shoes nearly six feet long, strode mightily out of the forest, and gazed across the treeless valley ahead.

"Hooraw! No choppin' for two mile!" he shouted.

"Hooraw! Bully! Hi-yi!" yelled the axe-men, Pierre, "Jawnny," and "Frawce," two hundred yards behind. Their cries were taken up by the two chain-bearers still farther back.

"Is it a lake, Baptiste?" cried Tom Dunscombe, the young surveyor, as he hurried forward through balsams that edged the woods and concealed the open space from those among the trees.

"No, seh; only a beaver meddy."

"Clean?"

"Clean! Yesseh! Clean's your face. Hain't no tree for two mile if de line is go right."

"Good! We shall make seven miles to-day," said Tom, as he came forward with immense strides, carrying a compass and Jacob's-staff. Behind him the axemen slashed along, striking white slivers from the pink and scaly columns of red pines that shot up a hundred and twenty feet without a branch. If any underbrush grew there, it was beneath the eight-feet-deep February snow, so that one could see far away down a multitude of vaulted, converging aisles.

Our young surveyor took no thought of the beauty and majesty of the forest he was leaving. His thoughts and those of his men were set solely on getting ahead; for all hands had been promised double pay for their whole winter, in case they succeeded in running a line round the disputed Moose Lake timber berth before the tenth of April.

Their success would secure the claim of their employer, Old Dan McEachran, whereas their failure would submit him perhaps to the loss of the limit, and certainly to a costly lawsuit with Old Rory Carmichael, another potentate of the Upper Ottawa.

At least six weeks more of fair snow-shoeing would be needed to "blaze" out the limit, even if the unknown country before them should turn out to be less broken by cedar swamps and high precipices than they feared. A few days' thaw with rain would make slush of the eight feet of snow, and compel the party either to keep in camp, or risk *mal de raquette*,—strain of legs by heavy snow-shoeing. So they were in great haste to make the best of fine weather.

Tom thrust his Jacob's-staff into the snow, set the compass sights to the right bearing, looked through them, and stood by to let Big Baptiste get a course along the line ahead. Baptiste's duty was to walk straight for some selected object far away on the line. In woodland the axeman "blazed" trees on both sides of his snow-shoe track.

Baptiste was as expert at his job as any Indian, and indeed he looked as if he had a streak of Iroquois in his veins. So did "Frawce," "Jawnny," and all their comrades of the party.

"The three pines will do," said Tom, as Baptiste crouched.

"Good luck to-day for sure!" cried Baptiste, rising with his eyes fixed on three pines in the foreground of the distant timbered ridge. He saw that the line did indeed run clear of trees for two miles along one side of the long, narrow beaver meadow or swale.

Baptiste drew a deep breath, and grinned agreeably at Tom Dunscombe.

"De boys will look like dey's all got de double pay in deys' pocket when dey's see *dis* open," said Baptiste, and started for the three pines as straight as a bee.

Tom waited to get from the chainmen the distance to the edge of the wood. They came on the heels of the axemen, and all capered on their snow-shoes to see so long a space free from cutting.

It was now two o'clock; they had marched with forty pound or "light" packs since daylight, lunching on cold pork and hard-tack as they worked; they had slept cold for weeks on brush under an open tent pitched over a hole in the snow; they must live this life of hardship and huge work for six weeks longer, but they hoped to get twice their usual eighty-cents-a-day pay, and so their hearts were light and jolly.

But Big Baptiste, now two hundred yards in advance, swinging along in full view of the party, stopped with a scared cry. They saw him look to the left and to the right, and over his shoulder behind, like a man who expects mortal attack from a near but unknown quarter.

"What's the matter?" shouted Tom.

Baptiste went forward a few steps, hesitated, stopped, turned, and fairly ran back toward the party. As he came he continually turned his head from side to side as if expecting to see some dreadful thing following.

The men behind Tom stopped. Their faces were blanched. They looked, too, from side to side.

"Halt, Mr. Tom, halt! Oh, *monjee,* M'sieu, stop!" said Jawnny.

Tom looked round at his men, amazed at their faces of mysterious terror.

"What on earth has happened?" cried he.

Instead of answering, the men simply pointed to Big Baptiste, who was soon within twenty yards.

"What is the trouble, Baptiste?" asked Tom.

Baptiste's face was the hue of death. As he spoke he shuddered:—

"*Monjee,* Mr. Tom, we'll got for stop de job!"

"Stop the job! Are you crazy?"

"If you'll not b'lieve what I told, den you go'n' see for you'se'f."

"What is it?"

"De track, seh."

"What track? Wolves?"

"If it was only wolfs!"

"Confound you! can't you say what it is?"

"Eet's de—it ain't safe for told its name out loud, for dass de way it come—if it's call by its name!"

"Windego, eh?" said Tom, laughing.

"I'll know its track jus' as quick's I see it."

"Do you mean you have seen a Windego track?"

"*Monjee,* seh, *don't* say its name! Let us go back," said Jawnny. "Baptiste was at Madores' shanty with us when it took Hermidas Dubois."

"Yesseh. That's de way I'll come for know de track soon's I see it," said Baptiste. "Before den I mos' don' b'lieve dere was any of it. But ain't it take Hermidas Dubois only last New Year's?"

"That was all nonsense about Dubois. I'll bet it was a joke to scare you all."

"Who's kill a man for a joke?" said Baptiste.

"Did you see Hermidas Dubois killed? Did you see him dead? No! I heard all about it. All you know is that he went away on New Year's morning, when the rest of the men were too scared to leave the shanty, because some one said there was a Windego track outside."

"Hermidas never come back!"

"I'll bet he went away home. You'll find him at Saint Agathe in the spring. You can't be such fools as to believe in Windegos."

"Don't you say dat name some more!" yelled Big Baptiste, now fierce with fright. "Hain't I just seen de track? I'm go'n' back, me, if I don't get a copper of pay for de whole winter!"

"Wait a little now, Baptiste," said Tom, alarmed lest his party should desert him and the job. "I'll soon find out what's at the bottom of the track."

"Dere is blood at de bottom—I seen it!" said Baptiste.

"Well, you wait till *I* go and see it."

"No! I go back, me," said Baptiste, and started up the slope with the others at his heels.

"Halt! Stop there! Halt, you fools! Don't you understand that if there was any such monster it would as easily catch you in one place as another?"

The men went on. Tom took another tone.

"Boys, look here! I say, are you going to desert me like cowards?"

"Hain't goin' for desert you, Mr. Tom, no seh!" said Baptiste, halting. "Honly I'll hain' go for cross de track." They all faced round.

Tom was acquainted with a considerable number of Windego superstitions.

"There's no danger unless it's a fresh track," he said. "Perhaps it's an old one."

"Fresh made dis mornin'," said Baptiste.

"Well, wait till I go and see it. You're all right, you know, if you don't cross it. Isn't that the idea?"

"No, seh. Mr. Humphreys told Madore 'bout dat. Eef somebody cross de track and don't never come back, *den* de magic ain't in de track no more. But it's watchin', watchin' all round to catch somebody what cross its track; and if nobody don't cross its track and get catched, den de—de *Ting* mebby get crazy mad, and nobody don' know what it's goin' for do. Kill every person, mebby."

Tom mused over this information. These men had all been in Madore's shanty; Madore was under Red Dick Humphreys; Red Dick was Rory Carmichael's head foreman; he had sworn to stop the survey by hook or by crook, and this vow had been made after Tom had hired his gang from among those scared away from Madore's shanty. Tom thought he began to understand the situation.

"Just wait a bit, boys," he said, and started.

"You ain't surely go'n' for cross de track?"
cried Baptiste.

"Not now, anyway," said Tom. "But wait
till I see it."

When he reached the mysterious track it
surprised him so greatly that he easily forgave
Baptiste's fears.

If a giant having ill-shaped feet as long as
Tom's snow-shoes had passed by in moccasins,
the main features of the indentations might
have been produced. But the marks were no
deeper in the snow than if the huge moccasins
had been worn by an ordinary man. They were
about five and a half feet apart from centres, a
stride that no human legs could take at a walking pace.

Moreover, there were on the snow none of
the dragging marks of striding; the gigantic
feet had apparently been lifted straight up
clear of the snow, and put straight down.

Strangest of all, at the front of each print
were five narrow holes which suggested that
the mysterious creature had travelled with bare,
claw-like toes. An irregular drip or squirt of
blood went along the middle of the indentations! Nevertheless, the whole thing seemed of
human devising.

This track, Tom reflected, was consistent with the Indian superstition that Windegos are monsters who take on or relinquish the human form, and vary their size at pleasure. He perceived that he must bring the maker of those tracks promptly to book, or suffer his men to desert the survey, and cost him his whole winter's work, besides making him a laughing-stock in the settlements.

The young fellow made his decision instantly. After feeling for his match-box and sheath-knife, he took his hatchet from his sash, and called to the men.

"Go into camp and wait for me!"

Then he set off alongside of the mysterious track at his best pace. It came out of a tangle of alders to the west, and went into such another tangle about a quarter of a mile to the east. Tom went east. The men watched him with horror.

"He's got crazy, looking at de track," said Big Baptiste, "for that's the way,—one is enchanted,—he must follow."

"He was a good boss," said Jawnny, sadly.

As the young fellow disappeared in the alders the men looked at one another with a certain shame. Not a sound except the sough

of pines from the neighboring forest was heard.
Though the sun was sinking in clear blue, the
aspect of the wilderness, gray and white and
severe, touched the impressionable men with
deeper melancholy. They felt lonely, masterless, mean.

"He was a good boss," said Jawnny again.

"*Tort Dieu!*" cried Baptiste, leaping to his
feet. "It's a shame for desert the young boss.
I don't care; the Windego can only kill me.
I'm going for help Mr. Tom."

"Me also," said Jawnny.

Then all wished to go. But after some par-
ley it was agreed that the others should wait
for the portageurs, who were likely to be two
miles behind, and make camp for the night.

Soon Baptiste and Jawnny, each with his
axe, started diagonally across the swale, and
entered the alders on Tom's track.

It took them twenty yards through the alders, to the edge of a warm spring or marsh
about fifty yards wide. This open, shallow
water was completely encircled by alders that
came down to its very edge. Tom's snow-shoe
track joined the track of the mysterious monster for the first time on the edge—and there
both vanished!

Baptiste and Jawnny looked at the place with the wildest terror, and without even thinking to search the deeply indented opposite edges of the little pool for a reappearance of the tracks, fled back to the party. It was just as Red Dick Humphreys had said; just as they had always heard. Tom, like Hermidas Dubois, appeared to have vanished from existence the moment he stepped on the Windego track!

The dimness of early evening was in the red-pine forest through which Tom's party had passed early in the afternoon, and the belated portageurs were tramping along the line. A man with a red head had been long crouching in some cedar bushes to the east of the "blazed" cutting. When he had watched the portageurs pass out of sight, he stepped over upon their track, and followed it a short distance.

A few minutes later a young fellow, over six feet high, who strongly resembled Tom Dunscombe, followed the red-headed man.

The stranger, suddenly catching sight of a flame far away ahead on the edge of the beaver meadow, stopped and fairly hugged himself.

"Camped, by jiminy! I knowed I'd fetch 'em," was the only remark he made.

"I wish Big Baptiste could see that Windego laugh," thought Tom Dunscombe, concealed behind a tree.

After reflecting a few moments, the red-headed man, a wiry little fellow, went forward till he came to where an old pine had recently fallen across the track. There he kicked off his snow-shoes, picked them up, ran along the trunk, jumped into the snow from among the branches, put on his snow-shoes, and started northwestward. His new track could not be seen from the survey line.

But Tom had beheld and understood the purpose of the manœuvre. He made straight for the head of the fallen tree, got on the stranger's tracks and cautiously followed them, keeping far enough behind to be out of hearing or sight.

The red-headed stranger went toward the wood out of which the mysterious track of the morning had come. When he had reached the little brush-camp in which he had slept the previous night, he made a small fire, put a small tin pot on it, boiled some tea, broiled a venison steak, ate his supper, had several good laughs, took a long smoke, rolled himself round and round in his blanket, and went to sleep.

Hours passed before Tom ventured to crawl forward and peer into the brush camp. The red-headed man was lying on his face, as is the custom of many woodsmen. His capuchin cap covered his red head.

Tom Dunscombe took off his own long sash. When the red-headed man woke up he found that some one was on his back, holding his head firmly down.

Unable to extricate his arms or legs from his blankets, the red-headed man began to utter fearful threats. Tom said not one word, but diligently wound his sash round his prisoner's head, shoulders, and arms.

He then rose, took the red-headed man's own "tump-line," a leather strap about twelve feet long, which tapered from the middle to both ends, tied this firmly round the angry live mummy, and left him lying on his face.

Then, collecting his prisoner's axe, snow-shoes, provisions, and tin pail, Tom started with them back along the Windego track for camp.

Big Baptiste and his comrades had supped too full of fears to go to sleep. They had built an enormous fire, because Windegos are re-ported, in Indian circles, to share with wild

beasts the dread of flames and brands. Tom
stole quietly to within fifty yards of the camp,
and suddenly shouted in unearthly fashion.
The men sprang up, quaking.

"It's the Windego!" screamed Jawnny.

"You silly fools!" said Tom, coming forward. "Don't you know my voice? Am I a
Windego?"

"It's the Windego, for sure; it's took the
shape of Mr. Tom, after eatin' him," cried Big
Baptiste.

Tom laughed so uproariously at this that the
other men scouted the idea, though it was quite
in keeping with their information concerning
Windegos' habits.

Then Tom came in and gave a full and particular account of the Windego's pursuit, capture, and present predicament.

"But how'd he make de track?" they
asked.

"He had two big old snow-shoes, stuffed with
spruce tips underneath, and covered with
dressed deerskin. He had cut off the back
ends of them. You shall see them to-morrow.
I found them down yonder where he had left
them after crossing the warm spring. He had
five bits of sharp round wood going down in

front of them. He must have stood on them
one after the other, and lifted the back one
every time with the pole he carried. I've got
that, too. The blood was from a deer he had
run down and killed in the snow. He carried
the blood in his tin pail, and sprinkled it behind him. He must have run out our line long
ago with a compass, so he knew where it would
go. But come, let us go and see if it's Red
Dick Humphreys."

Red Dick proved to be the prisoner. He
had become quite philosophic while waiting for
his captor to come back. When unbound he
grinned pleasantly, and remarked:

"You're Mr. Dunscombe, eh? Well, you're
a smart young feller, Mr. Dunscombe. There
ain't another man on the Ottaway that could
'a' done that trick on me. Old Dan McEachran will make your fortun' for this, and I don't
begrudge it. You're a man—that's so. If
ever I hear any feller saying to the contrayry
he's got to lick Red Dick Humphreys."

And he told them the particulars of his practical joke in making a Windego track round
Madore's shanty.

"Hermidas Dubois?—oh, he's all right," said
Red Dick. "He's at home at St. Agathe.

Man, he helped me to fix up that Windego track at Madore's; but, by criminy! the look of it scared him so he wouldn't cross it himself. It was a holy terror!"

THE RIDE BY NIGHT

MR. ADAM BAINES is a little gray about the temples, but still looks so young that few could suppose him to have been one of the fifty-three thousand Canadians who served Abraham Lincoln's cause in the Civil War. Indeed, he was in the army less than a year. How he went out of it he told me in some such words as these:—

An orderly from the direction of Meade's headquarters galloped into our parade ground, and straight for the man on guard before the colonel's tent. That was pretty late in the afternoon of a bright March day in 1865, but the parade ground was all red mud with shallow pools. I remember well how the hind hoofs of the orderly's galloper threw away great chunks of earth as he splashed diagonally across the open.

His rider never slowed till he brought his horse to its haunches before the sentry. There he flung himself off instantly, caught up his sabre, and ran through the middle opening of the high screen of sapling pines stuck on end, side by side, all around the acre or so occupied by the officers' quarters.

The day, though sunny, was not warm, and
nearly all the men of my regiment were in their
huts when that galloping was heard. Then
they hurried out like bees from rows of hives,
ran up the lanes between the lines of huts, and
collected, each company separately, on the edge
of the parade ground opposite the officers'
quarters.

You see we had a notion that the orderly had
brought the word to break camp. For five
months the Army of the Potomac had been in
winter quarters, and for weeks nothing more
exciting than vidette duty had broken the mo-
notony of our brigade. We understood that
Sheridan had received command of all Grant's
cavalry, but did not know but the orderly had
rushed from Sheridan himself. Yet we awaited
the man's re-appearance with intense curiosity.

Soon, instead of the orderly, out ran our
first lieutenant, a small, wiry, long-haired man
named Miller. He was in undress uniform,—
just a blouse and trousers,—and bare-headed.
Though he wore low shoes, he dashed through
mud and water toward us, plainly in a great
hurry.

"Sergeant Kennedy, I want ten men at once
—mounted," Miller said. "Choose the ten best

able for a long ride, and give them the best horses in the company. You understand,—no matter whose the ten best horses are, give 'em to the ten best riders."

"I understand, sir," said Kennedy.

By this time half the company had started for the stables, for fully half considered themselves among the best riders. The lieutenant laughed at their eagerness.

"Halt, boys!" he cried. "Sergeant, I'll pick out four myself. Come yourself, and bring Corporal Crowfoot, Private Bader, and Private Absalom Gray."

Crowfoot, Bader, and Gray had been running for the stables with the rest. Now these three old soldiers grinned and walked, as much as to say, "We needn't hurry; we're picked anyhow;" while the others hurried on. I remained near Kennedy, for I was so young and green a soldier that I supposed I had no chance to go.

"Hurry up! parade as soon as possible. One day's rations; light marching order—no blankets—fetch over-coats and ponchos," said Miller, turning; "and in choosing your men, favor light weights."

That was, no doubt, the remark which

brought me in. I was lanky, light, bred among horses, and one of the best in the regiment had fallen to my lot. Kennedy wheeled, and his eye fell on me.

"Saddle up, Adam, boy," said he; "I guess you'll do."

Lieutenant Miller ran back to his quarters, his long hair flying wide. When he reappeared fifteen minutes later, we were trotting across the parade ground to meet him. He was mounted, not on his own charger, but on the colonel's famous thorough-bred bay. Then we knew a hard ride must be in prospect.

"What! one of the boys?" cried Miller, as he saw me. "He's too young."

"He's very light, sir; tough as hickory. I guess he'll do," said Kennedy.

"Well, no time to change now. Follow me! But, hang it, you've got your carbines! Oh, I forgot! Keep pistols only! throw down your sabres and carbines—anywhere—never mind the mud!"

As we still hesitated to throw down our clean guns, he shouted: "Down with them—anywhere! Now, boys, after me, by twos! Trot—gallop!"

Away we went, not a man jack of us knew

for where or what. The colonel and officers, standing grouped before regimental headquarters, volleyed a cheer at us. It was taken up by the whole regiment; it was taken up by the brigade; it was repeated by regiment after regiment of infantry as we galloped through the great camp toward the left front of the army. The speed at which Miller led over a rough corduroy road was extraordinary, and all the men suspected some desperate enterprise afoot.

Red and brazen was the set of the sun. I remember it well, after we got clear of the forts, clear of the breastworks, clear of the reserves, down the long slope and across the wide ford of Grimthorpe's Creek, never drawing rein.

The lieutenant led by ten yards or so. He had ordered each two to take as much distance from the other two in advance; but we rode so fast that the water from the heels of his horse and from the heels of each two splashed into the faces of the following men.

From the ford we loped up a hill, and passed the most advanced infantry pickets, who laughed and chaffed us, asking us for locks of our hair, and if our mothers knew we were out,

and promising to report our last words faithfully to the folks at home.

Soon we turned to the left again, swept close
by several cavalry videttes, and knew then that
we were bound for a ride through a country
that might or might not be within Lee's outer
lines, at that time extended so thinly in many
places that his pickets were far out of touch
with one another. To this day I do not know
precisely where we went, nor precisely what
for. Soldiers are seldom informed of the meaning of their movements.

What I do know is what we did while I was
in the ride. As we were approaching dense
pine woods the lieutenant turned in his saddle,
slacked pace a little, and shouted, "Boys, bunch
up near me!"

He screwed round in his saddle so far that
we could all see and hear, and said:—

"Boys, the order is to follow this road as
fast as we can till our horses drop, or else the
Johnnies drop us, or else we drop upon three
brigades of our own infantry. I guess they've
got astray somehow; but I don't know myself
what the trouble is. Our orders are plain. The
brigades are supposed to be somewhere on this
road. I guess we shall do a big thing if we

reach those men to-night. All we've got to do
is to ride and deliver this despatch to the general in command. You all understand?"

"Yes, sir! Yes, sir! Yes, sir!"

"It's necessary you all should. Hark, now!
We are not likely to strike the enemy in force,
but we are likely to run up against small parties. Now, Kennedy, if they down me, you are
to stop just long enough to grab the despatch
from my breast; then away you go,—always
on the main road. If they down you after
you've got the paper, the man who can grab it
first is to take it and hurry forward. So on
right to the last man. If they down him, and
he's got his senses when he falls, he's to tear
the paper up, and scatter it as widely as he can.
You all understand?"

"Yes, sir! Yes, sir!"

"All right, then. String out again!"

He touched the big bay with the spur, and
shot quickly ahead.

With the long rest of the winter our horses
were in prime spirits, though mostly a little too
fleshy for perfect condition. I had cared well
for my horse; he was fast and sound in wind
and limb. I was certainly the lightest rider of
the eleven.

I was still thinking of the probability that I should get further on the way than any comrade except the lieutenant, or perhaps Crowfoot and Bader, whose horses were in great shape; I was thinking myself likely to win promotion before morning, when a cry came out of the darkness ahead. The words of the challenge I was not able to catch, but I heard Miller shout, "Forward, boys!"

We shook out more speed just as a rifle spat its long flash at us from about a hundred yards ahead. For one moment I plainly saw the Southerner's figure. Kennedy reeled beside me, flung up his hands with a scream, and fell. His horse stopped at once. In a moment the lieutenant had ridden the sentry down.

Then from the right side of the road a party, who must have been lying round the camp-fire that we faintly saw in among the pines, let fly at us. They had surely been surprised in their sleep. I clearly saw them as their guns flashed.

"Forward! Don't shoot! Ride on," shouted Miller. "Bushwhackers! Thank God, not mounted! Any of you make out horses with them?"

"No, sir! No, sir!"

"Who yelled? who went down?"

"Kennedy, sir," I cried.

"Too bad! Any one else?"

"No, sir."

"All safe?"

"I'm touched in my right arm; but it's nothing," I said. The twinge was slight, and in the fleshy place in front of my shoulder. I could not make out that I was losing blood, and the pain from the hurt was scarcely perceptible.

"Good boy! Keep up, Adam!" called the lieutenant with a kind tone. I remember my delight that he spoke my front name. On we flew.

Possibly the shots had been heard by the party half a mile further on, for they greeted us with a volley. A horse coughed hard and pitched down behind me. His rider yelled as he fell. Then two more shots came: Crowfoot reeled in front of me, and somehow checked his horse. I saw him no more. Next moment we were upon the group with our pistols.

"Forward, men! Don't stop to fight!" roared Miller, as he got clear. A rifle was fired so close to my head that the flame burned my back hair, and my ears rang for half an hour or more. My bay leaped high and dashed down a man. In a few seconds I was fairly out of the scrimmage.

How many of my comrades had gone down I knew not, nor beside whom I was riding. Suddenly our horses plunged into a hole; his stumbled, the man pitched forward, and was left behind. Then I heard a shot, the clatter of another falling horse, the angry yell of another thrown rider.

On we went,—the relics of us. Now we rushed out of the pine forest into broad moonlight, and I saw two riders between me and the lieutenant,—one man almost at my shoulder, and another galloping ten yards behind. Very gradually this man dropped to the rear. We had lost five men already, and still the night was young.

Bader and Absalom Gray were nearest me. Neither spoke a word till we struck upon a space of sandy road. Then I could hear, far behind the rear man, a sound of galloping on the hard highway.

"They're after us, lieutenant!" shouted Bader.

"Many?" He slacked speed, and we listened attentively.

"Only one," cried Miller. "He's coming fast."

The pursuer gained so rapidly that we looked

to our pistols again. Then Absalom Gray cried:

"It's only a horse!"

In a few moments the great gray of fallen Corporal Crowfoot overtook us, went ahead, and slacked speed by the lieutenant.

"Good! He'll be fresh when the rest go down!" shouted Miller. "Let the last man mount the gray!"

By this time we had begun to think ourselves clear of the enemy, and doomed to race on till the horses should fall.

Suddenly the hoofs of Crowfoot's gray and the lieutenant's bay thundered upon a plank road whose hollow noise, when we all reached it, should have been heard far. It took us through wide orchard lands into a low-lying mist by the banks of a great marsh, till we passed through that fog, strode heavily up a slope, and saw the shimmer of roofs under the moon. Straight through the main street we pounded along.

Whether it was wholly deserted I know not, but not a human being was in the streets, nor any face visible at the black windows. Not even a dog barked. I noticed no living thing except some turkeys roosting on a fence, and a white cat that sprang upon the pillar of a gateway and thence to a tree.

Some of the houses seemed to have been ruined by a cannonade. I suppose it was one of the places almost destroyed in Willoughby's recent raid. Here we thundered, expecting ambush and conflict every moment, while the loneliness of the street imposed on me such a sense as might come of galloping through a long cemetery of the dead.

Out of the village we went off the planks again upon sand. I began to suspect that I was losing a good deal of blood. My brain was on fire with whirling thoughts and wonder where all was to end. Out of this daze I came, in amazement to find that we were quickly overtaking our lieutenant's thoroughbred.

Had he been hit in the fray, and bled to weakness? I only know that, still galloping while we gained, the famous horse lurched forward, almost turned a somersault, and fell on his rider.

"Stop—the paper!" shouted Bader.

We drew rein, turned, dismounted, and found Miller's left leg under the big bay's shoulder. The horse was quite dead, the rider's long hair lay on the sand, his face was white under the moon!

We stopped long enough to extricate him, and he came to his senses just as we made out that his left leg was broken.

"Forward!" he groaned. "What in thunder are you stopped for? Oh, the despatch! Here! away you go! Good-bye."

In attending to Miller we had forgotten the rider who had been long gradually dropping behind. Now as we galloped away,—Bader, Absalom Gray, myself, and Crowfoot's riderless horse,—I looked behind for that comrade; but he was not to be seen or heard. We three were left of the eleven.

From the loss of so many comrades the importance of our mission seemed huge. With the speed, the noise, the deaths, the strangeness of the gallop through that forsaken village, the wonder how all would end, the increasing belief that thousands of lives depended on our success, and the longing to win, my brain was wild. A raging desire to be first held me, and I galloped as if in a dream.

Bader led; the riderless gray thundered beside him; Absalom rode stirrup to stirrup with me. He was a veteran of the whole war.

Where it was that his sorrel rolled over I do not remember at all, though I perfectly remember how Absalom sprang up, staggered, shouted, "My foot is sprained!" and fell as I turned to look at him and went racing on.

Then I heard above the sound of our hoofs the voice of the veteran of the war. Down as he was, his spirit was unbroken. In the favorite song of the army his voice rose clear and gay and piercing:—

> "Hurrah for the Union!
> Hurrah, boys, hurrah!
> Shouting the battle-cry of freedom!"

We turned our heads and cheered him as we flew, for there was something indescribably inspiring in the gallant and cheerful lilt of the fallen man. It was as if he flung us, from the grief of utter defeat, a soul unconquerable; and I felt the life in me strengthened by the tone.

Old Bader and I for it! He led by a hundred yards, and Crowfoot's gray kept his stride. Was I gaining on them? How was it that I could see his figure outlined more clearly against the horizon? Surely dawn was not coming on!

No; I looked round on a world of naked

peach-orchards, and corn-fields ragged with
last year's stalks, all dimly lit by a moon that
showed far from midnight; and that faint light
on the horizon was not in the east, but in the
west.   The truth flashed on me,—I was looking at such an illumination of the sky as would
be caused by the camp-fires of an army.

"The missing brigade!" I shouted.

"Or a Southern division!" Bader cried.
"Come on!"

"Come on!" I was certainly gaining on him,
but very slowly. Before the nose of my bay
was beyond the tail of his roan, the wide illu-
minations had become more distinct; and still
not a vidette, not a picket, not a sound of the
proximity of an army.

Bader and I now rode side by side, and
Crowfoot's gray easily kept the pace. My
horse was in plain distress, but Bader's was
nearly done.

"Take the paper, Adam," he said; "my roan
won't go much further. Good-bye, youngster.
Away you go!" and I drew now quickly ahead.

Still Bader rode on behind me. In a few
minutes he was considerably behind. Perhaps
the sense of being alone increased my feeling
of weakness. Was I going to reel out of the

saddle? Had I lost so much blood as that? Still I could hear Bader riding on. I turned to look at him. Already he was scarcely visible. Soon he dropped out of sight; but still I heard the laborious pounding of his desperate horse.

My bay was gasping horribly. How far was that faintly yellow sky ahead? It might be two, it might be five miles. Were Union or Southern soldiers beneath it? Could it be conceived that no troops of the enemy were between me and it?

Never mind; my orders were clear. I rode straight on, and I was still riding straight on, marking no increase in the distress of my bay, when he stopped as if shot, staggered, fell on his knees, tried to rise, rolled to his side, groaned and lay.

I was so weak I could not clear myself. I remember my right spur catching in my saddle-cloth as I tried to free my foot; then I pitched forward and fell. Not yet senseless, I clutched at my breast for the despatch, meaning to tear it to pieces; but there my brain failed, and in full view of the goal of the night I lay unconscious.

When I came to, I rose on my left elbow, and looked around. Near my feet my poor bay lay, stone dead. Crowfoot's gray!—where was Crowfoot's gray? It flashed on me that I might mount the fresh horse and ride on. But where was the gray? As I peered round I heard faintly the sound of a galloper. Was he coming my way? No; faintly and more faintly I heard the hoofs.

Had the gray gone on then, without the despatch? I clutched at my breast. My coat was unbuttoned—the paper was gone!

Well, sir, I cheered. My God! but it was comforting to hear those far-away hoofs, and know that Bader must have come up, taken the papers, and mounted Crowfoot's gray, still good for a ten-mile ride! The despatch was gone forward; we had not all fallen in vain; maybe the brigades would be saved!

How purely the stars shone! When I stifled my groaning they seemed to tell me of a great peace to come. How still was the night! and I thought of the silence of the multitudes who had died for the Union.

Now the galloping had quite died away. There was not a sound,—a slight breeze blew, but there were no leaves to rustle. I put my head down on the neck of my dead horse. Extreme fatigue was benumbing the pain of my now swelling arm; perhaps sleep was near, perhaps I was swooning.

But a sound came that somewhat revived me. Far, low, joyful, it crept on the air. I sat up, wide awake. The sound, at first faint, died as the little breeze fell, then grew in the lull, and came ever more clearly as the wind arose. It was a sound never to be forgotten,—the sound of the distant cheering of thousands of men.

Then I knew that Bader had galloped into the Union lines, delivered the despatch, and told a story which had quickly passed through wakeful brigades.

Bader I never saw again, nor Lieutenant Miller, nor any man with whom I rode that night. When I came to my senses I was in hospital at City Point. Thence I went home invalided. No surgeon, no nurse, no soldier at the hospital could tell me of my regiment, or how or why I was where I was. All they could tell me was that Richmond was taken, the army far away in pursuit of Lee, and a rumor flying that the great commander of the South had surrendered near Appomattox Court House.

"DRAFTED"

HARRY WALLBRIDGE, awaking with a sense of some alarming sound, listened intently in the darkness, seeing overhead the canvas roof faintly outlined, the darker stretch of its ridge-pole, its two thin slanting rafters, and the gable ends of the winter hut. He could not hear the small, fine drizzle from an atmosphere sur-charged with water, nor anything but the drip from canvas to trench, the rustling of hay bunched beneath his head, the regular breath-ing of his "buddy," Corporal Bader, and the stamping of horses in stables. But when a soldier in a neighboring tent called indistin-guishably in the accents of nightmare, Bader's breathing quieted, and in the lull Harry fancied the soaked air weighted faintly with steady picket-firing. A month with the 53d Pennsyl-vania Veteran Volunteer Cavalry had not quite disabused the young recruit of his schoolboy belief that the men of the Army of the Poto-mac must live constantly within sound of the out-posts.

Harry sat up to hearken better, and then concluded that he had mistaken for musketry the crackle of haystalks under his poncho sheet. Beneath him the round poles of his bed sagged as he drew up his knees and gathered about his shoulders the gray blanket damp from the spray of heavy rain against the canvas earlier in the night. Soon, with slow dawn's approach, he could make out the dull white of his carbine and sabre against the mud-plastered chimney. In that drear dimness the boy shivered, with a sense of misery rather than from cold, and yearned as only sleepy youth can for the ease of a true bed and dry warm swooning to slumber. He was sustained by no mature sense that this too would pass; it was with a certain bodily despair that he felt chafed and compressed by his rough garments, and pitied himself, thinking how his mother would cry if she could see him couched so wretchedly that wet March morning, pressed all the more into loneliness by the regular breathing of veteran Bader in the indifference of deep sleep.

Harry's vision of his mother coming into his room, shading her candle with her hand, to see if he were asleep, passed away as a small gust came, shaking the canvas, for he was instantly alert with a certainty that the breeze had borne a strong rolling of musketry.

"Bader, Bader!" he said. "Bader!"

"Can't you shut up, you Wallbridge?" came Orderly Sergeant Gravely's sharp tones from the next tent.

"What's wrong with you, Harry, boy?" asked Bader, turning.

"I thought I heard heavy firing closer than the picket lines; twice now I've thought I heard it."

"Oh, I guess not, Harry. The Johnnies won't come out no such night as this. Keep quiet, or you'll have the sergeant on top of you. Better lie down and try to sleep, buddy; the bugles will call morning soon now."

Again Harry fell to his revery of home, and his vision became that of the special evening on which his boyish wish to go to the war had, for the family's sake, become resolve. He saw his mother's spectacled and lamp-lit face as she, leaning to the table, read in the familiar Bible; little Fred and Mary, also facing the table's central lamp, bent sleepy heads over their school-books; the father sat in the rocking-chair, with his right hand on the paper he had laid down, and gazed gloomily at the coals fallen below the front doors of the wood-burning stove. Harry dreamed himself back

in his own chair, looking askance, and feeling
sure his father was inwardly groaning over the
absence of Jack, the eldest son. Then nine
o'clock struck, and Fred and Mary began to
put their books away in preparation for bed.

"Wait a little, children," Mrs. Wallbridge
said, serene in tone from her devotional reading. "Father wants that I should tell you
something. You mustn't feel bad about it.
It's that we may soon go out West. Your
Uncle Ezra is doing well in Minnesota. Aunt
Elvira says so in her letter that came to-day."

"It's this way, children," said Mr. Wallbridge, ready to explain, now that the subject
was opened. "Since ever your brother Jack
went away South, the store expenses have been
too heavy. It's near five years now he's been
gone. There's a sheaf of notes coming due
the third of next month; twice they've been
renewed, and the Philadelphia men say they'll
close me up this time sure. If I had eight
hundred dollars—but it's no use talking; we'll
just have to let them take what we've got.
Times have been bad right along around here,
anyhow, with new competition, and so many
farmers gone to the war, and more gone West.
If Jack had stopped to home—but I've had to

pay two clerks to do his work, and then they
don't take any interest in the business. Mind,
I'm not blaming Jack, poor fellow,—he'd a
right to go where he'd get more'n his keep,
and be able to lay up something for himself,—
but what's become of him, God knows; and
such a smart, good boy as he was! He'd got
fond of New Orleans,—I guess some nice girl
there, maybe, was the reason; and there he'd
stay after the war began, and now it's two
years and more since we've heard from him.
Dead, maybe, or maybe they'd put him in jail,
for he said he'd never join the Confederates,
nor fight against them either—he felt that way
—North and South was all the same to him.
And so he's gone; and I don't see my way now
at all. Ma, if it wasn't for my lame leg, I'd
take the bounty. It'd be *something* for you
and the children after the store's gone."

"Sho, pa! don't talk that way! You're too
down-hearted. It 'll all come right, with the
Lord's help," said Harry's mother. How
clearly he, in the damp cold tent, could see
her kind looks as she pushed up her spectacles
and beamed on her husband; how distinctly,
in the still dim dawn, he heard her soothing
tones!

It was that evening's talk which had sent
Harry, so young, to the front. Three village
boys, little older than he, had already contrived
to enlist. Every time he saw the Flag droop-
ing, he thought shame of himself to be absent
from the ranks of its upholders; and now, just
as he was believing himself big and old enough
to serve, he conceived that duty to his parents
distinctly enjoined him to go. So in the night,
without leave-taking or consent of his parents,
he departed. The combined Federal, State,
and city bounties offered at Philadelphia
amounted to nine hundred dollars cash that
dreadful winter before Richmond fell, and
Harry sent the money home triumphantly in
time to pay his father's notes and save the
store.

While the young soldier thought it all over,
carbine and sabre came out more and more
distinctly outlined above the mud-plastered
fireplace. The drizzle had ceased, the drip into
the trench was almost finished, intense stillness
ruled; Harry half expected to hear cocks crow
from out such silence.

Listening for them, his dreamy mind
brooded over both hosts, in a vision even as
wide as the vast spread of the Republic in

which they lay as two huddles of miserable men. For what were they all about him this woful, wet night? they all fain, as he, for home and industry and comfort. What delusion held them? How could it be that they could not all march away and separate, and the cruel war be over? Harry caught his breath at the idea,—it seemed so natural, simple, easy, and good a solution. Becoming absorbed in the fancy, tired of listening, and soothed by the silence, he was falling asleep as he sat, when a heavy weight seemed to fall, far away. Another—another—the fourth had the rumble of distant thunder, and seemed followed by a concussion of the air.

"Hey—Big Guns! What's up toward City Point?" cried Bader, sitting up. "I tell you they're at it. It can't be so far away as Butler. What? On the left too! That was toward Hatcher's Run! Harry, the rebs are out in earnest! I guess you did hear the pickets trying to stop 'em. What a morning! Ha—Fort Hell! see that!"

The outside world was dimly lighted up for a moment. In the intensified darkness that followed Bader's voice was drowned by the crash of a great gun from the neighboring fort.

Flash, crash—flash, crash—flash, crash succeeded rapidly.   Then the intervals of Fort
Hell's fire lengthened to the regular periods
for loading, and between her roars were heard
the sullen boom of more distant guns, while
through all the tumult ran a fierce undertone,—
the infernal hurrying of musketry along the
immediate front.

"The Johnnies must have got in close somehow," cried Bader.   "Hey, Sergeant?"

"Yes," shouted Gravely.   "Scooped up the
pickets and supports too in the rain, I guess.
Turn out, boys, turn out! there'll be a wild day.
Kid! Where's the Kid? Kid Sylvester!"

"Here!   All right, Barney; I'll be out in
two shakes," shouted the bugler.

"Hurry, then!   I can hear the Colonel
shouting already.   Man, listen to that!"—as
four of Fort Hell's guns crashed almost
simultaneously.   "Brownie!   Greasy Cook!
O Brownie!"

"Here!" shouted the cook.

"Get your fire started right away, and see
what salt horse and biscuit you can scare up.
Maybe we'll have time for a snack."

"Turn out, Company K!" shouted Lieutenant Bradley, running down from the

officers' quarters. "Where's the commissary sergeant? There?—all right—give out feed right away! Get your oats, men, and feed instantly! We may have time. Hullo! here's the General's orderly."

As the trooper galloped, in a mud-storm, across the parade ground, a group of officers ran out behind the Colonel from the screen of pine saplings about Regimental Headquarters. The orderly gave the Colonel but a word, and, wheeling, was off again as "Boot and saddle" blared from the buglers, who had now assembled on parade.

"But leave the bits out—let your horses feed!" cried the Lieutenant, running down again. "We're not to march till further orders."

Beyond the screen of pines Harry could see the tall canvas ridges of the officers' cabins lighted up. Now all the tents of the regiment, row behind row, were faintly luminous, and the renewed drizzle of the dawn was a little lightened in every direction by the canvas-hidden candles of infantry regiments, the glare of numerous fires already started, and sparks showering up from the cook-houses of company after company.

Soon in the cloudy sky the cannonade rolled about in broad day, which was still so gray that long wide flashes of flame could be seen to spring far out before every report from the guns of Fort Hell, and in the haze but few of the rebel shells shrieking along their high curve could be clearly seen bursting over Hancock's cheering men. Indistinguishably blent were the sounds of hosts on the move, field-guns pounding to the front, troops shouting, the clink and rattle of metal, officers calling, bugles blaring, drums rolling, mules screaming,—all heard as a running accompaniment to the cannon heavily punctuating the multitudinous din.

"Fwat sinse in the ould man bodderin' us?" grumbled Corporal Kennedy, a tall Fenian dragoon from the British army. "Sure, ain't it as plain as the sun—and faith the same's not plain this dirthy mornin'—that there's no work for cavalry the day, barrin' it's escortin' the doughboys' prisoners, if they take any?—bad 'cess to the job. Sure it's an infantry fight, and must be, wid the field-guns helpin', and the siege pieces boomin' away over the throops in the mud betwigst our own breastworks and the inner line of our forts."

"Oh, by this and by that," the corporal grumbled on, "ould Lee's not the gintleman I tuk him for at all, at all,—discomfortin' us in the rain,—and yesterday an illigant day for fightin'. Couldn't he wait, like the dacint ould boy he's reported, for a dhry mornin', instead av turnin' his byes out in the shlush and destroyin' me chanst av breakfast? It's spring chickens I'd ordhered."

"You may get up to spring-chicken country soon, now," said Bader. "I'm thinking this is near the end; it's the last assault that Lee will ever deliver."

"Faith, I dunno," said the corporal; "that's what we've been saying sinst last fall, but the shtay of them Johnnies bates Banagher and the prophets. Hoo—ow! by the powers! did you hear them yell? Fwat? The saints be wid us! who'd 'a' thought it possible? Byes! Bader! Harry! luk at the Johnnies swarmin' up the face of Hell!"

Off there Harry could dimly see, rising over the near horizon made by tents, a straggling rush of men up the steep slope, while the rebel yell came shrill from a multitude behind on the level ground that was hidden from the place occupied by the cavalry regiment. In the next moment the force mounting Fort Hell's slope fell away, some lying where shot down, some rolling, some running and stumbling in heaps; then a tremendous musketry and field-gun fire growled to and fro under the heavy smoke round and about and out in front of the embrasures, which had never ceased their regular discharge over the heads of the fort's defenders and immediate assailants.

Suddenly Harry noted a slackening of the battle; it gradually but soon dropped away to nothing, and now no sound of small-arms in any direction was heard in the lengthening intervals of reports from the siege pieces far and near.

"And so that's the end of it," said Kennedy. "Sure it was hot work for a while! Faix, I thought onct the doughboys was nappin' too long, and ould Hell would be bullyin' away at ourselves. Now, thin, can we have a bite in paice? I'll shtart wid a few sausages, Brownie, and you may send in the shpring chickens wid some oyshters the second coorse. No! Oh, by the powers, 't is too mane to lose a breakfast like that!" and Corporal Kennedy shook his fist at the group of buglers calling the regiment to parade.

In ten minutes the Fifty-third had formed in column of companies. "Old Jimmy," their Colonel, had galloped down at them and once along their front; then the command, forming fours from the right front, moved off at a trot through the mud in long procession.

"Didn't I know it?" said Kennedy; "it's escortin' the doughboys' prisoners, that's all we're good for this outrageous day. Oh, wirra, wirrasthru! Police duty! and this calls itself a cavalry rigiment. Mounted Police duty,— escortin' doughboys' prisoners! Faix, I might as well be wid Her Majesty's dhragoons, thramplin' down the flesh and blood of me in poor ould Oireland. Begor, Harry, me bhy, it's a mane job to be setting you at, and this the first day ye're mounted to save the Union!"

"Stop coddin' the boy, Corporal," said Bader, angrily. "You can't think how an American boy feels about this war."

"An Amerikin!—an Amerikin, is it? Let me insthruct ye thin, Misther Bader, that I'm as good an Amerikin as the next man. Och, be jabers, me that's been in the color you see ever since the Prisident first called for men! It was for a three months' dance he axed us first. Me, that's re-enlishted twice, don't know

the feelin's of an Amerikin! What am I here
for? Not poverty! sure I'd enough of that
before ever I seen Ameriky! What am I wal-
lopin' through the mud for this mornin'?"

"It's your trade, Kennedy," said Bader, with
disgust.

"Be damned to you, man!" said the corporal,
sternly. "When I touched fut in New York,
didn't I swear that I'd never dhraw swoord
more, barrin' it was agin the ould red tyrant
and oprissor of me counthry? Wasn't I glad
to be dhrivin' me own hack next year in Phila-
medink like a gintleman? Oh, the paice and
the indipindence of it! But what cud I do
when the counthry that tuk me and was good
to me wanted an ould dhragoon? An Amerikin, ye say! Faith, the heart of me is Amerikin, if I'm a bog throtter by the tongue. Mind
that now, me bould man!'

Harry heard without heeding as the horses
spattered on. Still wavered in his ears the
sounds of the dawn; still he saw the ghostlike
forms of Americans in gray tumbling back
from their rush against the sacred flag that had
drooped so sadly over the smoke; and still, far
away beyond all this puddled and cumbered
ground the dreamy boy saw millions of white

American faces, all haggard for news of the armies—some looking South, some North, yearning for the Peace that had so long ago been the boon of the Nation.

Now the regiment was upon the red clay of the dead fight, and brought to halt in open columns. After a little they moved off again in fours, and, dropping into single file, surrounded some thousands of disarmed men, the remnant of the desperate brigades that Lee had flung through the night across three lines of breastworks at the great fort they had so nearly stormed. Poor drenched, shivering Johnnies! there they stood, not a few of them in blue overcoats, but mostly in butternut, generally tattered; some barefoot, some with feet bound in ragged sections of blanket, many with toes and skin showing through crazy boots lashed on with strips of cotton or with cord; many stoutly on foot, streaming blood from head wounds.

Some lay groaning in the mud, while their comrades helped Union surgeons to bind or amputate. Here and there groups huddled together in earnest talk, or listened to comrades gesticulating and storming as they recounted incidents of the long charge. But far the

greater number faced outward, at gaze upon
the cavalry guard, and, silently munching thick
flat cakes of corn-bread, stared into the faces
of the horsemen. Harry Wallbridge, brought
to the halt, faced half round in the saddle, and
looked with quick beatings of pity far and wide
over the disorderly crowd of weather-worn
men.

"It's a Louisiana brigade," said Bader.

"Fifty-three, P. V. V. C.," spoke a prisoner,
as if in reply, reading the letters about the
little crossed brass sabres on the Union hats.
"Say, you men from Pennsylvany?"

"Yes, Johnny; we come down to wake up
Dixie."

"I reckon we got the start at wakin' you
this mornin'," drawled the Southerner. "But
say,—there's one of our boys lyin' dyin' over
yonder; his folks lives in Pennsylvany. Mebbe
some of you 'ud know 'em."

"What's his name?" asked Bader.

"Wallbridge—Johnny Wallbridge."

"Why, Harry—hold on!—you ain't the only
Wallbridges there is. What's up?" cried
Bader, as the boy half reeled, half clambered
from his saddle.

"Hold on, Harry!" cried Corporal Kennedy.

"Halt there, Wallbridge!" shouted Sergeant Gravely.

"Stop that man!" roared Lieutenant Bradley.

But, calling, "He's my brother!" Harry, catching up his sabre as he ran, followed the Southerner, who had instantly divined the situation. The forlorn prisoners made ready way for them, and closing in behind, stretched in solid array about the scene.

"It's not Jack," said the boy; but something in the look of the dying man drew him on to kneel in the mud. "Is it *you*, Jack? Oh, now I know you! Jack, I'm Harry! don't you know me? I'm Harry—your brother Harry."

The Southern soldier stared rigidly at the boy, seeming to grow paler with the recollections that he struggled for.

"*What's* your name?" he asked very faintly.

"Harry Wallbridge—I'm your brother."

"Harry Wallbridge! Why, I'm *John* Wallbridge. Did you say Harry? *Not Harry!*" he shrieked hoarsely. "No; Harry's only a little fellow!" He paused, and looked meditatively into the boy's eyes. "It's nearly five years I've been gone,—he was near twelve then. Boys," lifting his head painfully and casting his look slowly round upon his com-rades, "I know him by the eyes; yes, he's my brother! Let me speak to him alone—stand back a bit," and at once the men pushed back-ward into the form of a wide circle.

"Put down your head, Harry. Kiss me! Kiss me again!—how's mother? Ah, I was afraid she might be dead—don't tell her I'm dead, Harry." He groaned with the pain of the groin wound. "Closer, Harry; I've got to tell you this first—maybe it's all I've time to tell. Say, Harry,"—he began to gasp,—"they didn't ought to have killed me, the Union soldiers didn't. I never fired—high enough—all these years. They drafted me, Harry—tell mother that—down in New Orleans—and I—couldn't get away. Ai—ai! how it hurts! I must die soon's I can tell you. I wanted to come home—and help father—how's poor father, Harry? Doing well now? Oh, I'm glad of that—and the baby? there's a new baby! Ah, yes, I'll never see it, Harry."

His eyes closed, the pain seemed to leave him, and he lay almost smiling happily as his brother's tears fell on his muddy and blood-clotted face. As if from a trance his eyes opened, and he spoke anxiously but calmly.

"You'll be sure to tell them I was drafted
—conscripted, you understand. And I never
fired at any of us—of you—tell all the boys
that." Again the flame of life went down, and
again flickered up in pain.

"Harry—you'll stay by father—and help
him, won't you? This cruel war—is almost
over. Don't cry. Kiss me. Say—do you
remember—the old times we had—fishing?
Kiss me again, Harry—brother in blue—you're
on—*my* side. Oh I wish—I had time—to tell
you. Come close—put your arms around—
my neck—it's old times—again." And now
the wound tortured him for a while beyond
speech. "You're with me, aren't you, Harry?

"Well, there's this," he gasped on, "about
my chums—they've been as good and kind—
marching, us all wet and cold together—and
it wasn't their fault. If they had known—how
I wanted—to be shot—for the Union! It was
so hard—to be—on the wrong side! But—"

He lifted his head and stared wildly at his
brother, screamed rapidly, as if summoning all
his life for the effort to explain, "Drafted,
drafted, drafted—Harry, tell mother and
father *that.* I was *drafted.* O God, O God,
what suffering! Both sides—I was on both

sides all the time. I loved them all, North
and South, all,—but the Union most. O God,
it was so hard!"

His head fell back, his eyes closed, and
Harry thought it was the end. But once more
Jack opened his blue eyes, and slowly said in a
steady, clear, anxious voice, "Mind you tell
them I never fired high enough!" Then he lay
still in Harry's arms, breathing fainter and
fainter till no motion was on his lips, nor in his
heart, nor any tremor in the hands that lay in
the hand of his brother in blue.

"Come, Harry," said Bader, stooping tenderly to the boy, "the order is to march. He's
past helping now. It's no use; you must leave
him here to God. Come, boy, the head of the
column is moving already."

Mounting his horse, Harry looked across to
Jack's form. For the first time in two years
the famous Louisiana brigade trudged on without their unwilling comrade. There he lay,
alone, in the Union lines, under the rain, his
marching done, a figure of eternal peace; while
Harry, looking backward till he could no
longer distinguish his brother from the clay of
the field, rode dumbly on and on beside the
downcast procession of men in gray.

A TURKEY APIECE

Not long ago I was searching files of New York papers for 1864, when my eye caught the headline, "Thanksgiving Dinner for the Army." I had shared that feast. The words brought me a vision of a cavalry brigade in winter quarters before Petersburg; of the three-miles-distant and dim steeples of the besieged city; of rows and rows of canvas-covered huts sheltering the infantry corps that stretched interminably away toward the Army of the James. I fancied I could hear again the great guns of "Fort Hell" infrequently punctuating the far-away picket-firing.

Rain, rain, and rain! How it fell on red Virginia that November of '64! How it wore away alertness! The infantry-men—whom we used to call "doughboys," for there was always a pretended feud between the riders and the trudgers—often seemed going to sleep in the night in their rain-filled holes far beyond the breastworks, each with its little mound of earth thrown up toward the beleaguered town. Their night-firing would slacken almost to cessation for many minutes together. But after the b-o-o-oom of a great gun it became brisker usually; often so much so as to suggest that some of Lee's ragged brigades, their march silenced by the rain, had pierced our fore-front again, and were "gobbling up" our boys on picket, and flinging up new rifle-pits on the acres reclaimed for a night and a day for the tottering Confederacy.

Sometimes the *crack-a-rac-a-rack* would die down to a slow fire of dropping shots, and the forts seemed sleeping; and patter, patter, patter on the veteran canvas we heard the rain, rain, rain, not unlike the roll of steady musketry very far away.

I think I sit again beside Charley Wilson, my sick "buddy," and hear his uneven breathing through all the stamping of the rows of wet horses on their corduroy floor roofed with leaky pine brush.

That *squ-ush, squ-ush* is the sound of the stable-guard's boots as he paces slowly through the mud, to and fro, with the rain rattling on his glazed poncho and streaming corded hat. Sometimes he stops to listen to a frantic brawling of the wagon-train mules, sometimes to the reviving picket-firing. It crackles up to animation for causes that we can but guess;

then dies down, never to silence, but warns, warns, as the distant glow of the sky above a volcano warns of the huge waiting forces that give it forth.

I think I hear Barney Donahoe pulling our latch-string that November night when we first heard of the great Thanksgiving dinner that was being collected in New York for the army.

"Byes, did yez hear phwat Sergeant Cunningham was tellin' av the Thanksgivin' turkeys that's comin'?"

"Come in out of the rain, Barney," says Charley, feebly.

"Faith, I wish I dar', but it's meself is on shtable-guard. Bedad, it's a rale fire ye've got. Divil a better has ould Jimmy himself (our colonel). Ye've heard tell of the turkeys, then, and the pois?"

"Yes. Bully for the folks at home!" says Charley. "The notion of turkey next Thursday has done me good already. I was thinking I'd go to hospital to-morrow, but now I guess I won't."

"Hoshpital! Kape clear av the hoshpital, Char-les, dear. Sure, they'd cut a man's leg off behind the ears av him for to cure him av indigestion."

"Is it going to rain all night, Barney?"

"It is, bad 'cess to it; and to-morrow and the day afther, I'm thinkin'. The blackness av night is outside; be jabers! you could cut it like turf with a shpade! If it wasn't for the ould fort flamin' out wanst in a whoile, I'd be thinkin' I'd never an oi in my head, barrin' the fires in the tints far an' near gives a bit of dimness to the dark. Phwat time is it?"

"Quarter to twelve, Barney."

"Troth, then, the relief will be soon coming. I must be thramping the mud av Virginia to save the Union. Good-night, byes. I come to give yez the good word. Kape your heart light an' aisy, Char-les, dear. D'ye moind the turkeys and the pois? Faith, it's meself that has the taste for thim dainties!"

"I don't believe I'll be able to eat a mite of the Thanksgiving," says Charley, as we hear Barney *squ-ush* away; "but just to see the brown on a real old brown home turkey will do me a heap of good."

"You'll be all right by Thursday, Charley, I guess; won't you? It's only Sunday night now."

Of course I cannot remember the very words of that talk in the night, so many years ago.

But the coming of Barney I recollect well, and the general drift of what was said.

Charley turned on his bed of hay-covered poles, and I put my hand under his gray blanket to feel if his legs were well covered by the long overcoat he lay in. Then I tucked the blanket well in about his feet and shoulders, pulled his poncho again to its full length over him, and sat on a cracker-box looking at our fire for a long time, while the rain spattered through the canvas in spray.

My "buddy" Charley, the most popular boy of Company I, was of my own age,—seventeen,—though the rolls gave us a year more each, by way of compliance with the law of enlistment. From a Pennsylvania farm in the hills he came forth to the field early in that black fall of '64, strong, tall, and merry, fit to ride for the nation's life,—a mighty wielder of an axe, "bold, cautious, true, and my loving comrade."

We were "the kids" to Company I. To "buddy" with Charley I gave up my share of the hut I had helped to build as old Bader's "pard." Then the "kids" set about the construction of a new residence, which stood farther from the parade ground than any hut in the row except the big cabin of "old Brownie," the "greasy cook," who called us to "bean—oh!" with so resonant a shout, and majestically served out our rations of pork, "salt horse," coffee long-boiled and sickeningly sweet, hardtack, and the daily loaf of a singularly despondent-looking bread.

My "buddy" and I slept on opposite sides of our winter residence. The bedsteads were made of poles laid lengthwise and lifted about two feet from the ground. These were covered thinly with hay from the bales that were regularly delivered for horse-fodder. There was a space of about two feet between our bedsteads, and under them we kept our saddles and saddle-cloths.

Our floor was of earth, with a few flour-barrel staves and cracker-box sides laid down for rugs. We had each an easy-chair in the form of a cracker-box, besides a stout soap-box for guests. Our carbines and sabres hung crossed on pegs over the mantel-piece, above our Bibles and the precious daguerreotypes of the dear folks at home. When we happened to have enough wood for a bright fire, we felt much snugger than you might suppose.

Before ever that dark November began,

Charley had been suffering from one of those wasting diseases that so often clung to and carried off the strongest men of both armies. Sharing the soldiers' inveterate prejudice against hospitals attended by young doctors, who, the men believed, were addicted to much surgery for the sake of practice, my poor "buddy" strove to do his regular duties. He paraded with the sick before the regimental doctor as seldom as possible. He was favored by the sergeants and helped in every way by the men, and so continued to stay with the company at that wet season when drill and parades were impracticable.

The idea of a Thanksgiving dinner for half a million men by sea and land fascinated Charley's imagination, and cheered him mightily. But I could not see that his strength increased, as he often alleged.

"Ned, you bet I'll be on hand when them turkeys are served out," he would say. "You won't need to carry my Thanksgiving dinner up from Brownie's. Say, ain't it bully for the folks at home to be giving us a Thanksgiving like this? Turkeys, sausages, mince-pies! They say there's going to be apples and celery for all hands!"

"S'pose you'll be able to eat, Charley?"

"Able! Of course I'll be able! I'll be just as spry as you be on Thanksgiving. See if I don't carry my own turkey all right. Yes, by gum, if it weighs twenty pounds!"

"There won't be a turkey apiece."

"No, eh? Well, that's what I figure on. Half a turkey, anyhow. Got to be; besides chickens, hams, sausages, and all that kind of fixin's. You heard what Bill Sylvester's girl wrote from Philamadink-a-daisy-oh? No, eh? Well, he come in a-purpose to read me the letter. Says there's going to be three or four hundred thousand turkeys, besides them fixin's! Sherman's boys can't get any; they're marched too far away, out of reach. The Shenandoah boys 'll get some, and Butler's crowd, and us chaps, and the blockading squadrons. Bill's girl says so. We'll get the whole lot between us. Four hundred thousand turkeys! Of course there'll be a turkey apiece; there's got to be, if there's any sense in arithmetic. Oh, I'll be choosin' between breast-meat and hind-legs on Thanksgiving,—you bet your sweet life on that!"

This expectation that there would be a turkey apiece was not shared by Company I; but no one denied it in Charley's hearing. The boy held it as sick people often do fantastic notions, and all fell into the humor of strengthening the reasoning on which he went.

It was clear that no appetite for turkey moved my poor "buddy," but that his brain was busy with the "whole-turkey-a-piece" idea as one significant of the immense liberality of the folks at home, and their absorbing interest in the army.

"Where's there any nation that ever was that would get to work and fix up four hundred thousand turkeys for the boys?" he often remarked, with ecstatic patriotism.

I have often wondered why "Bill Sylvester's girl" gave that flourishing account of the preparations for our Thanksgiving dinner. It was only on searching the newspaper files recently that I surmised her sources of information. Newspapers seldom reached our regiment until they were several weeks old, and then they were not much read, at least by me. Now I know how enthusiastic the papers of November, '64, were on the great feast for the army.

For instance, on the morning of that Thanksgiving day, the 24th of November, the New York Tribune said editorially:—

"Forty thousand turkeys, eighty thousand turkeys, one hundred and sixty thousand turkeys, nobody knows how many turkeys have been sent to our soldiers. Such masses of breast-meat and such mountains of stuffing; drumsticks enough to fit out three or four Grand Armies, a 'perfect promontory of pope's noses, a mighty aggregate of wings. The gifts of their lordships to the supper which Grangousier spread to welcome Gargantua were nothing to those which our good people at home send to their friends in the field; and no doubt every soldier, if his dinner does not set him thinking too intently of that home, will prove himself a valiant trencherman."

Across the vast encampment before Petersburg a biting wind blew that Thanksgiving day. It came through every cranny of our hut; it bellied the canvas on one side and tightened it on the other; it pressed flat down the smoke from a hundred thousand mud chimneys, and swept away so quickly the little coals which fell on the canvas that they had not time to burn through.

When I went out towards noon, for perhaps the twentieth time that day, to learn whether our commissary wagons had returned from City Point with the turkeys, the muddy parade ground was dotted with groups of shivering men, all looking anxiously for the feast's arrival. Officers frequently came out, to exchange a few cheery words with their men, from the tall, close hedge of withering pines stuck on end that enclosed the officers' quarters on the opposite side of the parade ground.

No turkeys at twelve o'clock! None at one! Two, three, four, five o'clock passed by, and still nothing had been heard of our absent wagons. Charley was too weak to get out that day, but he cheerfully scouted the idea that a turkey for each man would not arrive sooner or later.

The rest of us dined and supped on "commissary." It was not good commissary either, for Brownie, the "greasy cook," had gone on leave to visit a "doughboy" cousin of the Sixth Corps.

"You'll have turkey for dinner, boys," he had said, on serving out breakfast. "If you're wanting coffee, Tom can make it." Thus we had to dine and sup on the amateur productions of the cook's mate.

A multitude of woful rumors concerning the absent turkeys flew round that evening. The "Johnnies," we heard, had raided round the

army, and captured the fowls! Butler's col-
ored troops had got all the turkeys, and had
been feeding on fowl for two days! The officers had "gobbled" the whole consignment for
their own use! The whole story of the Thanksgiving dinner was a newspaper hoax! Nothing was too incredible for men so bitterly
disappointed.

Brownie returned before "lights out"
sounded, and reported facetiously that the
"doughboys" he had visited were feeding full
of turkey and all manner of fixings. There
were so many wagons waiting at City Point
that the roads round there were blocked for
miles. We could not fail to get our turkeys
to-morrow. With this expectation we went,
pretty happy, to bed.

"There'll be a turkey apiece, you'll see, Ned,"
said Charley, in a confident, weak voice, as
I turned in. "We'll all have a bully Thanksgiving to-morrow."

The morrow broke as bleak as the preceding
day, and without a sign of turkey for our
brigade. But about twelve o'clock a great
shouting came from the parade ground.

"The turkeys have come!" cried Charley,
trying to rise. "Never mind picking out a

big one for me; any one will do. I don't
believe I can eat a bite, but I want to see it.
My ain't it kind of the folks at home!"

I ran out and found his surmise as to the
return of the wagons correct. They were
filing into the enclosure around the quartermaster's tent. Nothing but an order that the
men should keep to company quarters prevented the whole regiment helping to unload
the delicacies of the season.

Soon foraging parties went from each company to the quartermaster's enclosure. Company I sent six men. They returned, grinning,
in about half an hour, with one box on one
man's shoulders.

It was carried to Sergeant Cunningham's
cabin, the nearest to the parade ground, the
most distant from that of "the kids," in which
Charley lay waiting. We crowded round the
hut with some sinking of enthusiasm. There
was no cover on the box except a bit of cotton
in which some of the consignment had probably been wrapped. Brownie whisked this off,
and those nearest Cunningham's door saw disclosed—two small turkeys, a chicken, four
rather disorganized pies, two handsome bologna
sausages, and six very red apples.

We were nearly seventy men. The comical side of the case struck the boys instantly. Their disappointment was so extreme as to be absurd. There might be two ounces of feast to each, if the whole were equally shared.

All hands laughed; not a man swore. The idea of an equal distribution seemed to have no place in that company. One proposed that all should toss up for the lot. Another suggested drawing lots; a third that we should set the Thanksgiving dinner at one end of the parade ground and run a race for it, "grab who can."

At this Barney Donahue spoke up.

"Begorra, yez can race for wan turkey av yez loike. But the other wan is goin' to Char-les Wilson!"

There was not a dissenting voice. Charley was altogether the most popular member of Company I, and every man knew how he had clung to the turkey apiece idea.

"Never let on a word," said Sergeant Cunningham. "He'll think there's a turkey for every man!"

The biggest bird, the least demoralized pie, a bologna sausage, and the whole six apples were placed in the cloth that had covered the box. I was told to carry the display to my poor "buddy."

As I marched down the row of tents a tremendous yelling arose from the crowd round Cunningham's tent. I turned to look behind. Some man with a riotous impulse had seized the box and flung its contents in the air over the thickest of the crowd. Next moment the turkey was seized by half a dozen hands. As many more helped to tear it to pieces. Barney Donahoe ran past me with a leg, and two laughing men after him. Those who secured larger portions took a bite as quickly as possible, and yielded the rest to clutching hands. The bologna sausage was shared in like fashion, but I never heard of any one who got a taste of the pies.

"Here's your turkey, Charley," said I, entering with my burden.

"Where's yours, Ned?"

"I've got my turkey all right enough at Cunningham's tent."

"Didn't I tell you there'd be a turkey apiece?" he cried gleefully, as I unrolled the lot. "And sausages, apples, a whole pie—oh, say, ain't they bully folks up home!"

"They are," said I. "I believe we'd have

had a bigger Thanksgiving yet if it wasn't such a trouble getting it distributed."

"You'd better believe it! They'd do anything in the world for the army," he said, lying back.

"Can't you eat a bite, buddy?"

"No; I'm not a mite hungry. But I'll look at it. It won't spoil before to-morrow. Then you can share it all out among the boys."

Looking at the turkey, the sick lad fell asleep. Barney Donahoe softly opened our door, stooped his head under the lintel, and gazed a few moments at the quiet face turned to the Thanksgiving turkey. Man after man followed to gaze on the company's favorite, and on the fowl which, they knew, tangibly symbolized to him the immense love of the nation for the flower of its manhood in the field. Indeed, the people had forwarded an enormous Thanksgiving feast; but it was impossible to distribute it evenly, and we were one of the regiments that came short.

Grotesque, that scene? Group after group of hungry, dirty soldiers, gazing solemnly, lovingly, at a lone brown turkey and a pallid sleeping boy! Very grotesque. But Charley had his Thanksgiving dinner, and the men of

Company I, perhaps, enjoyed a profounder satisfaction than if they had feasted more materially.

I never saw Charley after that Thanksgiving day. Before the afternoon was half gone the doctor sent an ambulance for him, and insisted that he should go to City Point. By Christmas his wasted body had lain for three weeks in the red Virginia soil.

THE SWARTZ DIAMOND

THE Boer puzzled us. It was not because he loomed so big in the haze against the sunset; but he seemed at a mile's distance to detect us. We thought the cover perfect, for the hackthorn tops were higher than our horses' heads. If he from so far could see patches of khaki through bushes, his eyes must be better than our field-glasses. If he did not see us, why did he wave his hat as in salutation?

"Maybe he only suspect one patrol at de ford. Vat you t'ink, Sergeant McTavish?" said Lieutenant Deschamps to me.

"Perhaps he thinks some of his own kind may hold the ford," I suggested.

The others said nothing. They were fifteen French Canadians, including Corporal Jongers. We lay still behind our prone horses, and kept our Krags on the Boer.

He seemed to diminish as he advanced slowly from the mirage, but still he looked uncommonly big—and venerable, too. His hair and beard grew long and white, though he sat up as alert as any young man. At ten yards a pack-pony followed him. When half a mile away the burgher raised both hands above his head.

"He come for surrender, you t'ink, sergeant?" Lieutenant Deschamps is a gentleman. Because I was of another race he always treated me with more than the consideration due to a good non-com. Or possibly it was because he knew I had been advocate in Montreal before joining the mounted Canadian contingent.

"Better keep down and keep him covered," I replied. "That may be a signal." I stared about the horizon. The veldt was bare, except for the straggle of hackthorns fringing the curve about the ford. There could be no other Boer within three miles of us, unless hidden by the meanderings of the Wolwe, which runs twelve feet below the plain. But we had searched ten miles of its bed during the day. Westward lay the kopjes from among which the old Boer had apparently ridden.

He came calmly down the breach of the opposite bank and as far as the middle of the brawling shallow within fifty yards of us before Deschamps cried "Halt!" At the word we sprang up, accoutrements rattling, horses snorting. The old burgher looked up at us quizzically, passing his hand down his beard and gathering its length above his mouth before he spoke.

"Take care some of those guns don't go off," he said, with no trace of Dutch accent.

"You surrender?" Deschamps stepped forward.

"Sir, I am going to Swartzdorp. Did you not see me hold up my hands?"

"But for sure you could not see us here?"

He smiled and pointed up to the sky. In the blue a vulture swung wide above us. "So I knew," said the burgher, "Khakis were hiding. Boers would have come out. They would have recognized me."

"Your name?"

"Emanuel Swartz."

"*Bon!* The great landowner! I have much pleasure to see you. Come in, monsieur. Eef only you brought in your commando, how glad!"

"They may come yet," he said. "It depends." He shook his rein, and the big bay brought him up the breach into the midst of us. The pack-pony, which had imitated his halt, followed.

"You will not stop me. I have private business at Swartzdorp," he said.

"Truly I regret," said Deschamps. "But my orders! Here you must stay, monsieur, this night. To-morrow General Pole. He will be most glad to parole you, I have hope."

"Oh, very well, lieutenant," said Swartz, philosophically. "I dare say he won't send me to St. Helena." He dismounted, leaving his Mauser strapped to his saddle. Then he handed me his bandoleer. "I make you welcome to my pack also," he said hospitably. "There's some biltong and meal. Perhaps it will improve your fare."

"It will be poor stuff if it doesn't," I told him.

"You give your parole, sir?" asked Deschamps.

"For the night, yes. I will not try to escape."

His cordial, easy accents came with a certain surprising effect from one who was so unkempt and, in spite of his years, so formidable. I had never before seen one of the great Boer landowners. In his manner one could perceive, if not a certain condescension, at least the elevated kindness of a patriarchal gentleman accustomed to warm by affability the hearts of many descendants and dependents.   About Swartzdorp we had heard much of his English mother, his English wife, and his lifelong friendship with English officers and gentlemen.   It did not seem surprising that he should have come in voluntarily now that Bloemfontein and Pretoria were in Lord Roberts's hands.

It was cold for us in khaki that evening by the Wolwe, though we did not lack overcoats. The spruit tinkled icily along patches of gravel in the blue clay, and late June's high moon seemed pouring down a Canadian wintriness. "No fire," ordered Deschamps, lest far-sighted Boer parties, skilled in surprises, might locate us.   But the old burgher showed how to make small glowing heaps of dry offal, which had been plentifully left of old by troops of deer and antelope coming to drink at the spruit. Over one of these tiny smokeless fires our lieutenant sat with the prisoner.   I think I see again the reflection of the little flame flickering on the old giant's enormous beard and shapely outspread hands.

We had supped heavily on his meat and meal, but sleep in that nipping air came by dozes only, and drowsiness departed when digestion had relieved repletion. At midnight, when the vedettes were changed and the moon sagged low, we all were more wakeful than early in the evening. There had been little talk, and that in the low voices of endurance; but now Deschamps and Swartz fell into discourse about the Kimberley mines. This led to discussing the greater diamonds of South Africa, and so on till the burgher began a story stranger than fiction:

"One of the biggest stones ever taken from blue clay is still uncut. It has never been offered for sale. Near this very place it was found by Vassell Swartz, my cousin. The man is not rich even for a Free State burgher. He is fond of money. He believes his diamond to be worth twelve thousand pounds. No man could wish harder to sell anything. And yet he has not offered it. He has not even shown it. His wife has not seen it. He has had it constantly near him for eleven years. He has handled it frequently—in its setting. But he has not ventured to look at it since the morning after he found it. You wonder at that. Is it possible a rough diamond can shine so bright as dangerously to dazzle the eyes? No; Vassell would be glad to stare at it all day. But its

setting prevents him. And yet he set it himself."

The old burgher paused and looked about on
our puzzled faces with some air of satisfaction
at their interest.

"It is quite a riddle," said Deschamps.

"So it is. And I will make it harder. You
have been told that we Boers think nothing of
killing Kaffirs? But all Swartzdorp could tell
you that my cousin Vassell could scarcely bear
to let a Kaffir out of his sight. That is mysterious? Well, I will not go on talking in parables.
I will tell you the thing just as I heard it from
Vassell or know about it myself.

"Eleven years ago, Vassell and his brother,
my cousin Claas, went off as usual to Makori's
country beyond the Limpopo, elephant-hunt-
ing. Ivory was so plenty that they trekked
back a month earlier than they had expected.
On the return Vassell's riding-horse fell lame
not long after crossing this very Wolwe spruit
by a higher ford. My cousin gave the beast no
rest till evening, and no attention until after
they had made a laager against lions and had
eaten supper. Then he took a brand from the
fire and looked into the hoof. In it he found a
whitish stone of about the bigness of an ele-

phant-bullet of six to the pound. It was of the
colour of alum, and in the torchlight it glistened
as the scale of a fish.

"Vassell had never seen a rough diamond.
And he had heard of diamonds as brighter than
glittering glass. He thought only that the
pebble was a pretty stone. The man's heart
was soft with nearing his wife and children, so
he slipped the pebble into his empty elephant-
bullet pouch, thinking to give it for a toy to his
little Anna. There it lay forgotten until his
fingers went groping for a bullet at the next
daybreak. Kaffirs were then trying to rush my
cousins' laager.

"Wild Kaffirs these were, driven from Kimberley for unruliness in drink. They were
going back to their tribe; they had come far
without food, and they smelled the meat and
meal in the wagons—so Matakit afterward
told. But no hunger could have driven them
against a Boer laager. They mistook the wagons for the wagons of Englishmen."

The French Canadians smiled unoffended,
but my jaws snapped. Swartz turned to me
courteously:

"They mistook the wagons for those of English traders unskilled in arms and trekking pro-

visions to the mines. Though their first rush showed them their mistake, they went mad over their losses and came on twice more. Then they guessed, from the way my cousins reserved their fire, that their ammunition was low. So Matakit howled them on for a fourth rush.

"My cousins and their six Christian Kaffirs were now in alarm, for their cartridges were nearly all gone. It was then that Vassell's fingers groped in his elephant-bullet pouch, where he felt something rounding out the leather. That was the forgotten pebble. But its bigness was too great for the muzzle-loading elephant-rifle. So my cousin rammed it into the wide-mouthed, old-fashioned *roer,* a blunderbuss that our fathers' fathers praised because it frightened Kaffirs more than it hurt them. In justice to the roer it should have been loaded with a handful of slugs. But with only powder and the pebble it made such flash and noise that all the living wild blacks, but one, ran away howling. The one that fell before Vassell's pebble was the biggest of all, and their leader. There he lay kicking and bellowing like a buffalo bull, ten yards from the wagons.

" 'While he bawled we knelt in the laager,' Vassell told me, 'and we offered up thanks for this our deliverance, even like unto the deliverance of David by the pebble of the brook.'

"Then they ate breakfast while their Kaffirs inspanned, and still the wild one roared.

" 'It would be merciful, brother Vassell,' said Claas as they drank coffee, 'to put the Lord's creature out of his pain.'

" 'Nay,' said Vassell; 'my conscience will not consent to what Free State law might call murder. And, moreover, the Kaffir's pain is a plain judgment of the Almighty.' Vassell is a dopper, like Oom Paul, and a dopper is quick to see the Almighty operating through himself. So they left the black thief gnashing, with five more who lay still, meat for vultures' beaks or lions' jaws.

"In four or five hours' time my cousins were nigh to Truter's drift on the Modder. There they saw two Englishmen and one Israelite digging into the blue-clay shoal.

" 'Good day,' shouts Claas. 'What are you digging for?'

" 'Diamonds, Dutchman, d—n you,' said the Englishmen, laughing.

"They came up out of the river-bed and showed my cousins four small rough stones which they had found elsewhere.

"Vassell looked closely at the stones. Then he knew that his pebble had been a great gem. He put innocent, simple dopper questions about the value of diamonds. And the Israelite said that a first-rate stone of the bigness of more than an elephant-bullet would be worth from twelve to twenty thousand pounds. Vassell felt that Israelite's eyes piercing him, and so he gave no more sign of excitement than a skull. But he was wondering if the grandfathers' old roer had sent the pebble through the Kaffir, which seemed unlikely.

"My cousins traded the flesh of a springbok for cartridges, and the English went away up the spruit, while Claas got ready to cross at Truter's. But Vassell made delay; he said that hunger was rummaging his inside.

" 'And that was the truth, Emanuel,' he told me later, 'for we had trekked since dawn. But it is not always needful to tell all the truth. Was I to arouse in Claas a greedy desire to share in the diamond? True,' said Vassell, 'we had agreed to share and share alike in the hunt, but the stone was not ivory, skin, nor meat, and I alone found it. We are commanded to agree with our adversary "in the way with him." And by halting in that place for the boiling of coffee there would be time to pray for direction. If the Almighty would have us trek back to the wounded Kaffir, it would be wise to turn before crossing at Truter's.'

"Of course my cousin Claas, when he heard of Vassell's hunger, felt hungry too, and the Kaffirs were told to prepare the meal. Meantime Vassell took his Bible from the wagon-box and fell on his knees. He expected the Lord would order him back to the Wolwe, and so it happened. But to induce Claas to obey the Lord's direction without understanding the whole thing was the trouble.

"Like an inspiration a familiar text came to Vassell's mind. 'Blessed are the merciful: for they shall obtain mercy.' He showed this to Claas as his reason for turning about. The text had a new meaning for Vassell. I tell you again he felt that he had been inspired to remember it. You have to bear that in mind, or you will not rightly understand how his brain was afterward affected.

" 'But it would be foolishness to apply the text to a wild Kaffir four hours' trek back,' said Claas.

" 'Nay, not if the Kaffir be subdued,' said Vassell.

" 'He is more than subdued; he is dead,' said Claas.

" 'Nay, he may not yet have perished,' said Vassell. But he felt sure the black was dead. And he felt equally sure he had been inspired to understand that he himself should obtain mercy in the shape of the diamond if he returned even as the good Samaritan to the Kaffir fallen by the way. Still Claas was stiff-necked, until Vassell opened the Book at Jeremiah iii. 12: 'Return, . . . for I am merciful, saith the Lord.' He handed it to Claas without a word.

"Claas naturally supposed that Vassell had opened the Bible at random, as the doppers often do when they are seeking direction. And hence Claas saw in this text a clear leading back to the Wolwe. Yet he wished to rest and smoke tobacco for a long hour after eating. But Vassell was greatly inspired with texts that day. He pointed to I Samuel xx. 38: 'Jonathan cried after the lad, Make speed, haste, stay not.' Then he fell into such a groaning and sighing about it that Claas could not smoke in peace.

" 'Anything is better than your rumblings,' said Claas, and so they hastened on the back-

ward course. 'For,' as Vassell told me, 'I was
in deep tribulation of fear lest the vultures
might gulp down the diamond, or some beak
strike it afar.' "

Here the huge old burgher sat up straighter
and paused so unexpectedly that his sudden silence was startling. I imagined he listened to
something far off in the stillness of the waning moon. Lieutenant Deschamps and the
French Canadians sat indifferent, but I sprang
up and put hands to my ears. Nothing could I
hear but the occasional stamping of our horses,
the walking hoofs of our vedettes by the river's
bend, and the clinking of swift water over
gravel.

"Did you hear something strange?" the patriarch asked me.

"Did you?" I asked.

"Is it likely that a great-grandfather's ears
can hear better than a young man's?" he asked
courteously.

"But you stopped to listen," I replied.

Then he shamed me by saying gently: "An
old voice may need a little rest. But now I will
go on:

"My cousins trekked back as fast as their
oxen could walk. They found the Kaffir still

squirming, and covering his eyes from the vultures. This went to Vassell's heart. He could
not cut the diamond out of the living. And
perhaps it was not in the man. Vassell drove
away the vultures and examined the wound.
Then his heart was lifted up exceedingly, for
as he told me, 'fear had been heavy in me lest
the diamond had gone clear through the Kaffir
and been lost on the veldt. But now my fingers
felt it under the flesh of his back. An inch
more had sent it through. And it seemed so
sure the pagan must die before morning that
my conscience was clear against extracting the
stone in haste.'

"This Wolwe Veldt was then Lion Veldt,
and Vassell thought it prudent to carry the
Kaffir into the night-laager, for lions bolt big
chunks, and the diamond might be in one of
them. Claas consented, and so the tame Kaffirs
lugged the wild one into one of the ivory-
wagons, and left him to die at his leisure.

"Late in the night Vassell, wakened by Claas
snoring, felt a strong temptation. He might
get up and knife out the stone unseen. 'But I
put the temptation away,' he told me, 'for my
movement might waken Claas, or the Kaffir
might kick or groan under the knife, and my

brother might spy on me. So I mercifully
awaited the hour when the Lord would let the
diamond come into my hands without Claas suspecting anything. Besides, it was against my
conscience to cut the Kaffir up warm when it
seemed so sure he would be cold before morning.'

"But next morning the Kaffir was neither
dead nor alive. And my cousins were keen to
see their wives and children. They must trek
on. But Vassell could not leave the diamond.
'And to end the Kaffir's life was,' he told me,
'more than ever against my conscience. That
first text, "Blessed are the merciful: for they
shall obtain mercy," kept coming back into
my mind. It scared me. It seemed to mean
I should have the diamond to myself only if I
spared the Kaffir. If I killed him Claas might
see me extract the stone and claim half. Moreover, I felt sure the jolting of the wagon would
end the pagan soon.'

"So they trekked. When they outspanned
at Swartzdorp, two days later, the Kaffir was
more alive than on the first day. No reward
yet for conscientious Vassell! He stayed only
a day with his wife, and then trekked for
Bloemfontein with the Kaffir in his horse-

wagon. Claas stayed at Swartzdorp. And all at Swartzdorp thought Vassell had gone crazy about the black.

"I was then residing in Bloemfontein, attending a meeting of the Raad. There I saw Vassell gaping at me in the market-place. Never before had I seen trouble in the man's face. When he told me he had brought a hurt Kaffir all the miles from Swartzdorp I felt sure the man was mad.

" 'It may be the Kaffir saved your life from lions?' I asked him.

" 'Nay; I saved his life,' he groaned. 'For we are commanded to do good unto our enemies. And, moreover, this is the Kaffir I fired it into.'

" 'Fired what?' I asked, not then knowing a word of it all.

" 'Emanuel,' he said, 'my soul is deep in trouble, and surely God has sent you to counsel me. He commanded me to bring the Kaffir here. The text he put into my mind will not go out of my mind. I dream of it each night, and I dream of the Kaffir with it, so it must mean him. And to be merciful that I may obtain the promised mercy I have brought him to the hospital.'

" 'What does this rant mean?   Put it in plain Taal,' I said.

"Vassell looked all about the market-place, tiptoed his lips to my ears, and whispered, 'Come into my horse-wagon.'

"I climbed up in front under the cover, and then heard breathing behind the seat.   There lay the Kaffir.   I turned on Vassell with 'You said you brought him to the hospital.'

" 'I am afraid to take him there.'

" 'Afraid they will require you to pay?'

" 'Nay, that is not the trouble.   I will reveal all to you.'

"Then he whispered to me all that I have told you, my friends.

" 'It was borne in on me,' Vassell said, 'that the surgeons would cut out the diamond to save the Kaffir's life, and thus I should obtain the mercy.   But now I am in fear they will not let me be present at the operation.   They will keep the diamond if they get time to examine it.'

" 'Drive to the hospital,' I said.   'They will let you be present.   I will arrange that.   Have you money?'

"Yes; he had sold his four best tusks for English gold.   So he had plenty to pay the doctors if a bribe should prove necessary.

"But it was not needed. The house-surgeon had the Kaffir carried in, and they examined him in our presence. Then they told Vassell it was a beautiful case involving the kidneys in some extraordinary way, and they wished to watch what would happen if Matakit lived—that was the outrageous Kaffir's name. To cut the bullet out, they said—for you may be sure Vassell never mentioned diamond to them—would kill the Kaffir. And if they killed him quickly, medical science might forego valuable knowledge which it might gain if they didn't operate an hour before he was quite out of danger by the wound.

"Think of my conscientious cousin's sad situation!" The old giant gazed about on us as if without guile. "Twelve thousand pounds! And the surgeons would not let him take the Kaffir away. Nor would they let Vassell stay in the ward with his diamond! And he dared not tell the doctors why the operation would have comforted him, lest they should secretly explore the Kaffir as diamondiferous clay!"

Here again the tale paused. A sardonic tone had for an instant been steely in the genial voice. But the face of the old man was as in a placid dream. We volunteers, trust-

ing all to our vedettes, grinned, thinking only
of Vassell's dilemma. The burgher seemed to
ponder on it; or maybe, I thought, he was rest-
ing his voice again. So ten seconds passed.
Then I heard the rush and grunt of a flac-flarc,
the veldt pig. It seemed to have been startled
out of the spruit by a vedette, for we faintly
heard a horse snort and a man scold. The moon
was now very low, but all seemed unchanged
except for an increasing restlessness of the
picketed horses. They had replied to the snort
of the vedette's beast. In an interval of tense
silence, the old Africander stared about on our
faces with a curious inspection that I now think
of as having been one of such pity as the deaf
perceive in other men's faces. But at the time
I supposed he but wished to assure himself that
all were attentively awaiting the rest of his
story.

Yet when the old burgher spoke again he
seemed to have forgotten the great Swartz diamond.

"Such silence on this veldt!" he murmured.
"I remember it alive with great game. Not
twenty miles from here I have lain often awake
in the night to a concert of lions and hyenas
and jackals, with the stamping of wildebeests,

and the barking of quaggas, and the rushing away of springbok and blesbok as the breeze gave them our scent. Now we hear nothing, my friends—nothing whatever moving on the plain?"

"Only the horses and the pickets and the stream," said Deschamps.

"But I," said the old burgher, "hear more. I hear the sounds of ghosts of troops of great game. And I hear with those sounds other sounds as of the ghosts of a needless war." He sighed heavily, and seemed to sink into sad reverie.

Deschamps and his French volunteers would not interrupt him, but I was impatient. "How did your cousin get at the diamond?" I asked.

"He did not get at it." The whitebeard roused up amiably and resumed his tale:

"And yet he did not part with it. For six weeks the Kaffir improved in the Bloemfontein hospital. Then the day came when the surgeons told my cousin they could learn nothing more of the lovely case from outside. I do not know whether they really meant to vivisect the Kaffir, but Vassell was sure of it, for he had that diamond on the brain. He longed to have the Kaffir live out his allotted span—at Swartz-dorp.

" 'Surely I must be with Matakit at his end-ing,' said Vassell to me.

"Now Matakit had been told how Vassell had mercifully saved him, and he wished for nothing better than to be Vassell's man. So, in the night, after my cousin had whispered to the Kaffir that the surgeons meant to cut him open, Matakit jumped out of the hospital win-dow and hurried to Vassell's horse-wagon wait-ing on the Modder road.

"My friends, to tell you all the sad expe-rience of my cousin with that Kaffir I should need to be with you for a week. Our time for talk together is too short—indeed, I seem to hear it going in the hackthorn tops. But still I can give you a little more.

"Consider, then, that Vassell's family al-ready thought him demented for bringing the wild black from the Wolwe. Trekking with him to Bloemfontein was worse, and carrying him back appeared complete lunacy. But Vas-sell was the head of a Boer family and must be obeyed by his household, from Tante Anna, his wife, to the smallest Kaffir baby bred on his farm.

"He told no one but me of the battle in his soul. It was this: the more he longed to knife the diamond out, the more his conscience was warned with that text the Lord had sent him. He had now a fixed idea that he would somehow lose the diamond unless he was merciful to Matakit.

"Out of sight of the Kaffir my cousin could not be easy, he feared so much the black would run away. To prevent that, Vassell at first carried a loaded rifle all day long. At night he locked the Kaffir in the room partitioned from his own. Its windows he barred with iron bars. This was to save Matakit from the Christian Kaffirs on the farm. At first they were likely to kill him in the dark, such was their jealousy of the wild man honored by a bed in the house of the baas, while their own Christian bones had to rest in the huts and the sheds.

"But their jealousy changed to deadly fear of Matakit. They imagined that he had bewitched the baas. Matakit, being no fool, soon smelled out that fear. As a witch doctor he lorded it over them. He began to roll in fat, for they brought to his teeth the best of their food. As for their women!

"At last Tante Anna looked into this thing.

Then the blood of her mother of the Great Trek ran hot in her. I happened to be visiting there at the time. She herself went at the pagan with the sjambok. Vassell turned his back, for he approved the lashing, but the Kaffir so groveled and howled under the whip that my cousin's conscience rose up untimely. It told him that he would be guilty, for the diamond's sake, of complicity in the killing if he did not interfere. Whereupon he took the sjambok from Tante Anna's hands, and ordered her to deal kindly with the Kaffir, as before.

" 'Kindly! The black beast is destroying Christianity on our farm!' she wailed. 'I will slay him with my own hands. And I hope I have done it already!!'

" 'Alas! no, Anna,' said Vassell. 'He will live. You have given him a reason to run away.'

" 'Run away? I wish to the Lord he would run away!'

" 'No, no, my woman,' Vassell whispered. 'You do not understand. Tell it to nobody— but the Kaffir is worth twelve thousand English pounds to me!'

"She turned to me laughing. 'Twelve thousand pounds. My poor demented man!'

" 'When he dies I will prove it,' said Vassell.

" 'What! A dead Kaffir worth a fortune?' She was all contempt for Vassell's folly.

"Of course he wished to explain to her. But he had an opinion that Matakit's days might be few if Tante Anna came to understand the meaning of the lump on Matakit's black back. Vassell's uncontrollable conscience required her to be no more unmerciful to Matakit. If Anna's sjambok cut out the stone, it might be lost in the litter of the yard.

"Well, my friends, the word went up and down the Orange Free State, and far into the Colony, and away across the Vaal, that Burgher Vassell Swartz was crazy with kindness for a wild Kaffir! Of course I denied it, and that carried weight, but the mystery grew, for I could not explain the case, so strong was Vassell in holding me to secrecy. To get my cousin out of his trouble I advised him to lend Matakit to me, but he would not agree. Possibly he suspected me of wishing to dig for the diamond.

"Ten years this sorrow lasted, and all the time Matakit grew fatter, till he could scarcely walk. He was the most overbearing black in all South Africa. What he suspected I do not

know, but when he became sure Vassell would
not let him be hurt much he wantonly abused
the patience of even his devoted baas. Poor
Vassell! Sometimes, to ease his sorrows, he
used the sjambok on Matakit, but always too
gently. Often he raised his gun to end it all;
indeed, he got into a way of thinking that the
devil was continually instigating him to kill the
Kaffir. And every dopper knows that to yield
consciously to the devil is the unforgivable
sin."

The ancient burgher paused once more.
And again we, whose senses were trained but
to the narrow spaces between Canadian woodlands, heard nothing but a sudden louder
tumult of gathered horses, the hoofs of the
vedettes, and the tinkle of the spruit. I could
not guess why old Emanuel looked so well
pleased. He loomed taller, it seemed, as he
squatted. It was as if with new vivacity that
he spoke on:

"The strange things my poor cousin did! I
will tell you of at least one more. Five years of
Matakit went by, and never again had Vassell
gone hunting afar, for he could not leave the
fat Kaffir behind, and he feared Matakit would
run away if he got near the country of his tribe.

But in the sixth year a new inspiration came to Vassell. The Lord might send a lion if he took Matakit where lions might be convenient for sending. Doppers always regard lions as dispensations of Providence when they kill pagan Kaffirs. So he brought Matakit afar to the Lion Veldt. There Vassell would not let his men make a laager—he slept in a wagon himself. And the Lord *did* send a lion in the night. The blacks lay by the fire. And when it fell low that lion bore a man away out into the darkness at two leaps.

" 'Baas! baas!' Vassell heard his Kaffirs shout. 'Baas! The lion has taken Matakit!' For they had been dozing, and now missed the fat black.

"The Lord had sent the lion, but the devil was carrying away the diamond. Vassell must be in at the ending, as he had planned. So out with his rifle he sprang, seized a brand, and ran, whirling it into flame, on the dragged body's spoor.

" 'Come back! Oh, baas, come back! The veldt is full of lions!' So the Kaffirs shrieked. But twelve thousand pounds is not forsaken by a Boer hunter for fear of lions. On Vassell ran. He would beat off the lion with the torch.

Happy would be his rich life without Matakit!
Plainly the Lord would be merciful to him because he had been merciful as commanded by
the text.

"But from the wagons came now a bawl:
'Baas! Baas! I am here, I, Matakit! I was
in a wagon.' He had sneaked away from the
fire. 'It is but Impugan that the lion has
taken.'

"Back went Vassell in rage. Now he would
finish the Kaffir! For what would his other
Kaffirs, the Christians he had bred, his best
hunters, too—what would they think but that
he valued the accursed pagan above brave old
Impugan and all the rest of them? Yet he only
beat out his torch on Matakit's head before
the diseased conscience stayed his hand once
more."

Again the white-beard burgher paused. The
picketed horses were now still. The moon was
gone, and the spruit chattered in starlit darkness. There was no sound of the vedettes, but
that was not strange. Yet uneasiness came
over me. My comrades shared it. We all
stared at the gigantic prisoner with some suspicion that I could not define. He seemed un-
canny. From an old man, and especially an old

Boer, sneers seemed unnatural. Some diabol-
ical amusement seemed to animate him. As he
jeered his cousin he seemed to jeer us. At first
I had liked his genial tone. Now he gave me a
sense of repulsion. For this I was trying to
account when the old burgher stooped and
freshened the fire with mealie cobs. The sparks
flew high. In that momentary light he resumed his story:

"My cousin Vassell was of my Swartzdorp
commando when this war began, but he is now
a prisoner in St. Helena. Before he left home
with his boys he instructed his wife about Matakit.

" 'Be as good to him as you can,' Vassell ordered. 'But if he should come to his end before
I return, then be careful to bury him deeper
than jackals or hyenas dig. Bury him carefully by'—no matter where; Vassell showed
Tante Anna precisely the place.

"The woman wept and fell on her husband's
neck, and cried: 'Farewell, and fight well; and
God bring you and the boys back to me, Vassell, my old heart. You need have no fear but
I will carefully bury the Kaffir!'

"*Gentlemen!*" We all sprang up at the
change in the old voice. "*Gentlemen*—you are

my prisoners." The burgher rose up, very hard
of face.

Deschamps drew his pistol. I thrust mine
almost into the burgher's face. But he spoke
firmly:

"What! Shoot your prisoner, with his commando surrounding you. Fifty Mausers are
levelled on you. Pooh! No! It would be
the end of you all. Lieutenant, your horses
are seized. Your vedettes are prisoners.
They were knocked off their saddles long ago,
when you heard nothing but the horses stamping. There was a Boer among them then. He
provoked that stamping. It was the signal to
strike down your vedettes. Fifty burghers are
listening to my voice now. Here, men!" And
at the word the Boer surprise came on. "Oom
Emanuel! Oh, Oom Emanuel!" was the cry.

"I truly grieve for you, gentlemen," said the
old burgher ten minutes later. "You were such
good listeners—you had ears for nothing but
my story. And because of that I leave you
food for a whole day. It will be sufficient, if
you march well on foot, to take you to my old
friend General Pole. I beg you to give him
my compliments. But he will not be in good
humour to-morrow. Every one of his patrols

within twenty miles has been captured to-night, unless something has gone wrong with De Wet, which is unlikely. Do not be cast down, lieutenant. You were not to blame. Your ears were not trained to the veldt. Good-bye. I invite you to visit me, lieutenant, after this war ends, at my Swartzdorp farm. Then I will tell you the rest of the diamond story."

"But that is not fair, sir," said Deschamps, whimsically. "I have interest in de story, and I want to know how she end."

"It has no end yet." The old burgher smiled broadly. "I was on my way to end it when you stopped me. I hoped to get through more easily without my burghers' aid, but I told them to follow if they saw me stopped. You missed us in searching the spruit this morning.

"I have really private business at Swartzdorp. Word was brought to me three days ago that Tante Anna dutifully buried Matakit months ago. Vassell was the Kaffir's life; I will be his resurrection. A great diamond of the first water is very salable, and the treasury of the republic is running low."

"But it may not be a diamond of the first water," said I.

"It must be," said the patriarch. "Anything less would be too shabby a mercy to Vassell."

BOSS OF THE WORLD

ABOUT one-tenth of the people in Boston are British Canadians, mostly from the Maritime Provinces, an acquisitive prudent folk who see naught to be gained by correcting casual acquaintances who mistake them for down-east Yankees. Often, indeed, they are descendants of Hezekiahs and Priscillas who, having been Royalists during the War of Independence, found subsequent emigration to a British country incumbent on their Puritan consciences. These Americans, returned to the ancestral New England after four or five generations of absence, commonly find Boston ways surprisingly congenial, though they continue to cherish pride in British origin, and a decent warmth of regard for fellow natives of the Maritime Provinces. Hence a known Canadian is frequently addressed by an unsuspected one with, "I am from Canada, too." Having learned this from ten years' experience, I was little surprised when old Adam Bemis, meeting me on the corner of Tremont and Boylston Streets, in May, 1915, stopped and

stealthily whispered, "I am from Yarmouth,
Nova Scotia."

"Really! I have always taken you for one of
the prevalent minority, a man from the State of
Maine."

"Most folks do.   It doesn't vex me any
more.   But I've wanted to tell you any time
the last ten years."

"Then, why didn't you?"

"It's not my way to hurry.   You will understand that well when I explain.   I'm needing
friendly advice."

He had ever worn the air of preoccupation
during our twelve years' acquaintance, but that
seemed proper to an inventor burdened with the
task of devising and selecting novelties for the
Annual Announcement by which Miss Minnely's Prize Package Department furthers the
popularity of her famous Family Blessing.
The happy possessor of five new subscription
certificates, on remitting them to Adam's Department, receives by mail, prepaid, Number
1 Prize Package.   Number 2 falls to the col-
lector of ten such certificates; and so on, in
gradations of Miss Minnely's shrewd beneficence.   The magnifico of one thousand certificates obtains choice between a gasoline auto-

buggy and a New England farm. To be ever adding to or choosing from the world's changing assortment of moral mechanical toys, celluloid table ornaments, reversible albums, watches warranted gold filled, books combining thrill with edification, and more or less similar "premiums" to no calculable end, might well account for Old Adam's aspect, at once solemn and unsettled.

"What is your trouble?" I enquired.

"The Odistor. My greatest discovery!" he whispered.

"Indeed! For your Department?"

"We will see about that. It is something mighty wonderful—I don't know but I should say almighty."

"Goodness! What is its nature?"

"I won't say—not here. You couldn't believe me without seeing it work—I wouldn't have believed it myself on anybody's word. I will bring it on to your lodgings—that's a good place for the exhibition. No—I won't even try to explain here—we might be overheard." He glanced up and down Tremont Street, then across—"Sh—there she is herself!" He dodged into a drug store opposite the Touraine.

Miss Mehitable Minnely, sole proprietor of
The Family Blessing, was moving imposingly
from the Boylston Street front of the hotel
toward her auto-brougham. At the top step
she halted and turned her cordial, broad, dominant countenance in both directions as if to
beam on streets crowded with potential prize-
package takers. She then spoke the permit-
ting word to two uniformed deferential atten-
dants, who proceeded to stay her carefully by
the elbows, in her descent of the stone steps.
Foot passengers massed quickly on both sides
of her course, watching her large, slow progress
respectfully. When the porters had conveyed
her across the pavement, and with deferential,
persistent boosting made of her an ample la-
ding for the "auto," the chauffeur touched his
wide-peaked cap, and slowly rolled her away
towards Brimstone Corner *en route* to the
Blessing Building. Adam came out of the
drug store looking relieved.

"She doesn't like to see any of us on the
street, office hours," he explained with lips
close to my ear. "Not that I ought to care
one mite." He smiled somewhat defiantly and
added, "To see me dodging the old lady's eye
you'd never guess I'm *her* boss. But I am."

He eyed my wonder exultantly and repeated, "It's *so*. She doesnt know it. Nobody knows, except me. But I *am* her boss. Just whenever I please."

On my continued aspect of perturbation he remarked, coolly:—"Naturally you think my head is on wrong. But you will know better this evening. I'm the World's boss whenever I choose to take the responsibility. If I don't choose, *she* goes on being my boss, and, of course, I'll want to hold down my job. Well, good-day for the present. Or, say—I forgot—will it suit you if I come about half-past-five? I can't get there *much* earlier. She's not too well pleased if any of us leave before Park Street clock strikes five."

"Very well, Mr. Bemis—half past. I shall expect you."

"Expect a surprise, too."

He walked circumspectly across Boylston Street through the contrary processions of vehicles, to the edging pavement of the Common, on his way toward the new Old State House, and Miss Minnely's no less immense Family Blessing Building.

It was precisely twenty-six minutes past five when Adam entered my private office in the rear room of the ground floor of a sky-scraper which overlooks that reach of Charles River lying between the Union Boat Club House and the long, puritanic, impressive simplicity of Harvard Bridge. He did not greet me, being preoccupied with the brown paper-covered package under his left arm. With a certain eagerness in his manner, he placed this not heavy burden on the floor, so that it was hidden by the broad table-desk at which I sat. He stooped. I could hear him carefully untie the string and open the clattering paper.

He then placed on the green baize desk-cover a bulbous object of some heavy metal resembling burnished steel. It was not unlike a large white Bermuda onion with a protuberant stem or nozzle one inch long, half-an-inch in diameter, and covered by a metal cap. Obviously, the bulb was of two equal parts, screwed together on a plane at right angles to the perpendicular nozzle. An inch of the upper edge of the lower or basic part was graduated finely as a vernier scale. The whole lower edge of the upper half was divided, apparently into three hundred and sixty degrees, as is the horizontal circle of a theodolite. The parts were fitted with a clamp and tangent screw, by which the vernier could be moved with minutest precision along the graduated circle.

"I was four years experimenting before I found out how to confine it," said Adam.

"What? A high explosive!"

"No—nothing to be nervous about. But what it is I can't exactly say."

"A scientific mystery, eh?"

"It might be called so, seeing as I don't myself know the real nature of the force any more than electricians know what electricity is. They understand how to generate and employ it, that's all. Did you ever see a whirlwind start?"

"No."

"Think again. Not even a little one?"

"Of course I have often seen little whirlwinds on the street carrying up dust and scraps of paper, sometimes dropping them instantly, sometimes whirling them away."

"On calm days?"

"Really I can't remember. But I think not. It doesn't stand to reason."

"That's where you are mistaken. It is in the strongest kind of sunshine on dead calm days that those little whirlwinds *do* start. What do you suppose starts them?"

"I never gave it a thought."

"Few do. I've given it years of close think-ing. You have read of ships on tropic seas in dead calm having top-sails torn to rags by whirlwinds starting 'way up there, deck and sea quiet as this room?"

"I've read of that. But I don't believe all the wonderful items I read in the papers."

"There are more wonders than the papers print. I saw that happen twice in the Indian Ocean, when I was a young man. I have been studying more or less on it ever since. Now I will show you the remainder of my Odistor. I call it that because folks when I was young used to talk of a mysterious Odic force."

To the desk he lifted a black leather grip-sack, as narrow, as low, and about twice as long as one of those in which surgeons carry their im-plements. From this he extracted a simple-seeming apparatus which I still suppose to have been of the nature of an electric machine. Ex-ternally it resembled a rectangular umbrella box of metal similar to that of the bulb. It was about four feet in length and four inches in height and in breadth. That end which he placed nearest the window was grooved to re-ceive one-half the bulb accurately. Clamped longitudinally to the top of the box was a copper tube half-an-inch in exterior diameter, and closed, except for a pinhole sight, at the end farthest from the window. The other, or open end, was divided evenly by a perpendicular filament apparently of platinum.

Adam placed this sighted box on the green baize, its longer axis pointing across the Charles River to Cambridge, through the window. He carefully propped up the wire-net sash. Stooping at the desk he looked through the pin-hole sight and shifted the box to his satisfaction.

"Squint along the line of sight," he said, giving place to me. I stooped and complied.

"You see Memorial Hall tower right in the line?"

"Precisely."

"But what is nearest on the Cambridge shore?"

"The stone revetment wall."

"I mean next beyond that."

"The long shed with the big sign 'Builders' in black letters."

"All right. Sit here and watch that shed. No matter if it blows away. They were going to tear it down anyway." He placed my chair directly behind the sighted tube.

With an access of eagerness in his countenance, and something of tremor apparent in his
clutching fingers, he lifted the bulb, unscrewed
its metal cap and worked the tangent screw
while watching the vernier intently. He was
evidently screwing the basal half closer to the
nozzle-bearing upper portion.

From a minute orifice in the nozzle or stem
something exuded that appeared first as a tiny,
shimmering, sunbright, revolving globule. At
that instant he placed the bulb on its base in its
niche or groove at the outer or window end of
the sighted box. Thus the strange revolving
globule was rising directly in the line of sight.

"Watch that shed," Adam ordered hoarsely.

I could not wholly take my eyes off the singular sphere, which resembled nothing that I
have elsewhere seen so much as a focus of sun
rays from a burning glass. But this intensely
bright spot or mass—for it appeared to have
substance even as the incandescent carbon of
an Edison lamp seems to possess substance
exterior to the carbon—rose expanding in an
increasing spiral within an iridescent translu-
cent film that clung by a tough stem to the
orifice of the nozzle, somewhat as a soap-bubble
clings to the pipe whence it is blown. Yet this

brilliant, this enlarging, this magic globule was plainly whirling on its perpendicular axis as a waterspout does, and that with speed terrific. The mere friction of its enclosing film on the air stirred such wind in the room as might come from an eighteen-inch electric fan. In shape the infernal thing rapidly became an inverted cone with spiral convolutions. It hummed like a distant, idly-running circular saw, a great top, or the far-off, mysterious forewarning of a typhoon.

"Now!" Adam touched a button on the top of the metal box.

The gleaming, whirling, humming, prismatic spiral was then about eighteen inches high. It vanished without sound or spark, as if the film had been totally destroyed and the contained incandescence quenched on liberation. For one instant I experienced a sense of suffocation, as if all the air had been drawn out of the room. The inner shutters clashed, the holland sunshade clattered, the door behind me snicked open, air from the corridor rushed in.

"See the river!" Adam was exultant, but not too excited to replace the metal cap on the nozzle.

Certainly the Charles River was traversed by

a gust that raised white caps instantly. A bulk-headed sailing-dory, owned by a Union Boat Clubman whom I knew, lay over so far that her sail was submerged, and her centre-board came completely out of water. Only the head and clutching forearms of the two men aboard her could be seen. Afterward they told me they had been quite surprised by the squall. Beyond the Cambridge revetment wall a wide cloud of dust sprang up, hiding the "Builders" shed.

When this structure reappeared Adam gasped, then stood breathless, his countenance expressive of surprise.

He looked down at the Odistor, pondering, left hand fingers pressing his throbbing temple. Lifting the bulb he inspected the vernier, laid it down again, put on his spectacles and once more peered intently at the graduated scale.

"I see," he said, "I was the least thing too much afraid of doing damage in Cambridge back of the shed. But you saw the wind?"

"Certainly I saw wind."

"You know how it started?"

"I don't know what to think. It was very strange. What is the stuff?"

"Tell me what starts the whirlwind or the

cyclone, and I can tell you that. All I'm sure of is that I can originate the force, control it, and release it in any strength I choose. Do you remember the chap called Æolus we used to read about in the Latin book at school, he that bagged up the winds long ago? I guess there was truth at the back of that fable. He found out the secret before me, and he used it to some extent. It died with him, and they made a god out of his memory—they had some right to be grateful that he spared them. It must go to the grave with me—so far as I've reasoned on the situation. But that's all right. What's worrying me is the question—Shall I make any use of it?"

"I can see no use for it."

"What! Think again. It is the Irresistible Force. There is no withstanding it. I can start a stronger hurricane than ever yet blew. You remember what happened to that Hawaiian Island in the tornado last year? That was a trifle to what I can do. It is only a matter of confining a larger quantity in a stronger receiver and giving it a swifter send off with a more powerful battery. I can widen the track and lengthen the course to any extent."

"Suppose you can. Still it is only a de-
stroyer. What's the good of it?"

"What's the good of a Krupp gun. Or a
shell. Or a bullet?"

"They are saleable."

He looked keenly at me for some seconds.
"Do you see that far, or do you only *not* see
how it could be used as a weapon? That's it,
eh! Well, I'll tell you. There's England
spending more'n ten million dollars a day in
the war. Suppose I go to Lord Kitchener.
He's a practical, quick man—in half an hour
he sees what I can do. 'What will you give,'
I ask him, 'to have the Crown Prince and the
rest of them Prussians blown clear away?'
'What is your price?' he inquires. 'Ten million pounds would be cheap,' I reply. 'Take
five,' he says, 'we are not made of money.'
'Well, seeing it's you,' I tell him."

"It is a considerable discount, Adam. But
then you are a British subject."

"Yes—kind of. But the conversation was
imaginary. Discount or no discount, I feel no
special call to blow away whole armies of Germans. If I could set the Odistor on the Kaiser,
and the Crown Prince, and a dozen or so more
of the Prussian gang, I'd do it, of course. But

how could I find just where they were? Blowing away whole armies of men don't seem right
to me."

"But you needn't do that yourself. Sell your
secret outright to the British Government."

Adam stared as one truly astonished.

"Now what you think you're talking about?"
he remonstrated. "Can't you see farther than
that? Suppose I sell the *secret* to Kitchener.
Suppose he clears out all the Germans with it.
What next? Why, Ireland! Kitchener is a
Jingo Imperialist, which I never was and never
will be. I've heard of Jingoes saying time and
again that England's interests would be suited
if Ireland was ten feet under water. Or suppose he only blows the Irish out of Connaught,
just to show the others they'd better cut out the
Sinn Finn. What then? First place, I like
the Irish. My wife's Irish. Next, consider all
the world. Suppose England has got the irresistible weapon. There's no opposing it. Suppose France was to try, some time after this
war is over. Away go her cities, farms, vine-
yards, people, higher than Gilroy's kite. What
next? All the rest of the world then know they
must do what the English say—Germans, Ital-
ians, Russians, Yankees, Canadians. Now I'm

a cosmopolitan, I am. All kind of folk look good to me."

"But England ruling the world means universal peace," I said enthusiastically. "Free trade, equal rights, all the grand altruistic English ideals established forever and ever! Adam, let England have it! You'll be remembered as the greatest benefactor of humanity. A Bemis statue in Trafalgar Square, London! Sure! Think of that glory, Adam."

"For putting the English on top," he replied dryly. "I can't seem to want to. Not but what the English are all right. But *my* kind of Maritime Province Canadians are considerably more American than English, though they never rightly know it till they've lived here and in the old country. We're at home with Yankee ways and Yankee notions. In England we're only colonials. Not but what the war may change that a bit."

"Take your secret to Washington then. President Wilson will see that you get all that you can reasonably ask for it."

"Sure—but while the pro-German microbe is active in Washington, I will not offer the thing there. Yet my first notion was to let the United States have it—on conditions."

"What conditions?"

"Well, I'd bargain they must leave Canada alone. Woodrow would boss the rest of the world, I was thinking, just the way I'll do it myself if ever I *do* make up my mind. *No* bossing—everybody free and equal and industrious—no aristocracy, except just enough to laugh at—no domineering. But I ain't so pleased with Woodrow as I was when he started presidenting. He aint set the Filipinos free yet. And he knowing how bad they was treated by this Republic. Why, the worst grab ever England made wasn't a circumstance to Yankees allying with Aguinaldo, and then seizing his country."

"To what government will you sell?" I inquired patiently.

"Well, now, if I was going to sell to any government it would be Sir Wilfrid Laurier's. But he's got no government, now. Ontario folks beat him last election, for being too reasonable. If ever there was the makings of a good benevolent despot, Laurier's the man. I used to be saying to myself while I was perfecting the Odistor, says I inwardly, 'I'll give it to Laurier.' Of course, I was calculating he'd use it first thing to annex the United States

to Canada. That would be good for both
countries—if Laurier was on top. He'd give
this Republic Responsible Government, stop
letting it be run by hole-and-corner committees
and trusts and billionaires, and, first of all, he'd
establish Free Trade all over the continent.
That would be good for Nova Scotia apple-
growers, and, mind you, I'd like to do something for my native Province before I die.
Statue in Trafalgar Square, says you. Think
of a statue in Halifax—erected to me!
'ADAM BEMIS, BENEFACTOR OF
NOVA SCOTIA!' And a big apple-tree
kind of surrounding my figure with blessings!
Sounds kind of good, eh. Why don't I give it
to Laurier? Well he's getting old. He aint
any too strong in health, either. He mightn't
live long enough to get things running right.
And he'd be sure to tell his colleagues how the
Odistor is worked—he's such a strong party
man. That's the only fault he's got. Well,
now, think what happens after he drops out.
Why, some ordinary cuss of his Party takes
over the Bossdom of the world. Now, all ordinary Canadian politicians are hungry to be
knighted, or baroneted. Laurier's successor,
likely enough, would give away the Odistor to

England, in return for a handle to his name.
And once England got the Odistor—why, you
know what I told you before."

"Well, what Government will you sell
to?"

"To none. Germany's out of the question,
of course. France, Russia, Italy, Japan—
they're all unfitter than England, Canada or
the States. Once I planned to raise up the
people that are down—the Poles, Irish, Armenians, Filipinos, and so on. Then I got to
fancying the Irish with power to blow everything above rock in England out to sea. Would
they be satisfied with moving the Imperial
Parliament to College Green, giving England
a Viceroy and local councils, putting a Catholic
King in George's shoes and fixing the corona-
tion oath to abjuring Protestant errors? I
can't seem to think they'd be so mild. What
would the Poles do to the Prussians, Austrians,
and Russians; or the Armenians to the Turks,
if I gave them the Odistor? No—I won't take
such risks. If I gave the thing to one Nation
the only fair deal would be to give it to all, big
and little alike, making the smallest as powerful
as the biggest, everyone with power to blow all
the others off the footstool. What then?

Would mutual fear make them live peaceably?
I'm feared not. Probably every one would be
so afraid of every other that each would be for
getting its Odistors to work first. There'd be
cyclones jamming into cyclones all over out-
doors, a teetotal destruction of crops, and
everything and everybody blown clean away at
once. Wonder where they'd light?"

His query, did not divert me from the main
matter. "If you won't sell, how can you get
any money out of it?" I asked.

"No difficulty getting money out of it. Here
I am able to blow everything away—say Berlin
and thereabouts for a starter, just to show how
the thing works. Then all hands would know I
could blow away all Europe—except maybe
the Alps. I don't know exactly how strong
the Odistor could blow. Wouldn't all the Governments unite to pay me *not* to do it. See?
All the money John Rockefeller ever handled
wouldn't pay five minutes' interest on what I
ought to get for just *not* doing it. No harm in
not hurting anybody—see? And me working
for Miss Minnely for forty-five dollars a
week!"

"Resign, Adam," I said earnestly, for the
financial prospect was dazzling. "Take me in

as junior partner. Let us get at this thing together."

"What? Blackmailing the nations! And
you a professional Liberal like myself! No!
It wouldn't be straight. I can't have a partner
—you'll see that before I get through. But
now I suppose that you will admit that I *could*
get any amount of money out of the thing?"

"You have thought it all out wonderfully,
Adam."

"Wish I could stop thinking about it. I'm
only taking you gradually over the field—not
telling my conclusions yet—but only some of
my thoughts by the way. In fact it's years
since I gave up the notion of opening the secret
to any nation, or to all nations. For one thing
I couldn't get into any nation's possession if I
wanted to. Suppose, for instance, I offered it
to the Washington Administration. Naturally
the President orders experts to report on it—
say six army engineers. I show them how.
What happens? Why, those six men are bosses
of the Administration, the nation and all the
world. They can't but see that right away if
they've got any gumption. Will they abstain
from using the power? Scarcely. Will they
stick together *and* boss? They won't, because

they can't. It is not in human nature. Common sense, common logic, would compel each one to try to get his private Odistor going first, for fear each of the others might be for blowing him and the other four away in order to boss alone. Fact is, the moment I showed the process to any other man—and this is why I can't take *you* in as partner—I'd have to blow *him* straight away out beyond Cape Cod, for fear he would send me flying soon as he saw universal Bossdom in his hands."

"That seems inevitable," I admitted.

"Certainly. I can't risk the human race under any Boss except myself—or somebody that I am sure means as well as I do."

"Our political principles are in many respects the same," I suggested, hopefully.

"Will you—will any man except me—would even Laurier stay Liberal if he had absolute power? What would *you* do with the Odistor anyway?"

"Get a fortune out of it."

"How?"

"Well, we might try this scheme—detain ocean liners in port until the Companies agreed to pay what the traffic will bear."

"Gosh—you think I've got the conscience of

a Railway Corporation? No, sir! But what use in prolonging this part of our talk? I have thought of a thousand ways of using the thing on a large scale, but they are all out of the question, for one good and sufficient reason—folks would lock me up or kill me if I once convinced 'em of the power I possess. I couldn't blame them, they *must* do it to feel safe themselves. The only sure way for me to get big money out of it safely would be by retiring to a lonely sea island and advertising what I intended to do on a specified day—blow away some forest on the mainland, say, or send a blast straight overland to the Rockies and clear them of snow in a path fifty miles wide. Of course, folks would laugh at the advertisement—to say nothing of the expense of inserting it—and to convince them I'd have to *do* it. After that I might call on the civilised governments to send me all the gold, diamonds, and fine things I could think of. But what good would fine things do me? I should be afraid to let any ship land its cargo, or any other human being come on the island. I couldn't even have a cook, for fear she might be bribed to poison me or bust the Odistor—and I've got no fancy to do my own cooking. What good to Boss the World at that price? The

Kaiser himself wouldn't pay it. Universally
feared as he is already hated—but not bound
to live alone. For a while I was thinking to se-
clude myself that way in self-sacrifice to the
general good. I thought of issuing an order to
all governments to stop fighting, stop govern-
ing and just let real freedom be established—
the brotherhood of man, share and share alike,
equal wages all round, same kind of houses and
grub and clothes, perfect democracy! But suppose the Governments didn't obey? Politicians
are smart—they'd soon see I dursn't leave my
island to go travelling and inspecting what was
going on all over. I couldn't receive deputa-
tions coming to me for redress of grievances,
for fear they might be coming to rid the world
of its benevolent despot. Shrewd folks ashore
would soon catch on to my fix—me there all
alone, busy keeping ten or a dozen Odistors
blowing gales off shore for fifty miles or so to
keep people out of any kind of striking distance, and everlastingly sending hurricanes
upward to clear the sky of Zeppelins and aero-
planes that might be sent to drop nitro-glycer-
ine on me. Next thing some speculator
would be pretending to be my sole agent, and
ordering the world to fetch *him* the wealth.

How could I know, any more than God seems to, what things were done in my name?"

"Employ Marconi," I suggested; "have him send you aerial news of what's going on everywhere. Then you could threaten wrong-doers everywhere with the Odistor.

"Marconi is a good man, mebby, but think of the temptation to him. How could I be sure he was giving me facts. He could stuff me with good reports, and all the time be bossing the world himself, forcing the nations to give up to him by the threat that I'd back him and blow the disobedient to Kingdom Come. Besides, I don't know how to operate Marconi's instruments, and, if I did, all my time would be taken up receiving his reports. No, *sir*. There is no honest, safe, comfortable way for me to get rich out of the Odistor. I have known that for a considerable time."

"Then, why did you wish to consult me?"

"Well, first place, I wanted some friend to know what kind of a self-denying ordinance I'm living under. To be comprehended by at least one person is a human need. Besides that, I want your opinion on a point of conscience. Is the Odistor mine?"

"Yours? Isn't it your exclusive discovery?"

"But isn't it Miss Minnely's property? I experimented in her time."

"During office hours?"

"Mostly. And did all the construction in her workshop with her materials. She supposed I was tinkering up a new attraction for the Annual Announcement. Isn't it hers by rights? She's been paying me forty-five dollars a week right along. When she hired me she told me she expected exclusive devotion to the interests of the Family Blessing. And I agreed. Seems I'm bound in honour to give it up to her."

"For nothing?"

"Well, she's dead set against raising wages. But I *was* thinking she might boost me up to fifty a week."

"That seems little for making her Boss of the World."

"Oh, Miss Minnely wouldn't go in for *that*. A man would. A woman is too conservative. Miss Minnely's one notion is the *Blessing*. It's not money she is after, but doing good. She's sure the way to improve the world is to get the Blessing regularly into every family. I don't know but she's right too. It's harmless, anyway."

I could not but regard Adam's conscience as too tender. Yet it was pathetic to see this old man, potentially master of mankind (if he were not mistaking the Odistor's powers), feeling morally so bound by the ethics of the trusty employee. I had perused thousands of editorials designed to imbue the proletariat with precisely Adam's idea of duty to Capital. How to advise him was a serious problem.

"What would Miss Minnely do with it?" I inquired, to gain time.

"She would put it on the list of attractions in the Prize Package Department."

"Good heavens! And place absolute power in the hands of subscribers to the Blessing! Anarchy would ensue! They would all set about bossing the world."

"Not they," said Adam. "She would send out Odistors gauged to only certain specified strengths. For five subscription certificates the subscriber would get a breeze to dry clothes or ventilate cellars. Prize Odistor number two might clear away snow; number three might run the family windmill. Clubs of fifty new subscribers could win a machine that would clear fog away from the bay or the river, mornings. Different strengths for different premiums. See? It would prove a first-class attraction for the Announcement."

"Adam," I remonstrated, for the financial prospect was too alluring, "you are not required to give this thing to Miss Minnely. Resign. Remit a million as conscience money to her. Let us go into the manufacture together. You gauge the Odistors. I will run the business end of the concern."

"No! Miss Minnely has the first right. If anybody gets it she must. What bothers me most is this—will she bounce me if I tell her?"

"Bounce you? Why?"

"Think me crazy. I tell you she is *conservative*. And she is ready to throw me out— thinks I'm a back number. I can hardly blame her. Fact is, I have given so much time and thought to the Odistor of late years that I haven't found or invented half enough attractions for the Announcement. Last week she gave me an assistant—a Pusher. That means she is intending him to supersede me about two years from now. Yet I could invent a man with twice his brains in half the time. Sometimes I am tempted to put the Odistor on the small job of blowing him out into Massachusetts Bay. But he is not to blame for being

as God made him. Then, again, I think how
I could down him by simply showing the thing
to Miss Minnely. But the cold fit comes again
—what if she thinks me crazy? I'd lose my
forty-five dollars a week and might be driven
to Bossing the World. It's hard for old
men to get new jobs in Boston. They draw the
dead-line at fifty. Just when a man's got
some experience they put a boy of twenty-six
on top of him. On the other hand, suppose
she *does* consider it, and *does* see the whole
meaning of it. First thing she might do with
her Odistor would be to put a cyclone whirling
me." He sighed heavily. "Fact is I've got
myself into a kind of hole. What do you
advise?"

"Bury the Odistor. Forget it, Adam.
Then, with your mind free, you can invent new
things for the Announcement. I see no other
escape from your predicament."

"I expected you to advise that in the end,"
said Adam, and began repacking his singular
mechanism. "Bury it I will. But how can I
forget it? May be it has exhausted my inven-
tive powers. What then? I'm bounced. It's
tough to have to begin all over again at sixty-
three, and me Boss of the World if I could only

bring myself *to* boss. If I do get bounced and do get vexed, maybe I'll unbury it and show Miss Minnely what it *can* do. Well, good evening, and thank you for your interest and advice."

He departed with the old, solemn unsettled look on his honest Nova Scotian countenance.

Since that day I have frequently seen Adam, but he gives me no recognition. He goes about with eyes on the ground, probably studying the complicated and frightful situation of a World Power animated by liberalism and dominated by conscience. Some in the Blessing office tell me that Miss Minnely's disapproving eye is often on her old employee. They say she will soon lift the Pusher over Adam's white head.

What will he do then? I remember with some trepidation the vague threat with which he left me. At night, when a high gale happens to be blowing, I listen in wild surmise that Adam was bounced yesterday, and that the slates, bricks and beams of the Family Blessing Building are hurtling about the suburbs as if in signal that he has liberated a large specimen of the mysterious globule and embarked, of necessity, on the woeful business of bossing the world.

MISS MINNELY'S MANAGEMENT

I

GEORGE RENWICK substituted "limb" for "leg," "intoxicated" for "drunk," and "undergarment" for "shirt," in "The Converted Ringmaster," a short-story-of-commerce, which he was editing for "The Family Blessing." When he should have eliminated all indecorum it would go to Miss Minnely, who would "elevate the emotional interest." She was sole owner of "The Blessing," active director of each of its multifarious departments. Few starry names rivalled hers in the galaxy of American character-builders.

Unaware of limitations to her versatility, Miss Minnely might have dictated all the literary contents of the magazine, but for her acute perception that other gifted pens should be enlisted. Hence many minor celebrities worshipped her liberal cheques, whilst her more extravagant ones induced British titled personages to assuage the yearning of the American Plain People for some contact with rank.

Renwick wrought his changes sardonically, applying to each line a set of touchstones—

"Will it please Mothers?" "Lady school-teachers?" "Ministers of the Gospel?" "Miss Minnely's Taste?" He had not entirely converted The Ringmaster when his door was gently opened by the Chief Guide to the Family Blessing Building.

Mr. Durley had grown grey under solemn sense of responsibility for impressions which visitors might receive. With him now appeared an unusually numerous party of the usual mothers, spinsters, aged good men, and anxious children who keep watch and ward over "The Blessing's" pages, in devotion to Miss Minnely's standing editorial request that "subscribers will faithfully assist the Editors with advice, encouragement, or reproof." The Mature, with true American gentleness, let the Young assemble nearest the open door. All necks craned toward Renwick. Because Mr. Durley's discourse to so extensive a party was unusually loud, Renwick heard, for the first time, what the Chief Guide was accustomed to murmur at his threshold: "De-ar friends, the gentleman we now have the satisfaction of beholding engaged in a sitting posture at his editorial duties, is Mr. George Hamilton Renwick, an American in every ——."

"He *looks* like he might be English," observed a matron.

Mr. Durley took a steady look at Renwick: "He *is* some red complected, Lady, but I guess it's only he is used to out of doors." He resumed his customary drone:—"Mr. Renwick, besides he is American in every fibre of his being, is a first rate general purpose editor, and also a noted authority on yachting, boating, canoeing, rowing, swimming, and every kind of water amusements of a kind calculated to build up character in subscribers. Mr. George Hamilton Renwick's engagement by 'The Family Blessing' exclusively is a recent instance of many evidences that Miss Minnely, the Sole Proprietress, spares no expense in securing talented men of genius who are likewise authorities on every kind of specialty interesting, instructive, and improving to first-class respectable American families. Ladies and gentlemen, and de-ar children, girls, and youths, we will now pass on to Room Number Sixteen, and behold Mr. Caliphas C. Cummins, the celebrated author and authority on Oriental and Scriptural countries. Mr. Cummins is specially noted as the author of 'Bijah's Bicycle in Babylonia,' 'A Girl Genius at Galilee,' and many first-class serials published exclusively in 'The Family Blessing.' He may——"

Mr. Durley softly closed Renwick's door.

The Improving Editor, now secluded, stared wrathfully for some moments. Then he laughed, seized paper, and wrote in capitals:—

"When the editor in this compartment is to be exhibited, please notify him by knocking on this door before opening it. He will then rise from his sitting posture, come forward for inspection, and turn slowly round three times, if a mother, a school teacher, or a minister of the Gospel be among the visiting subscribers."

Renwick strode to his door. While pinning the placard on its outside he overheard the concluding remarks of Mr. Durley on Mr. Cummins, whose room was next in the long corridor: "Likewise talented editor of the Etiquette Department and the Puzzle Department. Mr. Cummins, Sir, seven lady teachers from the State of Maine are now honouring us in this party."

Renwick stood charmed to listen. He heard the noted author clack forward to shake hands all round, meantime explaining in thin, high, affable volubility: "My de-ar friends, you have the good fortune to behold me in the very act of composing my new serial of ten Chapters,

for 'The Blessing' exclusively, entitled 'Jehu
and Jerusha in Jerusalem,' being the experiences of a strenuous New England brother
and sister in the Holy Land, where our Lord
innogerated the Christian religion, now, sad to
say, under Mohammetan subjection. In this
tale I am incorporating largely truthful incidents of my own and blessed wife's last visit to
the Holy Places where——"

Renwick slammed his door. He flung his
pen in a transport of derision. Rebounding
from his desk, it flew through an open window,
perhaps to fall on some visitor to "The Blessing's" lawn. He hastened to look down. Nobody was on gravel path or bench within possible reach of the missile. Renwick, relieved,
mused anew on the singularities of the scene.

The vast "Blessing" Building stands amid a
city block devoted largely to shaven turf, flower
beds, grassed mounds, and gravel paths. It is
approached from the street by a broad walk
which bifurcates at thirty yards from the
"Richardson" entrance, to surround a turfed
truncated cone, from which rises a gigantic,
severely draped, female figure. It is that
bronze of Beneficence which, in the words of the
famous New England sculptress, Miss Angela

C. Amory Pue, "closely features Miss Martha Minnely in her grand early womanhood." In the extensive arms of the Beneficence a bronze volume so slants that spectators may read on its back, in gilt letters, "THE FAMILY BLESSING." Prettily pranked out in dwarf marginal plants on the turfy cone these words are pyramided: "LOVE. HEAVEN. BENEFICENCE. THE LATEST FASHIONS. MY COUNTRY, 'TIS OF THEE."

Not far from the statue slopes a great grassed mound which displays still more conspicuously in "everlastings," "THE FAMILY BLESSING. CIRCULATION 1915, 1,976,709. MONTHLY. COME UNTO ME ALL YE WEARY AND HEAVILY LADEN. TWO DOLLARS A YEAR."

The scheme ever puzzled Renwick. Had some demure humour thus addressed advertisements as if to the eternal stars? Or did they proceed from a pure simplicity of commercial taste? From this perennial problem he was diverted by sharp rapping at his door. Durley again? But the visitor was Mr. Joram B. Buntstir, veteran among the numerous editors of "The Blessing," yet capable of jocularities. He appeared perturbed.

"Renwick, you are rather fresh here, and I feel so friendly to you that I'd hate to see you get into trouble unwarned. Surely you can't wish Miss Minnely to see *that*."

"What? Oh, the placard! That's for Durley. He must stop exhibiting me."

"Mr. Durley won't understand. Anyway, he couldn't stop without instructions from Miss Minnely. He will take the placard to her for orders. You do not wish to hurt Miss Minnely's feelings, I am sure." Mr. Buntstir closed the door behind him.

"Bah—Miss Minnely's feelings can't be so tender as all that!"

"No, eh? Do you know her so thoroughly?"

"I don't know her at all. I've been here three months without once seeing Miss Minnely. Is she real? Half the time I doubt her existence."

"You get instructions from her regularly."

"I get typewritten notes, usually voluminous, signed 'M. Minnely,' twice a week. But the Business Manager, or Miss Heartly, may dictate them, for all I know."

"Pshaw! Miss Minnely presides in seclusion. Her private office has a street entrance. She seldom visits the Departments in office

hours. Few of her staff know her by sight.
She saves time by avoiding personal interviews.
But she keeps posted on everybody's work. I
hope you may not have to regret learning how
very real Miss Minnely can be. She took me
in hand, once, eight years ago. I have been
careful to incur no more discipline since—kind
as she was. If she sees your placard——"

"Well, what?" `

"Well, she can be very impressive. I fear
your offer to turn round before visitors may
bring you trouble."

"I am looking for trouble. I'm sick and
tired of this life of intellectual shame."

"Then quit!" snapped Buntstir, pierced.
"Be consistent. Get out. Sell your sneers at
a great established publication to some pam-
phlet periodical started by college boys for the
regeneration of Literature. Don't jeer what
you live by. That is where intellectual shame
should come in."

"You are right. A man should not gibe his
job. I must quit. The 'Blessing' is all right
for convinced devotees of the mawkish. But if
a man thinks sardonically of his daily work,
that damns the soul."

"It may be an effect of the soul trying to save

itself," said Buntstir, mollified. "Anyway, Renwick, remember your trouble with 'The Reflex.' Avoid the name of a confirmed quitter. Stay here till you can change to your profit. Squealing won't do us any good. A little grain of literary conscience ought not to make you *talk* sour. It's cynical to satirize our bread and butter—imprudent, too."

"That's right. I'll swear off, or clear out. Lord, how I wish I could. My brain must rot if I don't. 'The Blessing's' 'emotional'! Oh, Buntstir, the stream of drivel! And to live by concocting it for trustful subscribers. Talk of the sin of paregoricking babies!"

"Babies take paregoric because they like it. Pshaw, Renwick, you're absurdly sensitive. Writing-men must live, somehow—usually by wishy-washiness. Unpleasant work is the common lot of mankind. Where's *your* title to exemption? Really, you're lucky. Miss Minnely perceives zest in your improvements of copy. She says you are naturally gifted with 'The Blessing's' taste."

"For Heaven's sake, Buntstir!"

"She did—Miss Heartly told me so. And yet—if she sees that placard—no one can ever guess what she may do in discipline. You can't wish to be bounced, dear boy, with your family to provide for. Come, you've blown off steam. Take the placard off your door."

"All right. I will. But Miss Minnely can't bounce me without a year's notice. That's how I engaged."

"A year's notice to quit a life of intellectual shame!"

"Well, it is one thing to jump out of the window, and another to be bounced. I wouldn't stand that."

Buntstir laughed. "I fancy I see you, you sensitive Cuss, holding on, or jumping off or doing anything contra to Miss Minnely's intention." He went to the door. "Hello, where's the placard?" he cried, opening it.

"Gone!" Renwick sprang up.

"Gone, sure. No matter how. It is already in Miss Minnely's hands. Well, I told you to take it down twenty minutes ago."

"Wait, Buntstir. What is best to be done?"

"Hang on for developments—and get to work."

Buntstir vanished as one hastens to avoid infection.

II

Renwick resumed his editing of "The Converted Ringmaster" with resolve to think on nothing else. But, between his eyes and the manuscript, came the woeful aspect of two widows, his mother and his sister, as they had looked six months earlier, when he threw up his political editorship of "The Daily Reflex" in disgust at its General Manager's sudden reversal of policy. His sister's baby toddled into the vision. He had scarcely endured to watch the child's uncertain steps during the weeks while he wondered how to buy its next month's modified milk. To "The Reflex" he could not return, because he had publicly burned his boats, with the desperate valour of virtue conscious that it may weaken if strained by need for family food.

Out of that dangerous hole he had been lifted by the Sole Proprietress of "The Family Blessing." She praised his "public stand for principle" in a note marked "strictly confidential," which tendered him a "position." He had secretly laughed at the cautious, amiable offer, even while her laudation gratified his self-importance. Could work on "The Blessing" seem otherwise than ridiculous for one accustomed to chide presidents, monarchs, bosses, bankers, railway magnates? But it was well paid, and seemed only too easy, The young man did not foresee for himself that benumbing of faculty which ever punishes the writer who sells his facility to tasks below his ambition. At worst "The Blessing" seemed harmless. Nor could his better nature deny a certain esteem to that periodical which affectionate multitudes proclaimed to be justly named.

Renwick, viewing himself once more as a recreant breadwinner, cursed his impetuous humour. But again he took heart from remembrance of his engagement by the year, little suspecting his impotency to hold on where snubs must be the portion of the unwanted. Twelve months to turn round in! But after? What if an editor, already reputed impractical by "The Reflex" party, should be refused employment everywhere, after forsaking "The Blessing" office, in which "positions" were notoriously sought or coveted by hundreds of "literary" aspirants to "soft snaps"? So his veering imagination whirled round that inferno into which wage earners descend after hazarding their livelihood.

From this disquiet he sprang when his door was emphatically knocked. It opened. Mr. Durley reappeared with a throng closely resembling the last, except for one notable wide lady in street costume of Quakerish gray. Her countenance seemed to Renwick vaguely familiar. The fabric and cut of her plain garb betokened nothing of wealth to the masculine eye, but were regarded with a degree of awe by the other ladies present. She appeared utterly American, yet unworldly, in the sense of seeming neither citified, suburbanish, nor rural. The experienced placidity of her countenance reminded Renwick of a familiar composite photograph of many matrons chosen from among "The Blessing's" subscribers.

"Her peculiarity is that of the perfect type," he pondered while listening to Durley's repetition of his previous remarks.

At their close, he briskly said: "Mr. Renwick, Sir, Miss Minnely wishes you to know that your kind offer is approved. We are now favoured with the presence of four mothers, six lady teachers, and a minister of the Gospel."

Renwick flushed. His placard approved! It promised that he would come forward and turn round thrice for inspection. Durley had received instructions to take him at his word! Suddenly the dilemma touched his facile humour. Explanation before so many was impos-

sible.   Gravely he approached the visitors, held
out the skirts of his sack coat, turned slowly
thrice, and bowed low at the close.

The large lady nodded with some reserve.
Other spectators clearly regarded the solemnity
as part of "The Blessing's" routine. Mr. Durley resumed his professional drone:—"We will
now pass on to Room Number Sixteen, and behold Mr. Caliphas C. Cummins in——" Renwick's door closed.

Then the large lady, ignoring the attractions
of Mr. Cummins, went to the waiting elevator,
and said "down."

Renwick, again at his desk, tried vainly to
remember of what or whom the placid lady had
reminded him. A suspicion that she might be
Miss Minnely fled before recollection of her
street costume. Still—she *might* be. If so—
had his solemnly derisive posturing offended
her? She had given no sign. How could he
explain his placard to her? Could he not truly
allege objections to delay of his work by Durley's frequent interruptions? He was whirling
with conjecture and indecision when four measured ticks from a lead pencil came on his outer
door.

There stood Miss Heartly, Acting Manager

of the Paper Patterns Department. Her light blue eyes beamed the confidence of one born trustful, and confirmd in the disposition by thirty-five years of popularity at home, in church, in office. In stiff white collar, lilac tie, trig grey gown, and faint, fading bloom of countenance, she well represented a notable latter day American type, the Priestess of Business, one born and bred as if to endow office existence with some almost domestic touch of Puritan nicety. That no man might sanely hope to disengage Miss Heartly from devotion to "The Family Blessing" was as if revealed by her unswerving directness of gaze in speech.

"I have called, Mr. Renwick, by instruction of the Sole Proprietress. Miss Minnely wishes me, first, to thank you for this."

It was the placard!

Renwick stared, unable to credit the sincerity in her face and tone. She *must* be making game of him while she spoke in measured links, as if conscientiously repeating bits each separately memorized:

"Mr. Renwick—Miss Minnely desires you to know that she has been rarely more gratified— than by this evidence—that your self-identification with 'The Blessing'—is cordial and com-

plete. But—Miss Minnely is inclined to hope
—that your thoughtful and kind proposal—of
turning round for inspection—may be—modified—or improved. For instance—if you
would carefully prepare—of course for revi-
sion by her own taste—a short and eloquent
welcoming discourse—to visitors—that could
be elevated to an attraction—for subscribers—
of that she is almost, though not yet quite, fully
assured. Miss Minnely presumes, Mr. Renwick, that you have had the pleasure of—hearing Mr. Cummins welcome visitors. Of course,
Mr. Renwick, Miss Minnely would not have
asked you—but—as you have volunteered—in
your cordial willingness—*that* affords her an
opportunity—for the suggestion. But, Mr.
Renwick, if you do not *like* the idea—then Miss
Minnely would not wish—to pursue the suggestion further." A child glad to have repeated its lesson correctly could not have looked
more ingenuous.

In her fair countenance, open as a daybook,
Renwick could detect no guile. Her tone and
figure suggested curiously some flatness, as of
the Paper Patterns of her Department. But
through this mild deputy Miss Minnely must,
he conceived, be deriding him. With what

subtlety the messenger had been chosen! It seemed at once necessary and impossible to explain his placard to one so guiltless of humour.

"I hoped it might be understood that I did not intend that placard to be taken literally, Miss Heartly."

"Not literally!" she seemed bewildered.

"To be pointed at as 'a first class general purpose editor' is rather too much, don't you think?"

"I know, Mr. Renwick," she spoke sympathetically. "It sort of got onto your humility, I presume. But Miss Minnely thinks you *are* first class, or she would never have instructed Mr. Durley to *say* first class. That is cordial to you, and good business—to impress the visitors, I mean."

"Miss Minnely is very appreciative and kind. But the point is that I did not engage to be exhibited to flocks of gobemouches."

Miss Heartly pondered the term. "Please, Mr. Renwick, what are gobemouches?"

"I should have said The Plain People."

"Perhaps there have been rude ones—not subscribers," she said anxiously.

"No, all have acted as if reared on 'The Blessing.'"

She sighed in relief—then exclaimed in consternation:—"Can Mr. Durley have been— *rude?*" She hesitated to pronounce the dire word.

"Not at all, Miss Heartly. I do not blame Mr. Durley for exhibiting us as gorillas."

"But how *wrong.*" There was dismay in her tone. "Miss Minnely has warned him against the least bit of deception."

"Oh, please, Miss Heartly—I was speaking figuratively."

Her fair brow slightly wrinkled, her fingers went nervously to her anxious lips, she looked perplexed;—"Figuratively! If you would kindly explain, Mr. Renwick. I am not very literary."

"Do the ladies of the Paper Patterns Department *like* to be exhibited?" he ventured.

"Well, I could not exactly be warranted to say 'like'—Scripture has such warnings against the sinfulness of vanity. But we are, of course, cordially pleased to see visitors—it is so good for the Subscription Department."

"I see. And it is not hard on you individually. There you are, a great roomful of beautiful, dutiful, cordial young ladies. You keep

one another in countenance. But what if you
were shown each in a separate cage?"

Her face brightened. "Oh, now I understand, Mr. Renwick! You mean it would be
nicer for the Editors, too, to be seen all together."

Renwick sighed hopelessly. She spoke on
decisively: "That may be a valuable suggestion,
Mr. Renwick." On her pad she began pencil-
ling shorthand. "Of course I will credit you
with it. Perhaps you do not know that Miss
Minnely always pays well for valuable sug-
gestions." She wrote intently, murmuring:
"But is it practicable? Let me think. Why,
surely practicable! But Miss Minnely will
decide. All partitions on the Editorial Flat
could be removed! Make it cool as Prize
Package or Financial Department!" She
looked up from her paper, glowing with enterprise, and pointed her pencil straight at Renwick. "And so impressive!" She swept the
pencil in a broad half circle, seeing her picture. "Thirty Editors visible at one compre-
hensive glance! All so literary, and busy, and
intelligent, and cordial! Fine! I take the liberty, temporarily, of calling that a first-class
suggestion, Mr. Renwick. It may be worth

hundreds to you, if Miss Minnely values it. It may be forcibly felt in the Subscription List —if Miss Minnely approves. It may help to hold many subscribers who try to get away after the first year. I feel almost sure Miss Minnely *will* approve. I am so glad. I thought something important was going to come when Miss Minnely considered your placard so carefully."

"But some of the other Editors may not wish to be exhibited with the whole collection," said Renwick gravely. "For instance, consider Mr. Cummins' literary rank. Would it gratify him to be shown as a mere unit among Editors of lesser distinction?"

"You are most fore-thoughtful on every point, Mr. Renwick. That is so *fine*. But Mr. Cummins is also most devoted. I feel sure he would cordially yield, if Miss Minnely approved. I presume you will wish me to tell her that you are grateful for her kind message?"

"Cordially grateful seems more fitting. Miss Heartly—and I am—especially for her choice of a deputy."

"Thank you, Mr. Renwick. I will tell her that, too. And may I say that you will be pleased to adopt her suggestion that you dis-

course a little to visitors, pending possible
changes in this Flat, instead of just coming forward and turning around.   Literary men are so
clever—and—ready."   He fleetingly suspected
her of derision.

"Please say that I will reflect on Miss Minnely's suggestion with an anxious wish to emu-
late, so far as my fallen nature will permit, Miss
Heartly's beautiful devotion to 'The Blessing's'
interests."

"Oh, thank you again, so much, Mr. Renwick."   And the fair Priestess of Business
bowed graciously in good bye.

III

Renwick sat dazed.   From his earliest acquaintance with "The Family Blessing" he had
thought of its famous Editress and Sole Proprietress as one "working a graft" on the Plain
People by consummate sense of the commercial
value of cordial cant.   Now he had to conceive
of her as perfectly ingenuous.   Had she really
taken his placard as one written in good faith?
He remembered its sentences clearly:

" When the editor in this compartment is to be
exhibited, please notify him by knocking on this door
before opening it.   He will then rise from his sitting

posture, come forward for inspection, and turn slowly
around three times if a school teacher, a mother, or a
minister of the Gospel be among the visiting subscribers."

Miss Minnely took that for sincere! Renwick
began to regard "The Blessing" as an emanation of a soul so simple as to be incapable of
recognizing the diabolic element, derision. He
was conceiving a tenderness for the honesty
which could read his placard as one of sincerity.
How blessed must be hearts innocent of mock-
ery! Why should he not gratify them by dis-
coursing to visiting subscribers? The idea
tickled his fancy. At least he might amuse
himself by writing what would edify Durley's
parties if delivered with gravity. He might
make material of some of Miss Minnely's
voluminous letters of instruction to himself.
From his pigeon-hole he drew that file, inspected it rapidly, laughed, and culled as he
wrote.

Twenty minutes later he was chuckling over
the effusion, after having once read its solem-
nities aloud to himself.

"Hang me if I don't try it on Durley's next
party!" he was telling himself, when pencil
tickings, like small woodpecker tappings,

came again on his outer door. "Miss Heartly
back! I will treat her to it!" and he opened the
door, discourse in hand.

There stood the wide, wise-eyed, placid,
gray-clad lady!

"I am Miss Minnely, Mr. Renwick. Very
pleased to introduce myself to a gentleman
whose suggestion has pleased me deeply." Her
wooly voice was as if steeped in a syrup of
cordial powers. Suddenly he knew she had
reminded him of Miss Pue's gigantic bronze
Beneficence.

"Thank you, Miss Minnely. I feel truly
honoured." Renwick, with some concealed trepidation, bowed her to his revolving chair.

"Mr. Renwick." She disposed her ampli-
tude comfortably; then streamed on genially
and authoritatively, "You may be gratified to
learn that I was pleased—on the whole—by
your cordial demeanour while—er—revolving
—not long ago—on the occasion of Mr. Durley's last visiting party. Only—you will permit me to say this in all kindness—I did not
regard the—the display of—er—form—as precisely *adapted*. Otherwise your appearance,
tone, and manner were eminently suitable—
indeed such as mark you strongly, Mr. Ren-

wick, as conforming—almost—to my highest
ideal for the conduct of Editors of 'The Blessing.' Consequently I deputed Miss Heartly—
with a suggestion. She has informed me of
your cordial willingness, Mr. Renwick—hence
I am here to thank you again—and instruct.
Your short discourse to visitors will—let me
explain—not only edify, but have the effect of,
as it were, obviating any necessity for the—er
—revolving—and the display of—er—form.
Now, you are doubtless aware that I invariably
edit, so to speak, every single thing done on be-
half of our precious 'Family Blessing.' For
due performance of that paramount duty I
must give account hereafter. My peculiar gift
is Taste—you will understand that I mention
this fact with no more personal vanity that if
I mentioned that I have a voice, hands, teeth, or
any other endowment from my Creator—*our*
Creator, in fact. Taste—true sense of what
our subscribers like on their *higher* plane. My
great gift must be entitled to direct what we
say to visitors, just as it directs what 'The
Blessing' publishes on its story pages, its editorial columns, its advertisements, letter heads,
everything of every kind done in 'The Blessing's' name. I am thorough. And so, Mr.

Renwick, I desire to hear your discourse be-
forehand. What? You have already prepared
it? Excellent! Promptitude—there are few
greater business virtues! We will immediately
use your draft as a basis for further consulta-
tion."

So imposing was her amiable demeanour that
Renwick had no wish but to comply. He
glanced over what he had written, feeling now
sure that its mock gravity would seem nowise
sardonic to Miss Minnely.

"In preparing these few words," he remarked, "I have borrowed liberally from your
notes of instruction to me, Miss Minnely."

"Very judicious. Pray give me the pleasure."

He tendered the draft.

"But no, please *deliver* it." She put away
the paper. Suppose me to be a party of our
de-ar visiting subscribers. I will stand here,
you there. Now do not hesitate to be audible,
Mr. Renwick." She beamed as a Brobdig-
nagian child at a new game.

Renwick, quick to all humours, took position,
and began with unction: "Dear friends, dear
visitors——"

She interrupted amiably:—"De-ar friends,

de-ar visitors.   Make two syllables of the de-ar.
The lingering is cordial in effect.   I have observed that carefully—de-ar softens hearts.
Dwell on the word—dee-ar—thus you will
cause a sense of affectionate regard to cling to
visitors' memories of 'The Blessing's' editorial
staff.   You understand, Mr. Renwick?"

He began again: "De-ar friends, de-ar visitors, de-ar mothers, de-ar teachers," but again
she gently expostulated, holding up a fat hand
to stop his voice.

"Please, Mr. Renwick—no, I think not—it
might seem invidious to discriminate by speci-
fying some before others.   All alike are our
de-ar friends and visitors."

"De-ar friends, de-ar visitors," Renwick cor-
rected his paper, "I cannot hope to express adequately to you my feelings of delight in being
introduced to your notice as a first class general
purpose editor, and eminent authority on——"

She graciously interposed:—"It might be
well to pencil *this* in, Mr. Renwick, 'introduced
to you by our de-ar colleague, Mr. Durley, the
most experienced of our guides to the "Family
Blessing" Building, as general purpose editor,
etc.'   That would impress, as hinting at our
corps of guides, besides uplifting the rank of

our valued colleague, Mr. Durley, and by consequence 'The Blessing,' through the respectful
mention made of one of our more humble em-
ployees.   Elevate the lowly, and you elevate
all the superior classes—that is a sound American maxim.   In business it is by such fine attention to detail that hearts and therefore subscribers are won.   But, Mr. Renwick, *nothing*
could be better than your 'I cannot hope to express adequately my feelings of delight,' etc.—
that signifies cordial emotion—it is very good
business, indeed."

Sincerity was unclouded in her gaze.   He
pencilled in her amendment, and read on:—
"and eminent authority on water amusements
of a character to build up character in first-class
respectable American families."

"Very good—I drilled Mr. Durley in that,"
she put in complacently.

"Dear friends," he resumed.

"De-ar," she reminded him.

"De-ar friends, you may naturally desire to
be informed of the nature of the duties of a
general purpose editor, therefore——"

"Let me suggest again, Mr. Renwick.
Better say 'Dear friends, closely associated with
"The Family Blessing," as all must feel who

share the privilege of maintaining it, you will naturally desire to be informed,' etc. Don't you agree, Mr. Renwick? It is well to neglect no opportunity for deepening the sense of our de-ar subscribers that the 'Blessing' is a privilege to their households. I do everything possible to make our beloved ones feel that they *own* 'The Blessing,' as in the highest sense they do. They like that. It is remunerative, also."

Renwick jotted in the improvement, and read on: "A general purpose editor of 'The Blessing' is simply one charged with promoting the general purpose of 'The Blessing.' To explain what that is I cannot do better than employ the words of the Sole Proprietress, Miss Minnely herself, and——."

The lady suggested, *"I cannot do so well as to employ the words of*—it is always effective to speak most respectfully of the absent Proprietress—that touches their imagination favourably. It is good business."

"I appreciate it, Miss Minnely. And now I venture to adapt, *verbatim,* parts of your notes to me."

"It was forethoughtful to preserve them, Mr. Renwick. I am cordially pleased."

He read on more oratorically:—"De-ar
friends, 'The Blessing' has a Mission, and to
fulfil that Mission it must, first of all, entertain its subscribers on their *higher plane.* This
cannot be done by stimulating in them any
latent taste for coarse and inelegant laughter,
but by furnishing entertainingly the whole-
some food from which mental pabulum is absorbed and mental growth accomplished."

"Excellent! My very own words."

"The varieties of this entertaining pabulum
must be *conscientiously* prepared, and admin-
istered in small quantities so that each can be
assimilated unconsciously by Youth and Age
without mental mastication. Mind is *not* Character, and——"

"How true. Character-building publica-
tions must *never* be addressed to mere *Mind.*"

"The uplifting of the Mind, or Intellect,"
Renwick read on, "is not the general purpose
of 'The Family Blessing.' It is by the Literature of the Heart that Character is uplifted.
Therefore a general purpose editor of 'The
Blessing' must ever seek to maintain and to present the *truly cordial.* That is what most
widely attracts and pleases all these sections of
the great American people who are uncor-

rupted by worldly and literary associations
which tend to canker the Soul with cynicism."

"I remember my glow of heart in writing
those inspiring, blessed, and inspired words!"
she exclaimed. "Moreover, they are true.
Now, I think that is about enough, Mr. Renwick. Visitors should never be too long de-
tained by a single attraction. Let me advise
you to memorize the discourse carefully. It is
cordial. It is impressive. It is informative of
'The Blessing's' ideal. It utters my own
thoughts in my own language. It is admirably
adapted to hold former subscribers, and to con-
firm new. All is well." She pondered silently
a few moments. "Now, Mr. Renwick, I would
be strictly just. The fact that an editor, and
one of those not long gathered to our happy
company, has suggested and devoted himself
to this novel attraction, will have noblest effect
in rousing our colleagues of every Department
to emulative exertion. Once more, I thank you
cordially. But the Sole Proprietress of the remunerative 'Blessing' holds her place in trust
for all colleagues, and she is not disposed to
retire with mere thanks to one who has identi-
fied himself so effectually with her and its
ideals. Mr. Renwick, your honorarium—your

weekly pay envelope," again she paused reflectively, "it will hereafter rank you with our very valued colleague, Mr. Caliphas C. Cummins himself! No—no-no, Mr. Renwick—do not thank me—thank your happy inspiration—thank your cordial devotion—thank your *Taste* —thank your natural, innate identification, in high ideals, with me and 'The Family Blessing.' As for me—it is for me to thank you— and I do so, again, cordially, cordially, cordially!" She beamed, the broad embodiment of Beneficence, in going out of the room.

Renwick long stared, as one dazed, at the story of "The Converted Ringmaster." It related in minute detail the sudden reformation of that sinful official. The account of his rapid change seemed no longer improbable nor mawkish. Any revolution in any mind might occur, since his own had been so swiftly hypnotized into sympathy with Miss Minnely and her emanation "The Blessing." How generous she was! Grateful mist was in his eyes, emotion for the safety of the widows and the orphan whose bread he must win.

Yet the derisive demon which sat always close to his too sophisticated heart was already gibing him afresh:—"You stand engaged," it sneered, "as assistant ringmaster to Durley's exhibition of yourself!"

New perception of Miss Minnely and Miss Heartly rose in his mind. Could mortal women be really as simple as those two ladies had seemed? Might it not be they had managed him with an irony as profound as the ingenuousness they had appeared to evince?

www.ingramcontent.com/pod-product-compliance
Lightning Source LLC
Chambersburg PA
CBHW030345120726
47901CB00007B/1924